PRAISE FOR
THE SUGARLAND BLUE NOVELS

"Romance suspense at its best . . . a fantastic addition to this fabulous series." —The Reading Cafe

"Scorching hot." —*Publishers Weekly*

"This exciting contemporary romantic-suspense story continues the saga of the delicious detectives in the Sugarland Police Department . . . a thrilling story." —The Reading Addict

"A roller coaster of emotion and action that will keep you gripped until the last page . . . with just the right combination of both romance and suspense." —Cocktails and Books

"What's not to love about sexy men in blue with fast hands, true hearts, and the courage of their convictions? Davis certainly knows how to draw the perfect balance of vulnerability and strength. . . . She wraps it all up in an action novel that falls just shy of a police procedural, but with plenty of pure, steamy romance and family drama." —*RT Book Reviews*

"If you like romance, action, and mysteries, then you will love this book." —Once Upon a Twilight

continued . . .

"Four stars! A totally entertaining experience."
—*RT Book Reviews*

"Exhilarating [with] a two-hundred-proof heat duet . . .
a strong entry [and] a terrific, action-packed thriller."
—*Midwest Book Review*

"Jo Davis turns up the heat full-blast. Romantic suspense that has it all: a sizzling firefighter hero, a heroine you'll love, and a story that crackles and pops with sensuality and action. Keep the fire extinguisher handy or risk spontaneous combustion!"
—Linda Castillo, national bestselling author of
The Dead Will Tell

"One of the most exciting 'band of brothers' series since J. R. Ward's Black Dagger Brotherhood. It's sweet and sexy, tense and suspenseful." —myLifetime.com

"A poignant and steamy romance with a great dose of suspense." —Wild on Books

"Hot, sizzling sex and edge-of-your-seat terror will have you glued to this fantastic romantic suspense story from the first page to the final word."
—Romance Novel TV

ALSO BY JO DAVIS

Sugarland Blue Novels
On the Run
In His Sights
Hot Pursuit
Sworn to Protect
Armed and Dangerous (novella)

Firefighters of Station Five Novels
Ride the Fire
Hidden Fire
Line of Fire
Under Fire
Trial by Fire

BRING THE HEAT

A SUGARLAND BLUE NOVEL

JO DAVIS

A SIGNET ECLIPSE BOOK

SIGNET ECLIPSE
Published by New American Library,
an imprint of Penguin Random House LLC
375 Hudson Street, New York, New York 10014

This book is an original publication of New American Library.

First Printing, December 2015

For more information about Penguin Random House, visit penguin.com.

ISBN 978-0-451-47699-9

Printed in the United States of America
10 9 8 7 6 5 4 3 2 1

Penguin
Random
House

To my wonderful, dear friend Mary Anne Tafelski. You came into my life like a tornado, an unbelievable bundle of energy, and I was thankfully swept up in your path. When I'm down, you refuse to allow me to wallow, you make me laugh, you listen, and you're always ready to go out and cause some trouble with me! I'm so grateful to call you my "bestie."

Captain Austin Rainey's story is for you. I love you, girlfriend.

1

Austin Rainey hopped out of his truck, slammed the door, and strode up the walk, biting back a curse of aggravation. So much for what had been, until an hour before, a damn fine spring day off.

Except for his impending divorce from Ashley. The constant fighting over the details, every little thing from the pots and pans to who got the cat. Not to mention the one argument they hadn't seen eye to eye on from the beginning:

The baby Ashley was carrying. Austin's baby, a son he had always longed for so badly and she never wanted. And yet she was going to deny him custody.

Why? Out of spite?

He tried to tell himself it didn't matter. He was going to have a son, and he'd be a great hands-on dad. At least he was alive to bitch about the crap that was his life, unlike the poor bastard inside the condo.

Something told him that might be the only positive note this day had in store.

Out of habit, he glanced around at the condos and surrounding neighborhood, getting the feel. It was older, well established. Upper middle class. Mercedeses, BMWs, and fully decked-out SUVs. Not rich, but not hurting by any stretch.

As he neared the lower-level breezeway between two buildings, he spotted Lieutenant Daniel Coleman talking to Detective Shane Ford and a couple of uniformed Sugarland PD officers he'd never met. The younger man's normally cheerful face reflected the grim pall permeating the air. Arms crossed over his chest, Danny leaned his tall frame against the side of the building, shaking his head.

The quartet glanced up at his approach, and Danny straightened, green eyes widening as he read the declaration across Austin's T-shirt.

Gun Control Means Using Both Hands.

The cops chuckled and Danny shot him an exasperated glare.

"Good God, Rainey. If you're really dying for Chief Byrne to ream you, at least take him to dinner first."

"Fuck you, asshole. It's my day off, the Rangers were winning, and my goddamn beer's going flat as we speak," Austin announced. No one gave a damn. With a sigh, he got down to business. "What's so important that I needed to be called down here?"

Shane Ford stepped forward. The tall, brown-haired man was one of Austin's best homicide detectives and a superb leader on the force. "Trust us, Cap. You'll understand when you see the body."

"Who was the first on the scene?"

"We were," Shane confirmed, gesturing to his partner, Taylor Kayne, who had just stepped into their circle. "Victim inside is identified as a thirty-one-year-old male named Matthew Blankenship. Call came in to nine-one-one this morning shortly before noon, a Mr. Rick Yates screaming at the dispatcher that his friend was dead. I arrived to find Mr. Yates completely hysterical. Haven't been able to get much out of him yet."

"Where is he?"

Shane jerked a thumb toward the adjacent parking lot, where two squad cars were parked side by side. A dark-haired man in the backseat of one had his face buried in his hands. Austin winced, a wave of sympathy rolling through him. Even seasoned veterans often had a tough enough time mentally dealing with a murder scene. He'd been chasing monsters for most of his life, sifting through the aftermath of their cruel work because he was damn good at it . . . and because the victims' ghosts never let him rest. He couldn't imagine walking in to discover a friend or loved one brutally killed.

"We'll speak with him after he's calmed down," Austin told Shane. "Go on."

"We found Mr. Blankenship deceased, apparently murdered, in his bedroom. After getting a good look at the victim and his manner of death, we immediately called you."

Austin tensed. "Did either of you touch anything?" His men were too good to make rookie mistakes, but still, he had to ask.

"Not a thing," Taylor assured him. "We went in, saw what we're dealing with, and came outside to secure the crime scene."

"I haven't been inside yet," Danny muttered. "Laura Eden and the FU are en route."

Laura Eden. The striking, dark-haired medical examiner who was smart as hell, had a dry sense of humor, and a mouth like a sailor. For the past few years, Laura had worked alongside the department's Forensics Unit, sarcastically dubbed the FU, to solve homicides and unexplained deaths. She was highly respected in the community.

She was also the bane of Austin's existence. And the woman who secretly drove him crazy with desire.

With an effort, he snapped himself out of his mental lapse. Thoughts of Laura faded, as did his pitiful hope of getting back to the game and his beer, and he let them go. In his department, easy solutions were as scarce as winning lottery tickets. "Okay, I'm going in. Danny?"

"Hope you haven't eaten lunch." Taylor grimaced.

Actually, he had. Damn.

He and Danny entered Blankenship's condo, ducking under the yellow crime scene tape stretched across the doorway. Inside, they paused, studying the interior. Tasteful, clean, not your stereotypical bachelor pad. A Fender electric guitar and a large amp in one corner. A framed photo of an older couple on the fireplace mantel, likely the parents. Another shot of two young guys, one auburn haired and one with dark brown hair, singing in a rock band on a small stage, guitars slung low. Blankenship and Yates?

A short hallway off the small living room led to the bedroom. Danny on his heels, he covered the distance and paused a second before stepping inside. The stench of loosed bowels gagged him. Afternoon sunlight filtered through the blinds, illuminating the bound man on the bed.

Halting, he stared at the carnage.

"Mother of God," Austin whispered.

Beside him, Danny's voice shook. "Have you ever seen anything like that before?"

"Not personally, no." Suppressing a shudder, he glanced at his partner, who swallowed convulsively. "You okay?"

Danny heaved a deep breath, expression determined. "Better than *him*. Jesus."

Austin clapped him on the shoulder, then stepped closer to the bed, cataloging the gruesome details. The man's face was frozen in horror, wide blue eyes twin orbs of glass. A length of red silk parted his lips, tied snug around his head.

Blankenship was sprawled spread-eagle on his back, but, interestingly, his wrists and ankles weren't bound to the four posts on his bed. The tall man's sculpted body evidenced plenty of hours in the gym. Good looking, Austin supposed, though he wondered what role, if any, the man's physical characteristics played in his murder.

"What do the guys want me to see?" Austin mused, frowning.

"Not sure yet."

The upper half of the man's body was so mutilated, the torso and the sheets were saturated in blood. The deep slashes indicated stab wounds, but he couldn't make that call. That was Laura's area of expertise.

"Doesn't look like he struggled much, considering what happened to him," Danny observed.

Austin cocked his head. "The killer might've slipped a roofie into his beer," he said. "I saw two beer cans on the coffee table in the living room."

"Statistically, the killer is probably a man."

He shrugged, then gestured to the body. "Could be, but not necessarily. Put a sharp instrument like a knife in a person's hand, throw rage into the mix, and anyone could do this."

Danny wrinkled his nose in disgust. "There're some sick people in this world."

"Yeah. Let's talk to his friend Yates, his coworkers. Get a picture of what he was into sexually, though I'm not sure anything like that is at play in this case. We need a picture of his after-hours social life, bar acquaintances, etc."

Danny frowned at Blankenship with intense scrutiny for several long moments. Austin had come to understand that expression, the quiet stance, the stiff set of his shoulders. Other than the obvious terrible scene, something was bothering his colleague.

"What is it?"

Danny cocked his head. "You know, this guy looks a lot like you."

"The fuck he does." But as Austin stared at the corpse, a creeping sensation crawled down his spine. "Okay, maybe a little. But the others wouldn't have called me down here just because he resembles me."

"No, but that might yield a clue." Danny gestured to

a small square of cream paper on the nightstand, and Austin walked over to view it better.

The object was a brief note, handwritten in what he considered a man's blocky, messy style, though it would take an expert to weigh in on that. He read the missive without picking it up.

One down, how many more to go? How many wrongs have you dealt others, Captain? How great is the number of your sins? One body for each of them. Your price to pay.

"Danny, read this." Austin stepped aside to let his friend view the damning note.

"Christ." He breathed. "So that's why they called you."

"You really think I'm the captain he's referring to in the note?"

"I'm not sure, but I know one thing—we've officially got a fucking nightmare on our hands."

Rick Yates had managed to pull himself together somewhat, but shook violently throughout the interview. This had always been the part of an investigation Austin dreaded the most, even more than studying the actual crime scene. The victim was gone, and nothing would reverse whatever fateful decisions he'd made the night before.

But the survivors broke his heart, and with good reason. He'd never learned to harden himself against the loved ones' sorrow, and hoped he never would. The day he could look into the reddened eyes of the Rick Yateses of this world and feel nothing, he'd turn in his damn shield.

The information Yates provided seemed typical enough to begin with. The two were lifelong friends, had grown up in the Sugarland area together. They held different jobs—Rick worked for a local telecom company in fiber optics, Matt was a graphic artist—but played together in a rock band as a sideline, for enjoyment rather than any real hope they'd make it big. They'd played Spanky's, a club in Nashville, the night before. The mood had been rowdy, festive. Before Blankenship left, he'd made no bones about the fact that he'd planned to find some serious action.

"You didn't see whether Matt picked anyone up at the club?" Austin pressed, leaning against the squad car Yates had been sitting in. Danny hovered at his elbow.

"No—" He choked. "I wish to God I had. I told him to be careful. I *always* tell him to fucking be careful."

Yates squeezed his eyes shut, but a tear escaped to roll down one cheek. Grieving, in denial, referring to his friend in present tense, unable to make the horrible switch in his mind.

"I'm sorry, Rick," Austin said. "I know how hard this must be to talk about right now."

He gave a bitter laugh and opened his eyes. "Do you?"

"Yes. Now, why would you caution him? What kinds of things was Matt into that concerned you?"

"Picking up random people for one-night stands,

guys or girls. Doesn't matter to him. Lately, he'd done a couple of threesomes."

"Were you ever included?"

Yates looked genuinely shocked, and shook his head. "No. I've never been a part of that."

A bisexual player. Interesting. Blankenship had certainly made the killer's job a breeze.

"I've got one more question, Rick. Did Matt do drugs?"

"Not on a daily basis. He did ecstasy sometimes after we played, especially if he had sex planned for later. But that's it, I swear."

"All right." Austin dug out his wallet and removed one of his cards. "Keep this. Call me or anyone in Homicide if you think of anything, no matter how insignificant it may seem. We'll be in touch."

"Captain Rainey." Yates hesitated and pocketed the card, lips trembling. "Matt's parents, I c-can't tell them. M-Matt's all they h-had."

His eyes filled again and Austin's throat tightened. He reached out, squeezed the younger man's shoulder. "Do the Blankenships live in the area?"

"Yeah." The tears fell as he recited the address.

"Lieutenant Coleman and I will take care of it. We need to speak with them anyway."

He and Danny turned to leave, just in time to see the Forensics Unit pull in behind Austin's pickup. And behind that, the dark Mercedes belonging to Laura Eden.

His heart skipped several beats and he forced himself to remain impassive as she stepped from the vehicle and headed his way.

It was almost impossible to concentrate on what she

was saying as she stopped in front of him. Even with her long dark hair pulled back into a ponytail with a clip, and wearing a pair of conservative black pants and a blue blouse, she was beautiful. Her large brown eyes were expressive and intelligent, missing nothing.

She had a great sense of humor, but the frequent half smile, the sparkle in her gaze, was noticeably absent at the moment as she stood waiting for his response.

"I'm sorry. What?" he muttered, feeling his face heat.

"I asked you to fill me in," she replied, eyeing him curiously. "What's going on with you? Are you feeling okay?"

"Of course. I'm ready for a steak dinner after taking a look inside."

If she realized he was deflecting the question of his mental lapse, she didn't call him on it. Instead, she got down to business. "Victim?"

Quickly, he gave her the rundown of what they knew so far, plus the position and condition of the body. She merely listened, nodding, her sharp mind taking in every detail and cataloging it in that incredible brain of hers.

When he was done, she took a pair of latex gloves from her pocket and pulled them on. "Into the battle zone, then. Want to come with?"

"Sure."

Not because he wanted to return to the grisly scene—that was the very last thing he wanted. But he wasn't going to turn down the rare chance to watch Laura work, a privilege usually granted to his men in the field while he was stuck behind a desk.

Few people would consider watching a medical examiner conduct an investigation at a murder scene anything to write home about, but cops were a different breed. The need to protect and see justice served ran strong in Austin's veins, and when an expert like Laura had to be called in to help, his curiosity and need to see things through came to the fore.

Sure, a lot of his fascination was the woman herself. But not all.

"These are definitely stab wounds. Don't suppose you recovered the murder weapon?" she asked, interrupting his musings.

"I wish. Wouldn't that have been nice."

"Yeah." She paused, peering closer at the body. "This poor guy didn't even put up a fight. No defense wounds on his hands or arms. No scratches from fingernails on his skin, and no skin under his nails, either, that I can see."

"That's what we observed, too."

"Tests may show trace amounts. No obvious evidence of sexual activity, but again, we'll see." She stood staring at the body for a moment. "He could've been roofied, or completely sedated. I'll let you know what we find."

"Thanks."

At that exact moment, she spotted the note. Slowly, she skirted the bed, leaned over, and read the missive without touching it. Then she straightened and pinned Austin with a glare. "What the hell is this?"

"What it appears to be, unfortunately. An accusation, and a probable motive."

"The killer is referring to you?"

"My team seems to think so. That's why they called me over here." He nodded to the victim. "They think he resembles me, too."

For once, words seemed to fail the woman as she turned to study the body again. Then she looked back at Austin. "I hope with everything in me that this has nothing to do with you."

"Me, too. But I don't know what other captain he could be addressing."

"You're not the only captain at the department."

"I'm the only auburn-haired one who looks like *him*."

Neither of them had an answer for that.

They walked outside together, and Laura directed her team to get the body loaded as soon as Forensics was finished processing the scene. Then she turned to Austin and regarded him thoughtfully.

"Are you sure you're all right?"

He tried a smile. "Why would you ask that?"

"You're too quiet, Austin, and you don't look well. You're completely healed from the attack, right?" Her gaze sharpened.

"Yes," he answered truthfully. A few months earlier, he'd been stabbed and nearly killed while working a case with Tonio Salvatore, one of his detectives. "It took a while, but I'm totally well. I'm just dealing with some personal stuff, and frankly it's running me down a little."

"Your divorce?"

"You heard?" he asked in surprise.

"Yes," she said quietly. "One of your uniformed officers mentioned it at a scene we worked a couple of weeks ago. I'm really sorry to hear about it."

"Thanks." He made a mental note to have a word with the shift during the next briefing about flapping their loose lips. "It's for the best, though—believe me." He didn't know whether she'd heard about Ashley's pregnancy, and he wasn't about to bring it up.

"Well, I know it'll be rough for a while, but it'll work out. I'm here if you ever want to talk."

Their eyes met and held. It was Laura's turn to blush, and Austin stared at her, captivated. In the past few years since they'd met, this was the first time she'd extended a personal offer of friendship. He wasn't dumb enough to think the timing was a coincidence, and suddenly the day seemed a lot brighter than before.

"Thank you." He smiled. "I'll remember that."

"Take care, Austin."

"You, too."

Watching that woman walk away was getting more and more difficult to do.

Gripping the steering wheel, Douglas relived every moment of the scene he'd masterminded, unconcerned about the possibility of discovery. He was so easily overlooked. Always had been.

To everyone except his one true love.

And Austin had taken her away.

Closing his eyes against the pain, he recalled the loss. His love had wasted away without him while he tried desperately to do something for her. Anything. But he was powerless.

And lonely. Depressed and isolated. There were days he could barely get up in the morning, let alone function like a normal human being.

And it was all Captain Austin Rainey's fault. Now? *The asshole has everything within his grasp that should've belonged to me! He doesn't even know what he has, and he's ready to throw it all away.*

So I'll beat him to it. Show him how it feels to be brought to his knees.

Then he'll finally understand what he's done to me.

2

Austin hovered outside Byrne's office door for a few seconds before knocking. He couldn't help but smile a bit as he recalled his meeting with his boss and good friend the day after the Blankenship murder almost a week before.

Muffled snickers punctuated the sudden stillness at his back. Assholes. He threw an evil glare over his shoulder, squelching the laughter if not the childlike glee on some of his detectives' faces.

Except for Danny, he noted with gratitude. Seated at his desk, his friend looked up from the Blankenship file, expression sober, and mouthed, Good luck.

"Come in," Byrne's deep voice intoned, colder than the North Atlantic. "And close the door."

He did, pushing it shut behind him. Dammit, Glenn couldn't be that angry with him. As a captain, Austin did his best to keep his nose clean.

In the early days, Austin had been wary of Glenn, who was then a hard-as-nails captain. The kind that made the men sit up straighter and sweat a little when he walked into the room. It wasn't long, however, before Austin realized the older man possessed a brilliant mind and a warmer heart than he let on.

What the hell have I done to piss him off?

The man in question didn't bother to rise from his chair, but merely nodded. His dark eyes snapped with irritation and his mouth was pressed tight. "What the fuck was yesterday?"

"I have no idea what you're talking about," he confessed, gazing steadily at the chief. "I was called to the Blankenship murder scene because my detectives believe the killer might be focused on me somehow."

The chief's stony expression softened some. "I know that. I'm talking about the public image we have to maintain."

"What do you—"

"'Gun Control Means Using Both Hands'?"

"Oh. The T-shirt," Austin muttered, sitting back in his chair. "I was off duty, Glenn. They sounded so adamant I get there, I didn't think to change my shirt first. How did you find out about it?"

"On the six o'clock news," the chief said icily. "When I saw you walk across the lawn of the crime scene wearing it."

Shit. He blew out a breath. "Damn. I'm sorry I messed up, okay? I never even saw the reporters."

"Messing up is wearing one blue sock and one black sock. Judging from the number of messages on my voice mail—one from the mayor himself—your stupidity qualifies as a clusterfuck."

Austin winced. "It's done. I don't know what I can do about it."

Glenn ran a hand through his salt-and-pepper brown hair. "Me, either. The problem is, with the climate in the media so

BRING THE HEAT   17

*anticop right now, none of us can afford to step one toe out of
line, even with something as innocent as what's supposed to
be cop humor on a T-shirt. You understand what I'm saying?"*

"Yes, sir. Every single thing we do gets blown totally out
of proportion."

"And then some! Hopefully this will all blow over by tomorrow and they'll be focused on county taxes or some shit."

*He'd started to ask whether the comments on the news
were that bad, but decided he really didn't want to know.*

*They'd all been called on the carpet by Glenn at some
point. The media and the public wanted answers about the
murder—answers Austin and his men didn't have. Yet.*

Bracing himself, Austin brought himself back to the
present, knocked and walked inside, shutting the door
behind him. Glenn waved him in and sat back in his
chair, looking no less harassed than he had in the past
few days.

"Tell me something good," the chief said wearily.
"Anything."

Austin thought about that. "Not a single one of our
men has been caught on a cell phone video doing anything remotely inappropriate. This week, anyway."

"Aren't you hilarious?" Byrne huffed, glaring at him.
"I'm talking about the Blankenship investigation."

"I know." He shook his head. "Not much to go on
yet. The full report from Eden isn't back, and they're
swamped."

"Damn."

"But I've started a list of my former cases where the
perp I've put away might still hold a grudge. It's slow
going."

"All right. Keep me informed."

"You know it."

"How are things with you? Personally?" The question was genuine, Glenn's expression concerned.

"Not too bad, I guess. The baby's due in four weeks, and I'll admit I'm scared as hell."

His friend smiled. "And excited."

"That too."

Just then a loud knock sounded on the chief's door, startling Austin. As he turned in his chair, he wondered who would have the nerve—everyone knew better than to interrupt the chief in a meeting.

"What?" Glenn barked.

The door opened and Shane stuck his head in. His gaze found Austin sitting there, then skittered away without acknowledging him.

"Chief, I need to speak with you." Shane's voice was strained.

"Now?" Glenn swept a hand toward Austin. "You can see I'm busy at the moment."

"This is important, sir. I wouldn't interrupt otherwise." Something in his tone must've alerted the chief, because Glenn nodded.

"Fine. Come in, Detective."

"No, sir. I mean, I think it's best if you come out here."

The chief's brows rose to his hairline. But he did as he was asked, pushing his fit frame from his seat and leaving the office with Shane.

That's not strange or anything, Austin said to himself.

Shrugging, he pulled his iPhone from his pants pocket and checked his text messages. Two from Ashley, combative as usual, one from his mother asking when she and his dad could come for a visit.

After he responded to those, he surfed on his Facebook app for a few minutes. In fact, when several minutes went by and the chief hadn't reappeared, Austin frowned. What was keeping his boss? They all had shit to do, and Austin was no exception.

Patience finally expired, he got up and left the office. As luck would have it, the chief was on his way back, Shane and Taylor walking with him.

"Are we done with our talk?" Austin asked his boss. "Because I've got things to—"

"Son, I need for you to go back into my office with us." Glenn stopped in front of him and gestured in that direction.

Son. It was the way he'd said it. *That tone.* Austin knew that voice, had used it and heard it used many times in his career. But he didn't have to judge by that alone. Their faces were grim, etched with sympathy, their eyes telling him without words how very much they didn't want to say whatever must be said.

"What's going on?" he asked quietly.

"In the office," Shane insisted.

Panic seized his heart, started to claw its way up his throat. "Tell me now. What's happened? Taylor?"

The blond detective wouldn't look at him, just shook his head. "Cap, please—"

"Has there been an accident? Is it my parents?" He

stared at them, unable to figure out whether it *was* one of his parents, how they would've learned something before him.

"No, it's not your folks," Glenn said, taking his arm. "Come inside."

Austin jerked his arm from the chief's grasp, voice rising. "Tell me! Is it Ashley? Oh God." His frantic gaze darted between them. "Something's happened to Ash— and my baby. Christ, what's going on?"

By then he realized all activity around them had gone silent. Without waiting for an answer, he yanked his phone from his pocket again and tried to punch in his estranged wife's number. His shaking hands wouldn't cooperate, and when Shane's hand covered the phone, Austin froze.

"Austin."

That one word told him all he needed to know. "Where is she? At the house?"

"You are not to go out there. Do you hear me?" Glenn ordered.

"No." He couldn't think it. Refused to believe. Frantic, he dug his truck keys out of his pocket and turned, running for the front of the building. Despite the chief shouting for someone to stop him, nobody did. Most of them simply gaped in confusion, unsure what to do.

By the time anyone mobilized behind him and there were sounds of pursuit, he was almost to his truck. In short order he was tearing out of the parking lot, narrowly missing a squad car and someone's personal SUV.

He didn't care. The only thing that mattered was

getting to his house as quickly as possible. The house he still owned but no longer lived in because he was letting Ashley have it in the divorce. The house where she'd raise their son, and Austin would be a fixture in his life.

Please, let them be safe. Let my boy be unharmed. I've waited for him for so long.

"He'll be fine," he told himself. "They both will."

All the way out of town to his place, he told himself that. Even when a marked squad tried to intercept and pull him over, he told himself that didn't mean the worst had happened.

But when he skidded to a stop in his own front yard, saw the yellow crime scene tape stretched across the front porch, his world came crashing down. Leaving the keys in the ignition, the truck running, he jumped out. Detectives Tonio Salvatore and Chris Ford, Shane's cousin, were on him before he reached the porch, and Tonio wrapped him in a hold from behind, around his chest, with arms like steel bands. But that didn't stop him from fighting to get free.

"Let me go!" he yelled.

"Cap, you're not going in there," Tonio shouted back. "You can't."

Chris stepped around in front of Austin, hands out as though trying to deter a rabid animal. "We absolutely can't let you in there. Deep down, I know you understand that."

His heart was going to explode. "Ashley's gone?"

"Yes. I'm so sorry," Chris said softly.

Austin stared at the detective, who blurred as his

eyes welled with tears. "The baby? Please. They saved my son, right?"

Tonio's voice was quiet in his ear. The arms didn't let go. "They couldn't. I'm sorry."

"My son, too? My son is dead? But he was so far along," he heard himself beg. "He was due in four weeks. I don't understand."

"He didn't have a chance," Chris said, placing his hands on Austin's shoulders. "He was already gone when Ashley was found."

"Wh-what happened?"

"She was murdered. I'm so sorry."

"How?" The word emerged as a wail from deep within his soul. "Why?"

"We're right here with you," Tonio said instead of answering either question. "And we're going to find who did this."

Ashley and his baby. Dead.

Austin swayed on his feet, nearly went down. Would have if not for the men holding him upright. Distantly he was aware that they were guiding him away from the house, toward Tonio's car. Chris opened the passenger-side door and got Austin seated just as more vehicles arrived. Austin didn't look to see who it was, nor did he care.

The most precious person in his life had just been taken from him before he'd even gotten a chance to know him. His baby was gone.

And Austin wanted nothing more than to be wherever his little angel was right now.

*   *   *

Laura scanned the yard as she pulled up and parked. She'd known, the second the address had come in, along with the victim's name.

Hand trembling, she shut off the ignition. *Oh, Austin.*

She spotted him as soon as she got out, sitting in the front passenger seat of someone's car. Detective Chris Ford hovered nearby as a paramedic crouched inside the open car door and checked the police captain's vitals. Chris paced a little, worry and strain clear on his face and in every line of his tense body.

Approaching, Laura caught his attention and waved him over, careful to keep herself out of Austin's line of sight. She didn't want the man thinking about what she was doing there. Not right now, if he was even capable of thinking at all.

"How is he?" The detective didn't have to ask who she meant.

"In shock. He hasn't said a word since we made him sit down. Not one sound."

Her heart bled for the big captain. "That's not uncommon. Everyone reacts differently to this type of bad news."

"Yeah. And this is the absolute worst I've ever seen. My God, Laura, who does this to a pregnant woman?"

"Someone evil," she said. "And I'll do everything in my power to help you all catch him."

Chris nodded, then glanced back toward the car. "Are you going to talk to him?"

"After. I can't focus if I'm worried about Austin, and I don't want to miss any details."

"Just . . . do your best. This one is personal," he said hoarsely.

"I always do, but yes. It's *very* personal."

With that, she steeled herself and went on inside. There just wasn't any preparation for a scene like this one. Cases involving infant deaths were among the worst, but most of those were due to accidents or natural causes. Nothing like what awaited her in the entertainment room just off the den.

There was nothing accidental or natural about Ashley Rainey's death, or the death of her unborn child. The room was destroyed, the big-screen TV shattered and ripped from the wall, lamps broken, furniture shoved aside. The woman had put up a good fight, which was evidenced by the defensive wounds on her hands and arms as well.

Under her manicured fingernails, she'd torn what appeared to be a good chunk out of her assailant's flesh. *Good for you, honey,* she thought sadly. *We're going to catch the demon who did this to you and your baby.*

Ashley, once a pretty blonde, had been badly beaten, especially her face. But that wasn't what had caused her death. The man's belt wrapped around her neck and applied with force until she asphyxiated had been. Tests would prove it, Laura felt certain, given the facial skin condition and coloring, and the broken blood vessels in her eyes.

Once finished, which didn't take long, she headed back outside. Chris and Tonio met her a good distance from the car where Austin still sat.

"Strangulation is the cause of death?" Chris asked.

"Almost positive, but tests will probably bear it out. The scene looks pretty straightforward."

"Beating and strangling a pregnant woman to death, that's a crime of intense rage," Tonio said in disgust.

Chris shook his head. "Or just seriously crazy."

"I'd say both, but motives are your area of expertise." Glancing past them, she spotted the captain's still figure in the car and sighed. "Is someone taking Austin home, staying with him?"

"We're driving him home," Tonio said. "Not sure who's staying with him tonight, but he won't be alone. The paramedic gave him a sedative to help him sleep, too."

"Okay, good. I'm going to speak with him. I'll be in touch."

"Take care," Chris said, and Tonio echoed him.

With no small amount of dread, Laura walked over to the car. Austin's strong profile came into view, and she saw he was sitting upright, just staring out the front windshield. Sunlight glinted off his deep auburn hair, setting it on fire. He gave no indication that he heard her footsteps approaching, so she called out softly.

"Austin?"

No response. She called his name again, and when he still didn't answer, she crouched inside the door and touched his leg. Slowly, he turned his head and looked down at her. His brows drew together as if trying to figure out exactly why she was there.

Then recollection dawned in his green eyes, the hurt so deep and profound it took her breath away.

"They're dead," he whispered. Tears filled his beautiful eyes.

"Yes. I can't tell you how sorry I am."

His hand covered hers. "Help my men find out who did this."

"I'll do my best."

"Take care of them." His voice broke, and so did her heart.

"You know I will." She swallowed hard, determined not to lose it. "I'm here for you. Always."

"I know. Thank you."

He hung his head and didn't say any more, just gazed at the floorboard. After several more seconds of lending her silent support, she gave his hand a squeeze and stood. Forcing herself to walk away from him was the hardest thing she'd ever done.

It felt wrong on every level to leave him there. But he was in good hands for now.

And she had a job to do. For Austin, and his lost family.

Austin awoke to darkness. Somehow, he was in the bedroom of his rented house in Sugarland. In his bed.

Light from the hallway spilled through a crack in the door, partly illuminating the room. From the living room he heard the sound of the television. Quiet talking. It seemed there were at least two people in his home.

Not that this place would ever be *home*. Not really.

Nor would it ever be, not without his son.

No, the awful memory wouldn't stay away forever,

no matter how much he wished it gone. Wished it had never happened at all. Someone had taken his dreams. Stolen his soul.

Forcing himself from the bed, he shuffled from the room, feeling like an old man. He wasn't surprised to see that Danny, Chris, and Tonio had made themselves at home. Pizza boxes littered the coffee table, and soft drink cans. No beer, a first for this crew.

"Hey."

At once, all eyes were on him. Chris made room for him on the couch, and they all started trying to feed him and make him comfortable.

"Are you hungry?" Chris asked.

Tonio nodded. "You should eat something."

Danny was frowning. "Sit down. Are you cold? You're shivering."

"I'm fine. Not hungry, not cold. Thanks." But he did sit, contemplating the pizza. Then his stomach lurched and he gave up the idea of food.

They were all silent for a few moments before Danny spoke up. "I suppose you want to know how the investigation is going."

He had to give his friend credit for not beating around the bush. "Yes. Do they have any suspects?"

An uncomfortable silence descended, and his three companions shared a look. Of course. Austin gave a sad laugh. "Sure. I'm the primary one, right? Estranged husband going through a bitter divorce, custody-rights battle, doesn't get along well with the soon-to-be ex. How am I doing so far?"

Danny sighed. "You're a person of interest, not a suspect. Nobody believes you did it, but every angle has to be studied, to count you out if nothing else."

He knew that. But it still hurt.

"There must be more. What am I missing?"

"You don't want to hear about the details right now," Chris said. "Let it rest for tonight."

"You may as well tell me. I'm going to find out one way or another."

At his insistence, Chris relented. "The murder weapon was a man's belt. It's the same size as two other ones still in your closet over there."

The reality of that slid over him with cold horror. Ashley had been strangled, with an object that likely belonged to him. Someone really was out to destroy Austin's life.

So far, the bastard had done a good job.

"I think I'm going to lie back down," he told them, standing. Any second, he was going to be sick.

"There's a sleeping pill on the nightstand, next to a bottle of water," Tonio said. "In case you need it."

"Just one?"

"Yeah. Just one." Tonio's meaningful gaze told him that was all he was getting, too. They were watching him like a hawk, and self-destruction was not on the agenda.

Returning to his room, Austin shut them all out. Then he swallowed the pill and crawled under the covers. He waited a long time for the medication to take effect before he finally got sleepy.

But nothing would really help. Never again.

*   *   *

There wasn't a dry eye in the packed church—except Austin's.

He couldn't cry. Couldn't rage, eat, sleep, or function outside one single purpose. His sole focus had been on getting through five days of hell to plan the funeral for his wife and son. Glenn, Danny, Austin's men, the other officers, and his own parents had been solid rocks of support, and he was grateful.

But beyond today? Nothing. Tomorrow? More of nothing.

Ashley's parents wouldn't sit with him. Wouldn't even look at him. After the graveside service, he made the mistake of approaching her mother.

"Barbara, I'm so sorry—"

A resounding crack exploded against his cheek as the older woman slapped him with more force than he'd ever dreamed she was capable of. Stunned, he put his hand to the blazing flesh and stared at the woman he'd believed to be a second mother.

"If you'd been the husband she needed, if you hadn't left them, this never would've happened!"

And there it was. The blame. The guilt.

He couldn't even refute her. Hadn't the same accusation been forming in the back of his own mind, unspoken?

"I was going to do right by her and the baby, I swear," he whispered. "We just couldn't stay married."

"The only words I ever want to hear out of your mouth in the future are that you've caught the monster who murdered my daughter and my grandson,"

Barbara spat. "Then I never want to speak to you again."

She walked away, his former father-in-law holding her up. He knew he'd never see either of them again.

A hand on his back startled him, and he turned to find himself wrapped in his own mother's embrace. For a few moments he lost himself in her familiar scent. The softness of her arms. Then his dad was there, too, and he thought maybe he could survive this. *Maybe*.

And he kept thinking that—until it was time for everyone to go home.

His parents wanted to stay, but he had gently sent them on their way, insisting he was going to be fine. Same with his friends. The day after the funeral, his house was quiet for once. Austin was still on family leave, a good idea anyway because of the investigation. His detectives were chasing leads, though they called frequently to check on him.

And, inevitably, in the silence that followed, reality set in. Then the true darkness descended.

He should call a Realtor, put his and Ashley's house on the market. Get it cleaned out. But he couldn't bring himself to take that final step. Instead he went to the liquor store and bought a variety of painkillers in variously colored bottles.

At his rented non-home, he parked himself on the couch, set his bottles on the coffee table, and poured himself a glass of whiskey. It burned all the way down, but left a pleasant fog in its wake that he liked, a lot. So much that the second one went down even better. And the third.

If you hadn't left them, this never would've happened!

His brain wouldn't shut down. Even though his team wouldn't allow him into his house, he'd worked enough crime scenes to know what had happened. To Ashley and his innocent son.

When the next bottle was done, he stared at it blearily, head swimming. Should he go to bed now? Sure, not that he'd sleep.

There were more bottles for tomorrow, and the day after that.

He woke up on a hard surface. His body hurt all over. He pushed up, tried to stand. His legs were jelly and he nearly fell. He was on the floor? Where?

Holding on to the wall, he managed to stay vertical, just barely. His brain felt like it was on a roller coaster and nothing made sense. A dangerous rumble in his stomach alerted him that he was going to be sick, and he stumbled faster.

He'd no sooner made it to the toilet and fell to his knees than he lost what little was in his stomach. He heaved again and again until he thought the lining inside him must be raw and bleeding.

No liquor in the world was enough to dull the pain. He'd failed his family. His son.

They were dead because he hadn't been there to protect them.

End this. End the agony.

Staggering out, he weaved down the hallway. His vision doubled. Tripled. His foot connected with something and he lost his balance. Fell headlong into the end table, taking out the glass hurricane lamp with him. It shattered, but he hardly felt anything. Looking down, he saw crimson on his arm. A river of blood flowing from the nasty gash.

Ignoring it, he crawled around the table. A mess of empty bottles was strewn everywhere and he knocked them aside, scattering them in search of one that was still full. It took some time, but finally he wrapped his fingers around a bottle of something clear. Vodka? He was so far gone he couldn't read the label.

After fumbling several times, he got the top open. Tilted his head back and drank deeply. Somewhere in the distance he heard his cell phone ring, but ignored it. Didn't matter. Nothing did.

Gradually his arm became heavy. Still, he was a little surprised when the bottle fell from his grasp to land with a *thunk* onto the floor, and his body went limp. Somehow he found himself lying on his side, unable to move. To do anything but listen to the thump of his slowing heartbeat.

So sorry, baby boy. Daddy's sorry . . .

A tear trickled from the corner of his eye, ran across the bridge of his nose.

Then the pain finally, finally faded to nothing.

Laura paced her kitchen, coffee mug in hand.

She was getting worried. The funeral two days earlier had been just about as bad as it got. From the weight of the horrible tragedy right down to the flared tempers and unjust blame leveled on Austin's head.

She'd given the captain plenty of space, but something told her he could use a friend. A couple of her own friends knew the torch she carried for the man and might tease her for being self-serving, but she didn't see things that way. Austin had no lack of people in his circle, it was true. But she felt a connection to the man, even more so of late.

Now, unable to get him on the phone, she was worried. In the past few days, he had at least answered when she'd checked on him. Postfuneral depression was a notoriously bad reality for many, especially those who lived alone, and these were the worst of circumstances. Austin wasn't the self-destructive type, and yet . . .

A really bad feeling stole over her. That was enough to get her moving out the door and to her car. She would gladly own up to feeling foolish once she saw he was safe.

The drive to his rented house took almost twenty minutes from her place outside Nashville. She debated phoning one of his cop friends to meet her there, and feared they'd think she was overreacting. About ten minutes out she made a call anyway, to Detective Chris Ford. She'd worked with all of them at one time or another, but she liked Chris and knew he'd take her concern seriously.

Turned out she wasn't the only one worried.

"I'm glad you called," the detective said. "In fact, Shane and I haven't been able to get an answer, either. We were just about to head over there."

"See you in a few."

In all, it was the longest twenty minutes of her life.

She arrived before the cousins and saw that the captain's truck was parked in the driveway. She jogged to the front door, knocking loudly and calling out.

"Austin? Austin, open up!" She repeated the pounding and calling out twice more, and there was no answer. A quick peek at the windows was no help, since the blinds were drawn.

She paced the porch until a big black truck pulled up to the curb. Shane and Chris hopped out and hurried over to her.

"No answer?" Shane asked.

"None. His truck is here, but maybe he went somewhere and someone else drove?"

"Could be. Do we take that chance?"

Chris shook his head. "No. We have to get in there and be sure. I'll pay for the door one way or the other."

His cousin nodded. "I'll help. Okay, let's do this."

"I've got it."

Backing up, Chris delivered several solid kicks to the wood, close to the knob and the frame. It didn't take long before a crack sounded and the door gave way, banging against the inside wall. The trio spilled inside, calling Austin's name.

Utter devastation greeted them. The house was a complete disaster. Dust coated every surface, as did piles of mail. Trash and liquor bottles were strewn everywhere, and the air was stale. Heavy with despair.

In the middle of it all, lying on his side next to the coffee table, was Austin.

"Oh no."

Laura rushed over to him and dropped to her knees.

She gently turned him onto his back, noting his grayish pallor, blue lips. A gash on his right arm had bled profusely, soaking the carpet and his shirt. From the location of the cut, she could tell it wasn't self-inflicted, but that was cold comfort.

Taking his wrist, she checked his pulse and found it to be almost nonexistent. Stomach lurching, she looked up at her companions, but Shane was already on the phone calling an ambulance. Chris knelt on his captain's other side.

"Is there anything I can do?" he asked.

"Not at the moment."

"His pulse?"

"It's bad," she said softly, not letting go of Austin's wrist. Gazing into the man's handsome face, she felt a wave of sadness go through her like a cold wind. "Oh, honey, what have you done to yourself?"

"Just about drank himself to death, looks like," Shane said, putting away the phone. He appeared as anguished as she and Chris. "Hang on, Cap. Help is coming."

His pulse was so weak and thready by the time the paramedics arrived, Laura was almost certain they'd have to perform CPR before they got him to Sterling Hospital. She recognized the crew from Station Five, however, and knew he was in the best possible hands.

They started an IV right away, and Zack Knight said, "The captain's lost a lot of blood through that gash, but that's not our biggest concern right now. If he drank even a fraction of all this, we're looking at acute alcohol poisoning."

"Does he have any medical conditions any of you are aware of?" Eve Tanner, Zack's partner, asked.

Shane spoke up. "Nothing physical, except exhaustion. He's been depressed, though. His estranged wife and unborn son were murdered, and he just buried them a couple of days ago."

Zack's mouth flattened into a thin line as they prepped him to be moved. "I saw that on the news, and I was so sorry to hear about it. I hope they catch the sick bastard who did it."

"Me, too," Eve put in grimly. "Let's get our patient rolling."

They got Austin on a gurney, strapped him in, and hurried out with him as quickly as possible. Laura and the detectives stepped out onto the front porch to watch them load their patient.

"I'll stay behind and fix the door," Chris offered. "Then I'm going to get a head start on cleaning up that shithole in there. No way does he need to come home to that mess. You two go ahead to the hospital if you want."

Laura rubbed her arms to ward off the sudden chill. "I'm definitely going. I won't rest until I know he's out of the woods."

"Same." Shane clapped his cousin on the shoulder, then turned to Laura. "Need a ride?"

She thought about it. "That's okay. I'll take my car. Thank you for the offer, though. Once we find out he's recovering, I'll come back and help Chris."

"Sounds good," Shane said. "I'll stay with Austin."

She wanted to be the one to stay with the captain, but

could hardly say so. They didn't know each other that well, and these men were his close friends. They got to be near him every day, in a way she might never be.

Well, she intended to work on their friendship, so the man had to survive.

She wasn't going to accept any other outcome.

3

The waiting room was packed with cops.

The wait itself? Never ending.

Laura was about to crawl out of her skin, so she could only imagine how Austin's friends and colleagues felt. When his parents showed up, the older couple was whisked away to a private room to speak with the doctor, and frustration was evident in the sea of anxious faces. The guys knew what had happened only in a basic sense.

Laura, Chris, and Shane had told only Danny, Tonio, and Taylor the truth. The others had a pretty good guess as to what had gone down when they learned the captain was found unresponsive at home. When someone suggested a suicide attempt, Austin's closest friends were quick to squelch that rumor before it got started.

Anyway, she refused to believe that was true. Depression and pain had led him to drink far too much. But there was no way such a vital man had set out to take his own life.

From down the hallway, Mr. and Mrs. Rainey appeared, and the group snapped to attention. Mr. Rainey had his arm around his wife, whose eyes were red from crying. Mr. Rainey himself appeared pale and shaken, and twice as old as when he'd arrived. They shuffled toward everyone until finally stopping, visibly collecting themselves. The crowd gathered into a tight knot to listen to what they had to say.

Mr. Rainey was a tall man with graying auburn hair, and it was easy to see Austin in his father. He did the speaking in a strong but quiet voice. "Thank you all for being here. It means a lot to me and my wife." She let out a little sob and he squeezed her tightly before continuing.

"Our son is fighting for his life right now. He's suffering from alcohol poisoning and the next few hours are critical."

"Any prayers you can say would be welcome," his mother said, dabbing at her eyes. "He's been through so much."

Mr. Rainey took a deep breath. "We'll keep you informed, but if you could keep this in the family, so to speak, we'd appreciate it. Thanks again for your support."

Overwhelmed, the couple couldn't say more. They turned and went back in the direction from which they'd come. As they left, a nurse informed the others that visitors were restricted to family only for the time being, which was disappointing but not unexpected.

"I'll stay in case anything changes or the Raineys need anything," Shane said. "The rest of you can go home for now."

There was some grumbling, and cops started drifting

out reluctantly. They all wanted to do something for the captain, but there just wasn't anything to be done at the moment that wasn't already being handled. That time would come later, when he recovered.

"I'm going to head back to his house and help Chris finish cleaning," Laura said to Shane. "Let me know if anything changes."

"Will do."

Suddenly she found herself enveloped in a hug from the handsome detective, followed by Tonio and Taylor, which was nice. Really nice. In her line of work, she didn't often get the chance to bond with people. She wished it hadn't taken several tragedies to bring her closer to these wonderful guys.

Once back at Austin's house, she knocked on the newly repaired door. It opened after a few seconds and Chris let her in with a half smile.

"You sure you want to help me tackle this?"

"Absolutely. Where should I start?" She noted that he'd made progress on the living room. Bags of trash were bundled and sitting around the room, and he'd started dusting the furniture.

"The kitchen. Believe me, you'll be sorry you volunteered." Chris paused, grabbed his dust rag and the can of furniture polish. "Shane called. He said Austin's in rough shape."

"Yeah. He's critical."

Chris stilled, staring into space. "I never should've let him talk us into leaving. I shouldn't have left him alone."

"Hey, you didn't know this would happen," she

said, touching his arm. "Nobody did. He's normally such a strong man, but it leveled him, losing his family that way, especially the baby."

The detective shook himself from his gloom. "I know. All we can do now is make sure this place is welcoming when he gets back. Say, maybe you could give it a woman's touch? Sure looks like it could use some sprucing up."

Arching a brow, she put a hand on her hip. "Do I look like I spend my days decorating?"

"Oh, well, I—I didn't mean to sound sexist or anything—"

"Relax. I was just teasing." She winked. "Some flowers or something would be nice. Maybe a rug or three, and some pictures."

"Yeah," he said, clearly relieved. "Thanks."

Working together, they threw themselves into making Austin's home a space he could relax in, rather than a prison.

She just hoped with all her heart that he'd get to see it.

Consciousness returned slowly.

At first he wasn't sure where he was. Whether he was dead or simply drifting in some nebulous fog of alternate reality. But when he heard familiar voices talking, discussing his situation, heard his mother crying, he knew.

And he was ashamed.

Even though he couldn't move a muscle, or speak, he was aware enough to realize he'd been in real trouble. He'd caused the people he loved the most to feel pain, and that was something he would never wish to inflict on anyone.

"Austin? Baby, wake up, please," his mother entreated.

If he could've managed a smile, he would have. Forty-two and his mother still called him *baby*. His dad said something, and their voices faded in and out for a while. He drifted, dozing, and the next time he surfaced, he put more effort into opening his eyes.

At last he managed to crack them a bit, blinking against the sunlight in the room. God, his head was pounding. When his vision focused, he saw his dad sitting in a chair, staring at the silent television on the wall. Next to him, his mom was flipping through a magazine, not really reading it.

"Hey," he croaked. Both of his parents started and the joy on their faces, not to mention the exhaustion, tore at Austin's soul. Rushing over, his mom took his hand and peppered his face with kisses, smoothed back his hair.

"Oh, honey, we were so worried. Thank God you're awake."

She started to cry, and he awkwardly patted her back, though the IV and bandage on his arm restricted his movement. "I'm okay, Mom."

"You almost died, Austin." Pulling back, she gazed at him, tears running down her still pretty face. "This is the second time in less than a year we've almost lost you. My heart can't take any more of this."

Guilt nearly ripped him in half. "I'm sorry. I didn't mean for this to happen."

His dad scooted up his mom's chair for her, urging her to sit. Then he moved his own seat closer and put his hand on Austin's shoulder. "We know you didn't, son. Losing Ashley and the baby like that, it was too much. Hell, it would be too much for any man to handle, and we never should've left. Not so soon, anyhow."

He shook his head, and regretted it. The room spun for a few seconds and he waited for things to settle before answering. "No. I should've been stronger. I never should've let a drop of booze touch my lips when I was so raw and grieving. Once I started, I couldn't seem to stop."

His mom's lip quivered. "So you didn't mean to hurt yourself?"

"No," he said firmly. "No way. I'm *not* suicidal. I'm grieving, maybe even depressed, but I don't want to die. I want to find the scum who killed Ashley and my son and put him away for good."

His dad peered deep into his eyes for several long moments, and finally nodded in satisfaction. "I believe you, and I believe *in* you. You've got a whole lot of friends who do as well."

Austin swallowed hard. "Everyone knows?"

"Pretty much. Your buddies at the station have circled the wagons, refused to give a statement to the media on your personal situation. A couple of them even cleaned your house."

Shame warred with gratitude. Right now it was a draw as to which feeling was stronger. "I'll thank them when I get out of here."

"Oh, they're not going to wait that long to see you, trust me." His dad's mouth curved upward in a small smile. "They don't want any thanks, though—just for you to get better."

"A woman has come by a couple of times hoping to see you," his mother said, studying him closely. "Striking lady, long dark hair. Says her name is Laura."

Ah. A fishing expedition. He gave his mom a smile. "Laura Eden. Our paths cross through work, and she's a friend of sorts."

"Really? I like her. She's very nice."

"Yes, she is." He didn't want to give his mom more fuel, and really there wasn't more to tell. Except Laura's job, and he might as well be straight with them. "She's the medical examiner who works out of Nashville. Her office covers our county because we don't have one of our own."

It didn't take long for them to put two and two together. His dad spoke first. "So she's working with your detectives on trying to catch who killed Ashley and the baby?"

"Yes, as well as another case we have." He was *not* going to mention the auburn-haired victim from the other day—the one with the note that was likely addressed to Austin himself.

"I hope she helps to catch that animal," his mom spat. Then she stopped, took a deep, calming breath. "I'm sorry. You don't need to think about anything but getting better. I'm glad she's a friend."

"She is." Just then there was a knock on the door.

Austin sat up a bit, half expecting the visitor to be the subject of their conversation. So he was more than a little disappointed to see the chief walk into the room.

"Austin, it's good to see you awake." Glenn strolled over to the bed, held out his hand.

Austin shook the offered hand as best as he could. "Thanks."

His mom kissed his cheek and stood. "We're going to head out for a while, find a bite to eat. See you later, honey. Love you."

"Love you, too, Mom."

After clapping his shoulder, his dad followed her out. Austin watched them go, dreading this talk. He wished they had sent the chief away, anything to put off what he sensed was coming. Then again, might as well get it over with.

"How are you feeling?" Glenn asked.

"Go ahead and say what you came here to say," he snapped. "Don't insult my intelligence by beating around the bush."

Glenn stared at him, looking hurt. "Don't insult me by implying I don't care. I may be your boss, but we're friends and I have a great deal of respect for you."

That took the wind out of his sails and he sank into the pillows, closing his eyes. When he opened them again, the chief was simply waiting. "My apologies. I didn't mean to disrespect you, I'm just on edge."

"Anyone would be, after what you've been through." Glenn paused, face filled with sympathy. "Austin, you need time off."

"I knew that was coming. Especially after this," he said, indicating his current predicament.

"Yeah. I was going to suggest it anyway, with what happened to your family. And with you being too close to the case, there's just no way I can allow you to work it."

Officially. Unofficially, the chief wasn't going to stop him. Nobody would.

"Sure, I get it." *Say all the right things and he'll go away.*

"Take a month off and we'll reevaluate, see how you feel—"

"A *month*? I was thinking a couple of weeks." A ball of dread began to form in the pit of his stomach.

"Four. Get your head together—you've been through a lot."

"Is that an order?"

"If you want to put it that way, yes."

"What else is going on here, Glenn? The truth."

Sitting back in his chair, the chief met his gaze without flinching. "You're not an official suspect in Ashley's murder, but there's some circumstantial evidence that makes you someone we need to rule out."

Knowing that didn't make it easier to hear, and the dread became an iron weight around his neck. "What kind of evidence?"

"There was a hair found on your wife's body that DNA will probably show belongs to you. But hell, you lived in that house with her for years, so your DNA is all over that place."

"What else?"

"Your belt was used to strangle her," Glenn said grimly. "There were a couple of fingerprints on it. One of them matched your right index finger. However, it wasn't in the right hand position for the action of strangling her."

He wanted to be sick. "And the other print?"

"Unknown. That's the one we believe actually belongs to the assailant, but we need a damn suspect." Glenn paused. "You want to do something useful, come up with a list of anyone who might hold a grudge against you. Someone you've put away in the last few years who just got out of the joint is a good place to start."

A bitter laugh escaped Austin's throat. "That'll take some time."

"Well, you've got plenty."

Austin glared at his boss, to no effect. "How much of my vacation has to do with the department saving face with the press?"

Glenn sighed. "I'm not going to lie—they somehow got wind of your breakdown, or whatever, and the speculation is rampant. They're straddling the line between accusing you of Ashley's murder and your being a victim. You know how horrible the media has been toward cops lately, and this is a potential disaster."

"I'm innocent, Glenn," he stated, anger boiling under his skin. "You know that."

"I do. We just need to let this die down before it takes on a life of its own and you end up being tried and convicted on the ten o'clock news. Okay?"

"I hear you."

Fuck! More than twenty years as a cop, and now

someone was trying to destroy his life. He wasn't going to give the murdering bastard more rope to hang him.

"I'm behind you all the way," Glenn said, standing. "I'm glad you're all right. Get some rest and we'll talk soon."

"Thanks, Chief."

Frustrated, he watched his boss walk out the door. For a while he fumed, unable to do anything else. Then he got tired and slept for a while, and when he awoke, the sunlight had dimmed into afternoon. Stretching, he tried to clear the fog from his brain. His head didn't hurt as bad as before, and he decided he was mending, no thanks to his own stupidity.

"It's good to see you awake," a soft feminine voice said.

Turning his head, he smiled. Laura was sitting by his bed, looking like an oasis for a man who'd been lost in the desert for months. Her dark hair was loose around her shoulders, and she wore a pink V-neck T-shirt that hugged her breasts. Her long legs were encased in a pair of dark jeans.

"You look pretty," he told her. "I don't think I've ever seen you in street clothes."

She looked pleased at the compliment. "Thank you. You're looking better than you did last time I saw you, for sure."

"When did you see me?"

"I found you at home. Well, Shane, Chris, and I did," she amended.

The hits kept coming. He looked away from her and

cleared his throat. "I'm sorry you had to see me like that. I'm ashamed," he admitted.

Cupping his face, she made him look at her again. "No, none of that. How about you look forward from here on out? Think about what you *can* change instead of what you can't."

"You make it sound so easy." He found himself leaning into her touch. Her hand on his cheek felt so warm and welcoming. Much like the look in her eyes.

"It won't be, but taking control of your life again will be worth it. Believe me."

"You know something about that?"

"Just a little." Taking his hand, she lowered it to the bed, but didn't let go. "That's a story for another time."

He let it slide, for now. "Taking control sounds good. I've got plenty of time to get started, since the chief placed me on leave."

She winced. "Yeah, I kind of saw that coming."

"I did, too, but it stings." Questions burned in his gut, and as he stared at her, they wouldn't be denied. "I want you to give me your professional assessment of Ashley's murder."

"Austin, I don't think now is the time—"

"I need for you to tell me," he said quietly. "Please."

He'd never seen Laura struggle over discussing such things, but this situation was vastly, terribly different. He was asking as a friend, not a colleague. She hesitated, visibly torn between the truth and not wanting to hurt him more than he already had been.

"You already know she was strangled with a belt," she finally said.

"One of mine."

"Yes. Did they tell you about the two prints on it?" When he nodded, she went on. "The one that didn't match yours was in the correct position to commit the murder."

"Glenn didn't mention that, just that we don't know who the print belongs to yet."

"He might not have known. That will definitely help take the heat off you."

"Innocent until proven guilty. Right." He couldn't keep the bitterness from his tone.

"I agree it's not fair to have to prove it, but you *are* innocent. The evidence will bear that out, because there's more. The tissue under Ashley's fingernails belongs to a Caucasian, and I'm going to guess a male because of the sheer strength needed to kill in this way. It's actually very difficult to strangle a person."

Austin swallowed hard. "So she fought, scratched the hell out of somebody."

"Yes. You get a suspect and you're going to have him cold with the evidence."

"That's the problem, isn't it? Finding the monster who did this." Tears pricked his eyes and he shook his head. "We didn't have a very good relationship toward the end, but I never wanted anything bad to happen to her. Ever."

"I know, sweetie."

"She didn't even want our baby. Did you know that?"

Her eyes were pools of hurt—for him. "No, I didn't."

"The pregnancy was one of those surprises that happens after things get out of control. We got together one more time after I was almost killed a few months ago, but we knew it wasn't going to work. I was so happy about the baby, but she wasn't at *all*."

Laura frowned. "But she fought you for custody anyway?"

"Yeah. Because she could, and the courts favor the mothers. I don't like to speak ill of her, especially now, but she was pretty hateful. She wanted to put the screws to me."

"Then it's a good thing the evidence is steering the blame away from you—otherwise you'd have motive."

He shook his head. "I would never harm my son."

"I know that and so do your friends, but not everyone would be convinced. That won't be an issue, though. Facts are facts, and someone else did the crime."

"And what if you didn't have all the facts? What would your gut tell you about me?"

Her lips curved up. "You're a good man, Captain. I trust you completely."

He wasn't sure how good a man he was, but he knew one thing: he wanted to keep Laura around, get to know her much better.

Convincing his parents to go home this time had been twice the job it had been before.

Austin watched his dad pull out of the driveway, and waved at his teary mom until they disappeared around the corner. Then he went back inside.

Now it was just Shane, Danny, and himself. The duo had arrived together, right after his folks had gotten him home. Honestly, it had been sort of a relief because his friends had kept the mood light, and in turn had kept Austin's mom from coming unglued. Their visit had gone a long way to reassure his folks that there wouldn't be a repeat of Austin's breakdown.

Austin had done his best to reassure them of that, too.

"My son had his life taken from him before he got a chance to live," he'd told them. "Who am I to throw mine away? Trust me, please. I won't let you down again."

They had finally believed him. Now he had to make good on his promise.

"This place looks good," Austin said to his friends, indicating the spotless living room. "It hasn't been this clean since I moved in. And which one of you is the decorator? I didn't know you guys had the flair."

There were several accent rugs lying about, as well as framed pictures someone had dug out of the albums that had been in storage boxes. Some were of his parents, some of his older brother who'd been killed in Desert Storm. There were even a couple of accent lamps on the side tables.

Shane smiled. "Um, you know damn well none of us have a decorative bone in our bodies."

"Who did it, then?"

"Laura. She helped Chris whip this place into shape."

"Wow, that was nice of her." Warmth stole over him, settled in his gut. He liked how it made him feel that she'd been here, trying to make things better for him.

Danny and Shane smirked at each other, then at him.

Danny spoke up. "Something going on there we need to know about?"

"No. Not that it's any of your business."

"But you'd like for there to be," Shane said, grinning.

"You know, you may have tenure but I can still bust your ass back to investigating stolen bikes."

"Not at the moment, you can't."

"Watch me. The second I'm back on duty, you're in trouble."

"Whatever you say, Cap."

All around him was evidence that he was a lucky man. He had to remember that.

He couldn't allow his grief to keep him from living— or from putting a killer behind bars.

Austin nursed his second tonic—he wasn't sure when he'd ever want so much as a beer again—and shifted on the barstool, glancing around at the crowd.

The Waterin' Hole was packed tonight. People were playing pool, laughing, and talking. Taylor's girlfriend, Cara Evans, was setting up with her band, getting ready to play. They were a crowd favorite. Austin glanced around and didn't see Taylor, but he figured the man would show at some point.

Austin hadn't spoken with Laura in a couple of days, since his release from the hospital, and that bugged him, more than it should. His need to go slow with her was in direct odds with the desire to pick up the pace. Should he make the first call? Something told him she wasn't that old-fashioned—if she wanted to talk to him, she'd call.

Or maybe not. Hell if he knew what to do.

What was the oh-so-sweet Miss Eden up to right now? Was she on a date? Had he kissed her? Taken her home? Fuck.

"Hey, man. You gonna drink that tonic or what?"

Austin met the bartender's gaze. The man frowned at him, slung a hand towel over his shoulder, and braced his hands on the counter. The position caused his ripped biceps to bulge underneath his T-shirt, emphasizing his buff physique. The type of dude who was a magnet for anything female with a pulse, he'd bet *lonely* wasn't part of this guy's vocabulary.

"Yeah. What's your name?"

"Chandler," the man said, giving him a half smile.

"Well, Chandler, it's just been a long damn week." He rubbed his temples.

"Being an instant local celebrity doesn't agree with ya, huh? I saw the article in the paper, man. Sorry." The bartender waved a hand at the crowd. "Maybe what you need is some female company to cheer you up. There's several giving you the eyeball as we speak. Take that *Penthouse* beauty over there. She's practically burnin' a hole in your back, not that you'd ever notice." He waggled his dark brows and nodded to a table off in a corner.

Austin sighed. He wasn't in the mood to play tonight. Unless—what if Laura had shown up? Did she even know he came here? The lady was resourceful, so she'd have no trouble finding him.

The prospect of seeing her again appealed to him a great deal. His morose mood forgotten, he swung his gaze to the spot Chandler indicated. Instead of Laura, a voluptuous blonde bombshell a few tables away flashed him a welcoming smile and a generous amount of cleavage in her low-cut black dress.

Her smile deepened, revealing an alluring dimple at one corner of her generous mouth. Eyes never leaving his, she tilted a glass of white wine, wrapping it in slender fingers tipped with bloodred nails. She took a small sip, then licked an imaginary drop from her bottom lip, flicking it with a quick dart of her pink tongue. Message sent and received. His for the asking, and the bold invitation failed to stir his desire.

Christ, really? Compared with Laura, the woman was about as appealing as a wilted salad would be next to a filet mignon.

Because it seemed rude not to acknowledge the lady, he gave her a tight, polite smile—one clearly communicating, *No, thanks*—before turning around again.

As he did, he suddenly had the strangest feeling he was being watched. His gaze slid to a shadowy corner, but there was only Chandler clearing empty glasses off a table. The man barely glanced at him, then went back to his task. Still, a shiver danced along Austin's skin.

Must've been his imagination. The murders and what he'd been through had shifted his world slightly off its axis. Knocked him out of his groove. Everything would fall back into place tomorrow, after a good night's sleep. Dismissing the strange feeling, he turned his attention back to the bar as a startling realization punched him in the gut.

Finding the blonde, instead of Laura, smiling at him

had sent his spirits plummeting. He was more than ready to leave.

Chandler returned, took away his empty glass. "So? You gonna get a piece of that or what?"

"Nah. Too expensive. She's a Mercedes, I'm a Ford. Wouldn't work."

Chandler rolled his eyes. "Whatever."

"I'm a Mustang," a flirtatious voice said from next to Austin. "Plenty of speed and more bang for your buck. Will that rev your engine?"

Austin turned to see a twentysomething man with dark hair and big brown eyes grinning at him. The man was shorter than Austin, and slender. Something about the guy seemed familiar, but he couldn't place him. "Sorry, pal, but you're barking up the wrong tree. Or shopping at the wrong dealership, so to speak."

"Damn. All the good ones are taken or straight." The man actually pouted.

Just then Austin figured out where he knew him from. "Hey, I know you."

"You do?" The guy peered at him curiously, then grinned. "Hey! I hooked up your cable in your house! You're a cop or something, right?"

"Yeah, Sugarland PD." He held out his hand. "Austin Rainey. Good to see you again."

"Frankie Blair. You, too." They shook and Frankie eyed him closely. Austin could almost see the wheels turning in the man's head, and thought he saw a spark of something else in the man's eyes. But if Frankie recognized him from the recent tragic events that had made the news, the younger man was classy enough not to mention it.

"So, how's the cable business?" Austin asked. He didn't really care, but wanted to be polite.

The other man made a face. "That's not really what I'm going to do with the rest of my life. I'm in school for graphic design."

"Oh?"

"Yeah," Frankie said with enthusiasm. "I graduate at the end of May. Got a line on a job already from a friend of a friend."

"Hey, that's great. Congrats." He smiled, and Frankie returned it. Frankie was a likable guy, and Austin didn't mind the company.

"Thanks."

Frankie started to say something else, but a hand on Austin's shoulder interrupted their conversation. He swung his head around to find himself looking directly into the blonde's smoldering gaze. Lips tilted up, she eyed him from head to toe as though contemplating how he'd taste smothered in chocolate syrup and whipped cream. He must have been putting out some serious pheromones tonight. Or he looked as pathetically lonely and desperate for company as he felt. Jesus.

"Hello," the woman purred. "I'm Stacy. I couldn't help but notice that you're all by yourself."

Now she had a name. Super. "Well, actually, I was just talking to my friend here—"

"Buy a girl a drink?"

Hell. Austin glanced at Chandler and Frankie to see

them struggling to hide a smirk. His headache returned, pounding behind his eyeballs.

"Sure," he muttered, waving at the bartender. The
irony of the moment didn't escape him. If he'd located
his balls, he could've been buying a drink for Laura
right now.

Stacy was tall and busty. Her scrap of a dress barely
hid her nipples, whereas Laura always dressed in sleek
classy suits. This woman's hazel eyes were sharp, pred-
atory. Even cold. Not warm with intelligence like—

"Why don't we cut to the chase, honey?" Dropping
the preliminaries, she leaned against him, rubbing the
side of his body, arching like a cat. "Let's take this party
somewhere else, shall we?"

Chandler set a glass of wine in front of Austin's determined pursuer, shaking his head, then sauntered off.

Austin strove to maintain politeness. "Sorry, sugar. No
can do. I'm not in the mood, but thanks anyway. Enjoy
your wine."

Surprise flitted across her painted-doll face. But she
wasn't ready to give up. She laid a hand on his thigh,
sliding her fingers upward. There was no reaction from
his cock whatsoever. All he felt was disgust.

With a ripe curse, he bolted to his feet, grabbed his
tormentor's arms, and detached her. "I said *no, thank
you*. But I'm sure a pretty lady like you can find another
date." With Laura's beautiful image haunting him, he'd
nearly choked on calling this tramp a "lady."

Austin let out a huge sigh of relief as Stacy snatched
her purse and stalked off without even touching her
drink.

"Jeez, some people just don't know how to take no for an answer," Frankie said with a grimace.

Austin laughed. "Well, at least you do."

"I'm used to it, believe me."

"Now I don't buy that for a second. Me, I just don't swing your way, that's all."

"Poor pitiful me."

Austin shook his head, grinning. "And on that note, I'm out of here," he told Frankie. Digging out his wallet, he tossed down enough money for the drinks and a tip. "See you around."

"Sure thing. Take care."

"Same goes."

All the way home, Austin replayed the evening in his mind.

Something was bothering him. Something Frankie had said earlier, but he couldn't remember what. And for the life of him, he was too tired to think about it anymore.

Check out that asshole. How does he get women coming on to him? What makes that fucker so special?

The blond slut in the black dress wanted to take him home, but the cocky SOB had turned her away. Who does that?

Eyes narrowed, Douglas watched as the slut made her way to the bar with determination. Anger simmered as the bitch seated herself on a newly vacated stool on one side of the cop. The woman touched Rainey's shoulder, interrupting his conversation with the familiar dark-haired man. Leaned into him, smiling, rubbing her breasts against his arm. Sliding her hand to his crotch.

Ugly rage crushed his chest. For a few moments he couldn't breathe, couldn't think past the crimson haze. Blackness consumed his soul, choking his breath with the force of it.

Rainey didn't deserve the pleasure.

Not when I've been denied, and it's all his fault.

Then Rainey put his hands on the slut's shoulders and set her firmly away.

The wild cacophony in his head abated somewhat. Still, he'd have to teach the cop another lesson. He clearly hadn't learned well enough the first two times.

Cheeks flaming at his rejection, the blond slut clutched her fussy little purse and made for the exit, head down.

He couldn't leave right away, but he knew how and where to find her.

Calling it a night at last, he followed unnoticed through the sea of revelers.

Austin peeled off his clothes and slid naked between the crisp cotton sheets with a satisfied groan. Oh yeah, it felt nice to stretch out on his back. Sink into the soft king-sized mattress and let his bones melt. God, what a shitty couple of days it had been.

But the day can always get worse, he reminded himself.

The chirp of the cell phone on his nightstand jerked him from the pleasant fog of near sleep. Propping himself on one elbow, he peered at the caller ID. *BLOCKED*

NUMBER. For two seconds, he considered letting it go to voice mail. But in his line of work, the caller might be any number of people.

Son of a bitch, this better be important. He snatched the phone, imagining it was the caller's throat. "Hello?"

A low male voice sent a shiver down his spine. "I took care of her, the dumb bitch. She learned her lesson about getting near the likes of you."

"What?" He blinked in confusion. "I'm sorry. You must have the wrong number."

"Oh, I have the right number, Captain Rainey." A low laugh sounded from the other end. "I had to make my point, because you're just not getting it."

Cold fingers curled around his heart and squeezed. Austin sat up, the sheets falling to his hips. "Who the hell is this? *What* point?"

The voice tightened, became more clipped. "You ruined my life, and now I'm going to ruin yours."

He searched the shadows of his bedroom, the shrinking steel band constricting his lungs. "How did I ruin your life?"

The caller ignored the question. "I'm going to punish you until you can't take any more. Then I'm going to end you."

"Did you kill Matt Blankenship? My wife and son? Because I swear to God—"

"Sweet dreams, Rainey. I'm gonna sleep like a baby."

The line went dead.

Austin's thoughts shattered and he stared into nothingness. Blank with shock, unable to react. Phone in hand, he sat motionless, heart slamming in his chest.

Long after he should've called Glenn, Danny, and his detectives.

Long after the revelation froze his blood in horror, and he began to shake.

"Oh my God," he whispered, closing his eyes. "Oh God."

The monster on the phone had killed his family.

And his reign of terror had just begun.

4

Austin strode through the station, fielding the expected greetings from officers and other staff members who hadn't seen him since his major fuckup followed by the hospital stay.

It was humbling to say the least. He was not in the best of moods when he arrived at Glenn's office, shutting the door behind him. Danny was already there and the two men studied him in concern.

Danny frowned. "Jesus, you look terrible."

Austin snarled a curse and dropped into a chair next to his friend. He ran a hand down his face, drawn and haggard from little sleep. His knew his eyes were bloodshot and tired.

"The tap is in place on my phones, both here and at home," Austin announced. "For all the good it will do."

The chief leaned forward, all traces of his earlier humor vanished. "Do you have any idea at all how in the hell you picked up a stalker? Think back months, years. A strange case, or an altercation with one of your arrests that might not have seemed important at the time. Anything."

He shook his head. "All he said was that I ruined his life, and now he's going to ruin mine. I have no idea who he could be."

"Austin," Danny said gently. "What about Ashley? Could the caller have ties to her?"

He stared at the lieutenant. "What do you mean?"

"Do you think maybe she was seeing someone? Maybe she was having an affair and he blames you for ruining things when she got pregnant with your child?"

Those words hit his gut as though Danny had struck him. "No. Ashley wasn't seeing anyone," he insisted. "She's a *victim*. She's got nothing to do with this other than being used to punish me."

"All I'm suggesting is another angle. It's possible—"

"No!" Austin took a deep breath. "I know where you're going and I'm telling you to forget it. I won't accept that."

Glenn held up a hand. "All right. We'll table that discussion for now."

Austin let it drop, but figured Danny would still check out his theory. A good investigator never left any loose ends once a question was raised and Austin couldn't fault him for that. But he was also just as certain that road would go nowhere.

Glenn rose from his chair and skirted his desk, perching one hip on the corner, hands clasped in front of him. Sympathy warmed his gaze.

"Austin," Byrne began carefully. "You're a good cop and a terrific investigator. You know it's typical for a killer to stalk the object of his rage for years before giving in to the need to act on his fantasy. Given the nature and timing of your wife's murder, along with Blankenship's, the phone call? We can't ignore the fact that he's connected to you somehow."

"Yeah, I know. It's all we've got right now." Austin looked away, shaking his head. "God knows I keep searching for answers until I think I'll lose my mind. I've started looking at my past cases again, adding to the list of which criminals might've held a serious enough grudge against me to actually follow through with killing. But the idea that Ashley and my child were murdered because of me . . ."

He couldn't imagine anything more horrible and doubted he ever would. The pain was still so raw and consuming. Austin had fallen into a black pit in the weeks following Ashley's funeral. Now that he'd managed to start pulling himself together, he was determined to make her murderer pay for taking her life, and their child's.

"I know how you feel, but I *have* to look into Ashley's personal life and double-check for any connection to the Blankenship murder or her killer," Danny said quietly. "In fact, I already started."

A protest hovered on Austin's lips and he struggled with the suggestion, even though it was necessary. "I hate the fuck out of this."

"It has to be ruled out. Let Danny continue to handle it," Glenn urged. "If a connection exists, he'll find it. If not, there's no reason to put yourself through the pain."

Austin ran a hand through his hair, causing the auburn strands to poke in every direction. "All right. Thanks."

Glenn hesitated. "There's something else. I know you're still technically on leave, but I'm also not stupid enough to think you're going to back off from this case no matter what I say."

"Even if you threatened to fire me, I couldn't walk away from this."

"Exactly, but I don't want you to fuck up because you lost your objectivity."

"I won't. For God's sake, you know me better than that," Austin said, reining in his anger. "I'm not a maverick, and Danny and my detectives are with me every step of the way."

Glenn pinched the bridge of his nose with a heavy sigh. "This is much more serious than the shit I'll get from the mayor if he finds out one of my men is trying to track his own stalker. You fuck this up, you're *dead*."

"If someone else fucks this up, I'm dead anyway," Austin countered, not giving an inch. "I'd rather die because of my own stupidity, thank you very much."

"Christ," Glenn muttered. "I must be out of my mind. I'm rescinding your leave, effective immediately. If you're ready to return, that is. Believe me, there's no rush."

Austin released a pent-up breath. "Yes, I'm more than ready. I appreciate this."

"Well," Danny mused. "The obvious starting place is to establish whether Austin is the killer's next intended victim or if he plans to go for someone else."

Austin shook his head. "On the phone, he made it clear he wants me to pay. He'll go for me eventually, but I believe he'll try for other victims close to me first. He may have already."

"What do you mean?" Danny asked.

"A girl named Stacy tried to pick me up in the Waterin' Hole last night. The man who called me said he'd taught the 'dumb bitch' a lesson about getting near the likes of me. I think he was referring to her."

Danny swore. "Jesus, that means he was there watching you."

He shuddered. "Yeah."

"He's fixated on you," Glenn replied, grim. "You're his endgame."

Austin remained silent for a long moment.

"Then I've got to make sure my face stays in front of the killer."

"What do you have in mind?"

Determination steeled his resolve. "We're going fishing," he revealed. "With yours truly as bait."

Laura wheeled her Mercedes into a visitor's parking space, shouldered her purse, and dashed through the front doors of the police department. The voice message Austin had left on her cell phone this morning had taken her by surprise, to say the least.

He needed to see her, right away. He'd sounded upset, and that made her anxious. The man had suffered enough blows to last a lifetime, and she shuddered to think what else might have happened.

Inside, she was shown to the chief's office. Knocking, she peeked into the room to find Danny standing a few feet away, giving her a puzzled look. Beyond him, Glenn and Austin were seated, apparently surprised to see her as well.

"Laura! Come in. To what do we owe this pleasure?"

Hmm. So the call from Austin had been a personal one. Still, speaking with them about the case couldn't hurt.

Danny ushered her inside and she did a double take at him. When had Coleman become so buff? All that gorgeous dark brown hair and spectacular sea foam green eyes. If Austin didn't occupy every spare thought, she might've noticed before.

"I was just dropping by to see Austin. By the way, you're looking good, Danny," she said sincerely. "Been working out?"

The lieutenant flushed to the roots of his hair. "Ah, some, thanks. Have a seat—" He gestured.

Laura grinned. *What a dear, lovely man.* She glanced at Austin, who was glowering at her, eyes narrowed. Unlike Danny, he looked like he'd been trampled by a herd of elephants. She took the empty chair next to him and gave the captain a tentative smile.

"Can I get you a soda?" Danny offered politely.

"Why, yes—that would be wonderful! I've been running all morning and I'm parched. Something diet and caffeine-free, if you have it?"

"Why bother?" Austin grouched.

"You've got it. Be right back."

Danny gave her a shy smile, and she couldn't help but notice how beautifully it transformed his angular face. Why hadn't some pretty lady gobbled up this man?

"Laura, how are you?" the chief asked warmly.

"I'm doing well, thanks. I just stopped by to see Austin, but it's good to see you, too."

A heavy silence descended while they waited for

Danny to fetch her soda. She scrutinized Austin, taking in his disheveled appearance. He sat upright in the chair, both feet flat on the floor, gripping the armrests so hard his knuckles were white. His face was fraught with tension, eyes haunted. Foreboding knotted her stomach.

Danny returned and she thanked him, taking the chilly can and popping the top. "So, what's going on? I get the distinct impression something else has happened."

Glenn clasped his hands atop the desk, his tone serious. "Something has, and I'll let Austin tell you about that later. You have anything new for us from your office?"

"I wish I did," she said regretfully, casting a glance at Austin. "I have fibers and some prints, but we need a suspect to match them with. The best news to date, though, is that the forensic evidence just doesn't point to Captain Rainey as a viable suspect."

"That's a damn good thing, too. I've just reinstated him." He paused, letting that tidbit sink in.

Laura perked up. "That's great news. Isn't it?"

"It's sooner than I'd planned but it has to do with what's happened," the chief continued. "We're going to have Austin be our media liaison on the case."

Her mouth fell open. "You're kidding me. Not to be rude, but why would you do that? Isn't that dangerous on several levels?"

"We're hoping to keep the killer's focus on me," Austin said. "Seeing my face may goad him into making a move. Plus, as much as I hate the media at times, there's the sympathy factor with the widower demanding justice."

"That's really risky," she protested. "Can't someone else do it?"

"Unfortunately, the spokesman has to be me." His tone was apologetic as he gazed at her. "Otherwise it defeats the whole purpose."

She didn't like this. At all.

Rainey sighed, looking drained. "What we need is a friendly face in the newsroom. Someone who's on our side and will turn the tide of public opinion toward us."

Laura thought about that. "I have a friend who's an anchor for Channel Eight. Her name is Joan Peterson. I've given her statements from the ME's office before, which is how we got to know each other."

"She's a good egg?" the chief asked.

"One of the best. If anyone will give you guys a fair shake and some good airtime, it's Joan. If you want, I'll have her call you."

Glenn nodded, appearing pleased. "That would be great, thank you. But the information doesn't leave this group, including Joan Peterson."

"And my detectives," Austin put in.

Glenn stood, signaling an end to the conversation. Taking the hint, Laura rose as well and said her goodbyes. "I'm sure she'll call you soon, gentlemen. I'll see myself out."

Austin took her arm. "Wait. Can I talk to you for a second?"

"Sure." She gave him a smile, which he returned halfheartedly.

She and Austin exited the office, pulling the door shut on their way out. As he walked with her toward the front of the building, she worried about what was wrong. As they stepped outside and faced each other, he shoved his hands in his pockets.

"Are you busy for lunch?"

Laura studied him. His green eyes were tired and that bothered her more than anything. Sadness lurked in their depths, so immense she could drown in them.

"I don't have any plans. Want me to meet you here?"

He shook his head. "No, not here. I just got here and the walls are already closing in. By lunch I'll be ready to get out of this place for a while before I lose my mind."

"Okay. What time?"

"I'll pick you up at your office around noon, if that's okay."

Her heart did a funny flip. "That's fine. I'll see you then."

Taking a chance, she leaned forward and bussed his cheek. Just the slightest kiss, lingering a bit too long to be strictly friendly, yet not so long as to be inappropriate on the steps of the station with his colleagues around. Pulling back, she felt a little thrill at the dazed expression on his face.

"See you later," she said. Then winked, and walked away.

Noon couldn't come fast enough.

Austin gazed after Laura. Seemed all he did was watch the delectable backside of that woman walk away. But that kiss! *Damn*. His cheek still burned from the sensation of her lips against his skin. He walked to his desk, feeling off-kilter, like a man underwater.

He'd asked Laura to lunch. And she'd accepted. He felt in his soul they wanted to explore the attraction between them, as unwise as it was right now with everything that was going on in his life. Must be the lack of sleep that had lowered his guard. Or perhaps the threat of impending death. Christ.

"If you don't hurry up and make a move, I'm going to ask her to dinner," Danny said, leaning back in his chair, hands clasped behind his head.

Austin frowned, casting about the room for the object of his partner's affections. "Who?"

"Laura, who else?"

"No." The word burst from his lips as he scowled. "You won't."

Danny grinned at him. "Finally getting your head out of your ass? It's about time."

"Maybe. But that's beside the point. A classy professional woman like Laura eats Boy Scouts like you for breakfast."

His friend was unfazed. "You can be a real bastard, Rainey. Just giving you notice: if things don't work out with you two, I'm asking her to dinner. And for the record, Laura Eden can have me for breakfast any day of the week she prefers. If she doesn't, at least I tried."

With great dignity, Danny strode away. His declaration reverberated through Austin's brain.

Freaking fantastic.

He'd made a lunch date with a gorgeous siren, been

challenged for her affections by his good friend, and been marked for death.

And it wasn't even noon yet.

"Son of a bitch."

Laura hovered near Toby Baxter's desk in his cubicle, leaning against the wall. From there, she could see the lobby and the doors beyond. A case of nerves had her stomach performing double back flips as she waited for Austin. Laura had been invited to join the assistant and two other doctors on their lunch hour but had to decline. Knowing the nosy group, she realized they were stalling, scouting for Laura's mysterious lunch date.

Conversation halted as though someone had flipped an off switch. In perfect harmony, all heads swiveled toward the glass double doors of the lobby.

"Wow," Toby said. "Who's the hunka burnin' love?"

"I dunno, but he can eat crackers in my bed anytime. Jeez Louise." A younger doctor smacked her gum harder, no doubt in time to her pulse.

"Forget the crackers," a third chimed in. "Bring on the whipped cream!"

Laura didn't need three guesses to figure out who had raised the room temperature. Sure enough, Austin was crossing the lobby with long strides. He'd donned a jacket with his dark jeans and wore his light blue button-up shirt open at the throat. The butt of his gun could be seen in its holster underneath his jacket as he strode forward. Ultradark sunglasses completed the ensemble, framed by tousled auburn hair.

He looked totally manly, sexy, and he was here for her.

He strode straight to Laura, ignoring the open stares of his admirers. "Ready to go, sweetheart?"

Laura blinked up at him, warmed to her toes by the endearment he'd used in front of everyone. "Sure."

"Laura, sweetie, I'd skip the main course and go straight for dessert," Toby quipped. The women dissolved into giggles.

She rolled her eyes and spun on her heel as Austin fell into step beside her, grinning. "Sorry about that. We don't exactly get a lot of excitement around here."

"In a morgue?" he drawled. "You don't say."

She was immensely glad there wasn't too much awkwardness about her job that might come between them. "Right? It's not exactly a hotbed of fun in this place." She waggled her brows, making him laugh. The deep, rich timbre rumbling from his chest made her ache, and intensified the longing she'd been fighting forever.

They walked out together, his hand coming to rest at the small of her back, gently guiding. Every nerve ending sizzled with awareness, and she stifled a sigh, allowing herself to bask in his touch, the wonderful spicy scent of him, the closeness of his warmth at her side.

She told herself not to get her hopes up. Austin simply needed her help, and he had something vitally important to discuss at lunch. Now that Rainey had been forced into a position of constant contact with her because of this case, he was doing his job. Because she'd supported him when he went off the deep end, they had a friendship as well. Perhaps that was all it would be.

He opened the passenger door of his truck for her, offering a hand to help her in. She took it, glancing at him, electrified by the contact and the strength of his fingers swallowing hers.

"Thank you," she managed, easing onto the seat.

His lips hitched up in a faint smile and he shrugged. "I'm so used to jumping in, I'd forgotten this monster isn't a low-slung Mercedes. Besides, I didn't want you to mess up your pretty suit."

Austin released her and shut the door, then trotted around to his side. He climbed in and they were on their way. Carefully, he merged into the heavy noon traffic.

"Any preferences for lunch?" he inquired, keeping his attention on the road.

"Nothing too heavy, or I'll fall asleep at my desk this afternoon."

"Okay. I know just the place on Preston Road," he said, nodding. "Salads, sandwiches, and stuff. It has a patio area outside, decorated like a garden. We can sit out there and talk, if that sounds okay with you."

Laura couldn't contain herself one second longer. In spite of the grand entrance he'd made in the lobby, the stress still rolled off him in waves. "Are you going to tell me what's wrong now?"

"It's that obvious, huh?" He sounded tired. Sad.

"Very," she assured him.

A long, long silence.

"I'm sorry about dragging you into my crap."

Although she couldn't see his eyes behind the dark sunglasses, his mouth was set in a grim line.

"Why would you say that? I'm right where I want to be."

"You don't want to run? If you did, I wouldn't blame you."

"I wouldn't do that, or even want to. I want to help you solve this and get on with your life. Everybody wins."

"Everybody except the people who've been murdered." He let out a weary breath, but offered no censure.

Mortified at her blunder, Laura stared blindly out the window. How could she have forgotten the victims, the real reason she got dressed and went to work every day? His wife and child? Maybe she'd grown callous in her career, having seen too much.

Then she thought of her estranged older brother, Grayson, and the churning self-doubt eased. No, she'd never forget the family tragedy that had shaped her career path. Her burning desire to help others escape horror and, if possible, find solace.

Austin shut off the ignition. "Here we are."

He led her inside the small, trendy restaurant and gave the hostess his name. Immediately, they were escorted outside to a table in a quiet, shady corner of the garden. The place was packed, and Laura knew he'd had this planned all along and must've called ahead. Otherwise, they couldn't have secured such a great spot on a beautiful spring day during the lunch rush. Once more, his thoughtfulness confounded her.

A cute blond waitress, who couldn't have been a day over twenty, handed them menus, giving Austin a serious once-over and a huge smile. He never spared the girl a glance. Deflated, she took their drink order and disappeared.

Austin removed his sunglasses and tucked them into his jacket, rubbing his face. Resting his elbows on the table, he returned Laura's gaze, his handsome face the picture of exhaustion, eyes troubled. Sparring with her wasn't on the agenda. Whatever was going on had shaken him badly.

"Before whatever is developing between us continues, and I start doing the news segments with your contact, there's something you need to know." He paused, trying to find the right words. "You're putting yourself at great risk just being around me. In fact, I'm having second thoughts about it."

"Oh no you don't," she interjected, holding up a hand. "I should've known where you were going. I'm a big girl and you're not getting rid of me so easily."

Instead of getting angry, his voice softened. "I'm not jerking you around, sugar. When I do the news spot, the extra exposure will put you in more danger than you are now."

"I'm already in the public eye," she countered. "I'm in the news every time there's a big case involving a death. There's always an inherent risk— Austin, what's wrong?"

He looked away, his expression wretched. "Off the record. What I'm about to tell you stays between us. I mean, my team and my boss know, but nobody on the outside."

Her heart seized. "Of course. You're scaring me."

"Last night, some new evidence came to light involving the murders. We know why the victims are connected. Now we just have to find the culprit to prove it."

She nodded. "But that's a major break! Why so grim?"

"Because the killer's teaching me a lesson," he said quietly.

"What?" The truth sank in slowly, horror seeping through her veins like poison. This was what she'd been afraid of all along. "He's stalking you."

"Yes. Jesus." He closed his eyes.

"No—" Laura gasped. She cast about for an explanation. *Anything but this.* "How do you know for sure? Maybe there's some mistake."

The waitress brought their drinks. They ordered grilled-chicken salads, though Laura suspected neither of them had much of an appetite. Austin waited until the waitress moved away before continuing.

"I spent some time at the Waterin' Hole last night, and this girl tried to pick me up. I declined and she left, alone."

As much as it infuriated her to think of some woman hitting on him, it made her feel good that he'd turned her down. If he said it was true, she believed him.

He took a deep breath, continuing. "Anyway, after I got home, the killer called me. He'd been watching me. Said the girl had been taught a lesson about hanging around with the likes of me. I think he might've done something terrible to her."

"Oh no. That's horrible." Her appetite fled.

"Yeah. He ended with basically threatening to kill me when he's done fucking up my life."

Her mind reeled. "You think he's going to come after you."

"Eventually. I'm hoping the news segments will

keep his attention focused on me, rather than on taking another innocent life."

"This is what pushed you into dangling yourself as bait." She placed her hand over his. "Please don't do this. It's too dangerous."

Taking her hand in his, he studied her from under long lashes. "The killer is going to make a move on me. I can't change that, but I can try to push him into acting sooner, maybe even making a mistake. The problem is, I don't want you caught in the cross fire. Just being near me—let alone working with me—could cause him to turn his attention to you. If you got hurt, I couldn't live with that."

Laura gaped at him, stunned. He'd just learned his life was in danger, yet his concern wasn't all for himself. He was worried about her. She fumbled to gather her scattered wits.

"I'm not going to get hurt. If you insist on doing the news, Joan won't mention my name as medical examiner on the case and she'll make sure we don't appear together on camera. This should disassociate me from you personally. Will that help alleviate your concern?"

"That helps. I still think you should stay away from me, though."

"I don't care." She squeezed his hand. "Is there any way I can talk you out of doing this? If the killer guesses what you're doing—"

"Even if he does, his twisted mind will turn it around and consider it a challenge." He shook his head. "I don't have a choice, Laura. I have to do this."

The idea of Austin baiting a maniac filled her with dread. "When?"

"This afternoon, if possible."

Every instinct screamed against Austin's plan, but if she didn't help, he'd enlist someone else. *No way in hell*.

"When we leave here, I'll call Joan and see if she can meet us in front of your building in a couple of hours. That should give you time to rehearse what you want to say. You light a fire under your killer and she gets a scoop. Then you can go on your way and forget all about me."

His lips twitched. "Fat chance. Not a damn thing about you is forgettable, lady."

And then he smiled. A big, beautiful, full-fledged smile that stole the oxygen from her lungs. French-fried her brain cells. Drove her blood pressure into stroke territory.

Speech deserted her, rescuing her from uttering something stupid. She smiled back uncertainly, giving silent thanks when their salads arrived. Not particularly hungry, she dug in, grateful to have something else to focus on besides the sexy contradiction across the table.

Between bites, Austin watched her intently, a question in his gaze. He held his silence as they ate, his open perusal making her squirm. Determined not to let him unnerve her, she straightened her spine and met his eyes, lowering her fork.

"Spit it out, Rainey. Your thoughts are blasting at me with Dolby sound."

Austin swallowed a bite, hesitated. He chose his words with care. "I know it's none of my business, but would you mind telling me whether you're involved with anyone?"

She stilled. "No, of course not. Do I strike you as the sort of person who'd send out signals that I'm interested in someone if I'm already dating another guy?"

"No," he said. "I just wanted to be sure. And there's Danny to consider. He's planning to ask you out, if I don't get my ass in gear."

"What?" Her tea glass paused halfway to her lips, and she set it down again. "Danny? I had no clue he was interested."

"Are *you* interested?"

Laura studied his fierce scowl. *Why, Austin is jealous!* The idea flooded her with prickly heat . . . and a smidgen of mischief. She smiled, unable to resist goading him.

"Danny's a sweet man. Cute, too. Why wouldn't I want to find out if we're compatible?"

Austin's face darkened. *Oh, that look!* She'd poked a sleeping lion with an electric cattle prod.

"Danny's an innocent kid," he ground out.

"I'd hardly use that term to describe a police lieutenant. I have a feeling the man doesn't get the credit he deserves. Anyway, I'm not interested in Danny, but thanks for the heads-up."

Austin graced her with that slow smile again, and her insides flipped. Then he attacked the remainder of his salad, spearing lettuce and chicken with vicious fervor. He really had been anxious at the idea of her going out with Danny. She felt bad for teasing him.

They polished off their meal, relaxing the rest of the

time with unimportant talk about this and that. The check arrived and Austin snagged it, refusing to let her pay half.

"I asked you to lunch," he insisted.

Laura shrugged. "Okay, thanks. I'll be glad to return the favor next time."

His eyes crinkled and lit with happiness. "Next time. Right."

Austin seemed distracted as they walked back to his truck, and no wonder. It occurred to Laura that he hadn't slept in almost twenty-four hours. She couldn't imagine the turmoil in his mind, knowing a killer pasted his face on each victim he tortured and killed. Knowing he burned to culminate his sick fantasies by doing the same to Austin.

He opened the passenger door for her, but instead of climbing in, Laura turned to face him. On impulse, she reached up and brushed his cheek with her fingers, stood on tiptoe, and placed a gentle kiss there. The quick intake of breath betrayed his surprise.

She pulled back just enough to peer into those incredible green eyes, swirling with emotion. Steeling herself, she spoke before her nerve fled.

"Austin, I don't want anything to happen to you, because if it did, who would drive me crazy?" she murmured with a half smile, playing with a lock of hair at his collar. The strands curled around her finger, like dark fire.

"Laura." He groaned, closing his eyes.

"Who would make me so damn nuts I can't see straight? Who would—"

Without warning, Austin pulled her against the hard length of his body and crushed his mouth down on hers. Not a soft kiss, but the hungry kiss of a starving man, tempted beyond reason.

Laura melted into him as he backed her against the side of the truck. He spread his legs, fitting them together intimately, his mouth never leaving hers. Big hands cupped her head, buried themselves in her hair. She opened herself to him and his tongue swept inside. Hot, demanding, erotic. Deeper.

Oh yes. Her body sought his, pressing as close as possible, loving his strength and heat wrapped around her. His erection ground into her stomach, seeking sanctuary. Her hands skimmed the nape of his neck, face, and broad shoulders. Wishing them away from here. Someplace where they'd make love for days, and he would be safe from a monster.

Austin broke the kiss, breathing like an Olympic runner, eyes glazed with desire. He shook his head. "God, Laura. I—I'm sorry," he said in a hoarse whisper. "I didn't mean to—"

She placed a finger over his lips. "Don't apologize. That was the most awesome kiss I've ever experienced. Gave the term *spontaneous combustion* a whole new meaning."

"I shouldn't have done that." But he was still attached to her like shrink-wrap.

Laura smiled. "But you did it very well."

He dropped his hands, backed away a couple of steps. "I shouldn't let that happen again, for your sake."

Uh-oh. He had that deer-in-the-headlights expression, morphing fast into full retreat mode. "Too bad, Captain Rainey," she said, climbing into the truck. "Because you're going to."

He moved to stand in her door, preventing her from shutting it, a mock scowl furrowing his brow. "You think so, do you?"

"I know so."

To prove it, she pulled him in for another blistering kiss designed to curl his toes and leave him wanting much more. She wanted him thinking of her tonight, and anytime he was alone.

His cell phone interrupted with the quirky tune from *Inspector Gadget*. Pulling away with a muttered apology, he snatched the thing from inside his jacket and answered. He walked to the front of his truck, but she overheard anyway.

"Rainey." Austin paused. As he listened, his mouth tightened. "What was her name? Physical description, clothing . . ."

The color drained from his face. "I'll be there soon." He braced his hands on the hood of his truck and lowered his head. "Jesus Christ."

Laura leaped out of the truck and hurried to his side, laying a hand on his sleeve. "What's happened?"

He raised tortured eyes to hers. "What I was afraid of. The girl from the Waterin' Hole. She's dead."

5

Austin had once been called to the scene of a suicide. The man had jumped off an overpass into a gulley some forty feet below. He often wondered what had gone through the man's mind in those final moments.

Austin didn't want to die, but he was falling, and the ground was rushing up with alarming speed.

When Ashley had been murdered, she'd clawed furrows in her own neck, desperate to breathe as the belt choked her. The knowledge of the terror she must've suffered as she died had nearly driven him insane. And her estranged husband, the police captain, hadn't been there to save her. His grief and remorse had almost killed him.

Now another woman was dead, and his carelessness might've put Laura's life in danger. If the woman's ID checked out, Stacy Mead had been brutally murdered for much less than a kiss.

A kiss that had set his blood on fire. Had made his lonely broken heart slam in his chest. He'd looked into Laura's perfect face, buried his hands in dark silk, pressed the curve of her lush body to his, and God, it was as if he'd waited a lifetime to feel whole again. How had the woman trampled his defenses into dust?

For Laura's sake, he couldn't let it happen again, no matter what she claimed. Even if the idea of her going out with Danny—perhaps sharing her fiery kisses with his friend—caused inky black rage to spread through his soul.

How rich that he'd been putting off acting on his feelings for her for so long. Just when they found their way to each other, the reason they did meant they had to stay apart.

Austin shook himself back to the present. After insisting on accompanying him to the scene to meet up with Forensics, Laura had fallen silent. Austin didn't want her anywhere near the killer's handiwork, couldn't stand the thought of evil brushing against her. But this was her job, and nobody did it better. They had no room for mistakes.

Danny met them at the entrance to the alley, and they went in together. Austin tried to block the scattered images of the last time his footsteps had made a walk like this. And failed.

Sweat rolled between his shoulder blades, down the side of his face. *You've seen dead women before. This one's no different.*

Before they entered the room, Danny briefed him. "Our officer who responded said city workers showed up behind the Waterin' Hole to empty the garbage. Found her body stashed beside the Dumpster. I won't lie to you. This could be rough."

"Why?"

"She was strangled."

His gut churned. "I can handle it."

Laura cut a curious look at him as Danny clapped him on the shoulder. Austin approached first. The sharp tang of garbage mingled with the foul stench of death assailed his nostrils. Cool air whispered over his damp skin, causing him to shiver. Or maybe it was the awful reminder that, in the end, no one escapes this fate. Such a stark, impersonal tomb. A cold, undignified period at the end of lives once filled with sorrow, joy, hope.

Like Ashley and his baby. *Why?*

He and Danny flashed their shields at the officer who'd been awaiting their arrival. Satisfied, the guy indicated the body draped with a sheet.

"Some bastard really did a number on the poor girl," he said in disgust. "Ready?"

Danny nodded. "Go ahead."

The cop pulled back the sheet and Austin recognized her immediately.

"Yeah, that's the girl from the club. Stacy." His voice wavered.

"Jesus," Danny muttered.

Long blond hair, low-cut black dress, generous breasts. His gaze slid to her hands. Bloodred fingernails that had been curled around her wineglass. Her neck . . .

A deep purple line bisected the creamy softness of her throat just under the jawbone. She'd clawed her neck. Fought for her life.

Oh God. Her mottled face became Ashley's. Then the

face morphed into Laura's striking, angular features surrounded by long dark hair. He began to shake. The ground rocked under his feet and he clutched his roiling stomach.

"Austin, are you okay?" Laura cried.

Danny grabbed his arm. "Easy, buddy. Need to step away?"

"Yeah."

The unruffled assistant jerked a thumb. "The back door to the club is open at the moment. Men's restroom is down the hall on the left."

Austin staggered inside and down the corridor, burst into the restroom. He stumbled into a stall, sank to his knees, barely making the toilet before his stomach rejected its contents. Hugging the rim, he coughed and gagged, unable to dispel the horrid mirage of Laura's face superimposed over Stacy Mead's.

How long he knelt there trembling, he wasn't sure. Long enough for the tread of hesitant footsteps on cold tile. Danny's steady voice, rife with worry.

"Is there anything I can do?"

"Just give me another minute," Austin rasped.

"You've got it." But he didn't leave.

Finally, Austin stood on rubbery knees, flushed the toilet, and wobbled to the sink. He splashed water on his face, rinsed the foulness from his mouth. Danny came to stand beside him, lending strength in his quiet way.

"I've never lost anyone as close to me as you have," his friend said at last. "But I know about loss. I understand what it means to have your heart ripped out, and to learn the past won't stay buried. I'm here for you now, whatever you need."

Austin glanced at him, blinking water from his eyes. At least he *hoped* the moisture was water. "Thanks. And for the record, I'm falling for Laura."

"You don't say." Danny crossed his arms. "Took you long enough to admit it."

"Doesn't matter. You saw what happened to Stacy Mead. A relationship is out of the question." Saying that aloud caused a terrible ache in his chest.

"I agree, keeping an emotional distance from her is for the best, until your stalker is caught. But once this is over—" His friend shrugged, letting the statement hang.

"We'd kill each other inside of a week." He didn't really believe that, though.

"Fine. Be an idiot and lose a fantastic lady to a man who'll treat her like a queen, the way she deserves. Because I'm warning you, if you fuck around with Laura's feelings and she ends up hurt, *I'll* whack off your balls."

Austin winced. "Jesus. You're supposed to be on *my* side."

"I always have been, my friend." He squeezed Austin's shoulder. "Let's get the hell out of here."

With pleasure. His exhausted brain couldn't handle another nasty shock. They'd pummeled him for hours, one after another, until his insides felt bruised and bleeding.

Only burying himself in Laura's heated kiss had soothed the pain.

But once more, the gods had played a cruel joke on him. Laura Eden was a sweet, magical elixir he couldn't afford to sip.

And Laura's life was a price he'd never pay.

Austin's official statement from the Sugarland PD announcing the serial murders aired at five o'clock. At his insistence, an unhappy Laura stayed at the station, but not before putting up a fuss. Austin refused to argue the matter.

The cameraman zoomed in for a close-up of Austin standing on the steps of the police department building. Austin relayed only the most basic facts to the public. No frills.

The killer, a male, had lured a man named Matt Blankenship from a local bar, followed him home, and murdered him. Evidence also had tied him to the murder of a local pregnant woman, whom Austin admitted was his own wife. His voice wavered, and he bitterly wondered whether sympathetic viewers would go easier on the police.

All men and women should exercise good common sense. *Don't pick up strangers. Guard your beverages carefully; never leave them unattended. Use the buddy system—make sure your friends know when you leave and who you're with.* He'd have more updates as the case developed.

Stacy Mead's murder and her connection to the case were kept under wraps. Austin wanted the caller, the man he believed to be the killer, to admit to the murder. Plus, the police always kept some details from the press and general public that only the killer would know.

Afterward, he called Danny, asked if he'd follow Laura home from work and see her safely inside her condo.

"Me?" his friend asked in surprise. "You don't want to do it?"

"No."

"Ah, okay. Remember what I said?"

"Yeah, I remember," he snapped.

Danny agreed to the favor with no further questioning. Austin knew his smitten partner wouldn't waste a second asking Laura to dinner. And she'd accept.

"Goddammit." A shitty end to a crazy roller coaster of a day.

Exhausted and strung out, Austin headed home a little early. Normally, he enjoyed the peace and solitude of the drive. Loved the power of the big truck wrapped around him, Aerosmith pumping from the stereo. Today, the loud music only added to the static in his head, and he shut it off.

Once home, he trudged inside, up the stairs. In his bedroom, the boots came off first, followed by the rest of his clothing. Naked, he flopped onto the bed, thinking he should take a quick shower, get something to eat.

Then the day caught up with him, and he fell headfirst into the welcome abyss that swallowed him whole.

Chest heaving, he wept beside Ashley's casket, two of his detectives holding him upright.

I'm so sorry. For you, our baby. Oh God, no no.

Tears of bitter grief streamed down his face. Sorrow wrapped his body in chains, sank him to the depths of the ocean. He longed to suck the water into his lungs, let the darkness drown him. Only one thing stopped him.

She had fought for survival, for their child, with every ounce of her strength. He wouldn't make a mockery of their lives by so easily giving up on his own.

He'd drag himself from the darkness, and when he did, he'd find the bastard who'd cut their lives short. Tear him apart, one limb at a time.

I'll find him, he cried. I swear.

Austin awoke with a start, chest aching, throat burning. Tears dampened his cheeks, his hair. He rolled to his back, wiped an arm across his face. God, how long had it been since he'd had the nightmare? Weeks.

Shadows cloaked his bedroom. He'd slept straight through the afternoon and into the night, without setting the frigging security system. Jesus. Drawing a shaky breath, he rose, yanked on a pair of cutoff shorts, grabbed his gun, and made a sweep through the house, switching on lights as he went.

Nothing. Satisfied, he set the alarm and was heading through the living room when the phone rang.

His pulse did a funny leap. Calls this late never brought good news. Especially now. His false sense of safety vanished as he moved to the phone resting on the table by his favorite recliner. *BLOCKED NUMBER.*

"Shit." He breathed. Either the killer had struck again or Austin's appearance on the news had shaken his world. Or, God help him, both. His brilliant plan hadn't included what he'd say to the bastard if he called again. Every muscle tense, he pressed record on the small black unit hooked to the phone, then picked up the receiver. "Rainey."

"Stupid cop," the man snapped. "What sort of game do you think you're playing?"

Oh Christ. This conversation was going to be like creeping through a minefield. Blindfolded. The killer's voice sharp as the sting of a blade at his throat.

"Playing games is your forte, asshole. Why don't we end this? You think you're so tough, let's meet and you can take your best shot."

Silence. He heard rapid breathing, pictured him trying to assimilate the curveball he'd thrown, force his words into his narrow perception of reality. And he hoped to hell the guys had time to trace the call. But he doubted the killer would be so careless.

"Like I said, stupid," the caller hissed. "Dumb as that blond bitch who came on to you the other night. Told you she learned, didn't I?"

Stacy Mead. Not exactly a confession, but close enough to remove any lingering doubts.

His blood chilled. Did the bastard understand that he'd committed murder but honestly have no remorse? If so, he wasn't dealing with a psychopath, but a true sociopath. An individual capable of distinguishing right from wrong, fantasy from reality, but possessing no conscience. The real deal.

"There's no need to involve anyone else in this. I'll be at the Waterin' Hole tomorrow night, waiting for you. You want me, come and get me."

The man laughed. "Tempting. Maybe I'll show, maybe I won't. You'll just have to be surprised. And come alone."

"I'll be there." *Damn*.

"Sweet dreams, Captain." The caller hung up.

Austin dropped heavily into the recliner, replacing the receiver in its cradle. Less than ten seconds later, it rang again.

"Rainey."

"Not enough time, man. We almost had the fucker."

"I figured as much. Thanks anyway, Jamie." Austin sighed.

"You bet. We'll nail this guy—don't worry."

Hanging up, Austin clasped his trembling hands. Christ, what had he done? Made a date with a killer. Yep, that ranked high on the list of Top Ten Dumb-Ass Stunts Austin Has Pulled. Funny thing was, he couldn't remember the last time he'd given a rat's ass whether one of those stunts got him killed or not. Until recently.

Until a dark-eyed beauty got under his skin, shook his dull, colorless existence, and roused him back to life. Along with his raging desire.

But he wouldn't let her into his heart. He'd given that part of himself once, only to have it ripped beating from his chest and handed back to him on a platter. He'd never survive the agony again.

A bullet to the brain would be quicker, and much kinder.

"You've lost your fucking mind," Danny grumbled. "Too many things can go south. What if we can't get to you in time?"

The possibility scared the hell out of Austin. God, he was so tired. Two nights virtually without sleep had left him feeling like he'd been run over and backed over again for good measure. He leaned back in his chair, waving off Danny's worry with a show of false bravado.

"You and Shane will be parked only one block from the club. I'll be wired and fitted with a tracking device. Nothing will go wrong."

"If he realizes that we're there, one block is too damn far away."

Austin slapped the files spread across his desk. "What else do you suggest? That I hide while he traps another poor, unsuspecting victim and hacks him or her to pieces? Forget it."

"Better him than you."

"You don't mean that."

"No, but I hate this."

Austin heard the defeat in Danny's surly tone. He'd go along with the plan, but he'd hate every second. *Well, that makes two of us, my friend.*

Austin turned his attention to the Blankenship file, burning to know whether his friend had asked Laura to dinner. Danny hadn't brought it up, and Austin didn't want to seem as though he gave a shit. Which he did, especially with the memory of Laura's hot, sweet mouth responding to his. Electrifying his starved senses.

Son of a bitch.

Danny pulled a folding chair close to Austin's desk and sat so they could review the file again, nodding to a photo of Blankenship's nude body, peppered with stab wounds. "Hell of a price to pay. Jesus, his parents."

"Yeah." The scene had been bad. The worst. Betty

Blankenship's screams haunted every waking moment. They'd torment him for months, until they faded enough for him to seal them in that tight compartment reserved for awful things best forgotten.

"No parent should have to learn their child has been murdered, much less how this guy died."

"Damn," Danny muttered. "I've wondered if his closest coworkers knew about his bisexuality, or if he kept that part of his life totally private except for life-long friends like Rick Yates."

"Probably irrelevant, but it won't hurt to check."

"I'll do some more poking around. What company did he work for again?"

Austin flipped through the report, scanning. "Here. Dynamic Media Creations in Nashville, near the new movie studio."

"That's quite a trek from his apartment in Sugar-land," Danny observed thoughtfully. "Plenty enough distance to keep his nightlife separate from his job."

His job. Blankenship had worked as a *graphic artist.* Austin was struck by the detail. He'd heard that term recently, in connection to someone besides Blankenship. But to whom?

The memory returned full force, and he stiffened. *Frankie Blair.*

Danny stretched his long legs out in front of him, arching a brow. "What is it?"

"God, I must be losing it." He raked a hand through his hair in annoyance. "I ran into my cable guy, Frankie Blair, in the Waterin' Hole the night Stacy Mead was murdered. Blair said he's in college to become a graphic artist. Graduates at the end of May."

"So?"

"He claims he has a line on a job from a 'friend of a friend.'"

"And you think maybe that was Blankenship? Pretty big coincidence."

"Maybe, maybe not. I intend to find out."

"Think he'll level with you?"

"Yeah," Austin mused. "Actually, I do. Think I'll leave him a message at work, maybe drop by his place later for a chat."

"I'll go with you, after I've paid a visit to Dynamic Media."

Austin nodded absently, instincts humming. Danny, sharp as he was, had a lot to learn. Coincidences didn't exist in this job. Ever. A few days earlier, Austin had never met a graphic artist. Now he'd run across two in a very short time span. A fluke? Not frigging likely.

"I've got the ME's report on Blankenship," Shane announced, brandishing a file as he strode toward them at a brisk pace.

Austin tensed and Danny straightened in his chair. Hurt went through him that Shane had received the file and not him, that Laura hadn't even called, but he told himself it didn't matter. Their normally cool, composed detective vibrated with excitement.

Shane plunked the file on Austin's desk without ceremony. "You're not gonna believe this shit. There wasn't a lot of forensic evidence at the scene, but what

Laura found—" He tapped the folder. "Look for your-selves."

Austin opened the folder, peering down at the re-port. Danny scooted close, following the text with his finger.

"One strand of black hair, thirteen inches in length, collected from the abdomen," the lieutenant read aloud. "A trace of Rohypnol found in the victim's bloodstream—no surprise there—but no evidence of sex. The black hair was synthetic. A wig, then."

"Austin," Danny whispered. "The report says it matches a strand of long black synthetic hair wound in the belt around Ashley's neck."

Austin stared at the damning words, felt the blood drain from his face. None of them had seen this one coming, not in their worst nightmares.

"Oh my God." He closed his eyes, feeling sick. "The killer was wearing a disguise."

"He's changing his appearance, possibly to look less threatening as a woman," Danny pointed out. "If we proceed with your fishing expedition tonight, the drag-net around you has to be tightened. No room for a clus-terfuck."

Danny shook his head. "This is ten kinds of fucked up. It feels wrong and I think we should call it off."

"I disagree," Austin said. "I say we go through with it—we just have to be cautious."

Glenn spread his hands to indicate the evidence in front of them. "Cautious is an understatement. The fact is, Blankenship was lured to his death. Drugged and murdered by someone wearing a wig, probably a man.

Whether or not anyone else is involved, we just don't know. Either way, he's just as dead, and God knows what the bastard has planned for Austin."

Silence ensued, the truth weighing heavy between them. Cold gripped him, settling into the marrow of his bones.

Is that the way I'm destined to die? At the hands of my family's killer?

"I want DNA run on all of it," Austin managed. "Especially the hair and the tissue under Ashley's fingernails."

"Already in the works. I put a rush on the testing, but they're backlogged by months. If I have to get nasty, I will." Shane shrugged.

Austin didn't doubt he'd follow through. "Do it. And I want to go ahead with tonight's setup."

"You sure about this?" Danny gave him a hard stare.

"Positive. I'll arrive at the club around nine tonight, wearing the wire. You and Shane will listen in the van, which will be parked across the street. Watch everyone who comes and goes through the front entrance. Chris will cover the service entrance at the back alley, Tonio the parking lot."

"Okay, we'll give it two hours. The killer doesn't make contact, your ass is out of there."

"And if he does, he may try to ensure my cooperation by slipping something in my beer before taking me from the club to another location, like he did with Blankenship."

"Shit," Danny groused. "This sucks."

Shane's mouth flattened. "There's no other way if

we hope to catch him before he kills again. But this monster won't get the chance to hurt Austin. We'll be on him like white on rice before that happens, you have my word."

Somehow, Austin didn't find that very comforting. Best-case scenario, the bust would go down as planned, his buddies finding him drugged to the gills and trussed like a Thanksgiving turkey. Worst case?

In truth, he'd die regretting that he'd tasted no more than a single kiss from Laura Eden's lips.

Laura was tired and heartsick.

Seemed Austin's news spot had generated quite the blowup with the other news stations, and quite a few reporters wanted a comment from the ME's office. More than she'd expected. Poor Toby had been going crazy fielding the calls, as the phone hadn't stopped ringing.

Not a single call had been from Austin, though. Laura hadn't heard a peep from him since he'd dropped her off at the station yesterday after lunch and promptly ordered Danny to follow her home.

Stupid, stupid. Just because he'd kissed her like a man dying of thirst, rocked her world like no man ever had, didn't mean he'd do it again. In fact, he'd backed way off, and the reason why couldn't be more clear.

"We'll darned well see about that."

Austin's violent reaction to the dead woman behind the club bothered Laura, because she realized he was internalizing the murder. Perhaps feeling guilty, wanting to protect Laura from the same fate.

When he'd stood looking down at Mead's corpse, the dark emotions swirling in Austin's laser green eyes delved much deeper than simply *upset*.

He'd been haunted. Destroyed.

After he'd staggered to the men's room and hadn't emerged for a good fifteen minutes, Danny had gone to check on him. Lord knew what had transpired, but the guys didn't show for another five minutes, Austin's face white as snow. She'd felt so bad for him. Still did.

She'd gain Austin's trust. Melt his resolve, layer by layer, and expose the passionate, wonderful man she'd glimpsed before. She'd be there for him as a friend whether he wanted her to or not. As a lover if he desired, and at least part of him did. If he'd give, just a little, she'd fix that sexy smile permanently on his face before he knew what hit him.

First, she had to get him to stop avoiding her like the bubonic plague. Considering how well they'd gotten along yesterday, there was no time like the present to take advantage of the brief thaw. He'd be reluctant to get close, especially with a psycho thrown into the mix.

Tough.

Starting tonight, she'd turn up the heat on her sexy captain. When she'd run an errand at the station earlier, she'd overheard one of the detectives saying something about Austin being at the Waterin' Hole tonight. Perfect.

"Because that's exactly where I'll be, too."

6

Austin got out of his truck, locked it, and pocketed the keys.

He smoothed the front of his shirt, impressed with their techie's skill. The tiny wire and tracking device were sewn into the seam next to the row of buttons on his shirt. Gotta love technology. Especially when two pieces of fiber optics, each one no thicker than a human hair, were all that stood between him and a grisly death.

"Everybody fuckin' pay attention," he muttered, loud enough for the team to hear. "I'd appreciate waking up in the morning with my balls intact."

He strode for the entrance to the club, secure in the knowledge that everyone was listening. His only lifeline. Not being able to hear a direct response creeped him out, but Danny had promised to call his cell phone, should a problem arise.

Problem. Right. What an understatement.

He chose his usual spot at the bar, rather than sitting at the back as he'd started to do. Best to stick to his routine. Looking around, he noted that Chandler wasn't working tonight. There was a different bartender on duty, a guy named Bryce who made a damn good drink.

He ordered a beer and settled in. Alcohol was the last thing he wanted, but it was a tempting lure for a killer. Now there was nothing else to do but wait.

His thoughts turned briefly to Frankie Blair. He'd left a message for Blair at the cable company, but the guy hadn't returned his call. Hopefully, he'd manage to pay Blair a visit tomorrow.

No one approached him as half an hour ticked by. Eventually, the bartender returned, took his empty bottle, and replaced it with another cold one. The second brew proved normal as well, and Austin took more time with it. Despite the onetime binge that had landed him in the hospital, he wasn't used to drinking more than this in one sitting. One more and he'd have to stay the night with one of the guys, drugged or not. No way would he get behind the wheel of his truck drowning in alcohol.

The hour mark came and went. "Two brews. Danny, hope your spare bed has clean sheets. Looks like I'm crashing with you."

Frustration was settling in. It was starting to look like their guy wasn't going to show after all. He'd stay a little longer, but it looked like he'd miscalculated.

Dammit to hell.

Taylor Kayne pulled into his driveway, into the garage, and shut off the ignition. He blew out a long breath, just sitting for a few seconds.

Christ, it had been a hell of a day. As much as he wanted to assist on the stakeout and help Austin, a small part of him had been glad he'd been opted out. They had plenty of guys there to handle it. He was looking forward to a beer, a hot shower, and his sexy girlfriend, and not necessarily in that order. As soon as he could stir his ass out of the car, that is.

With a groan, he got out and hit the lock button, then started across the garage toward the door that led inside to the kitchen. He could almost taste his sweet Cara's lips, her body against his. Yeah, maybe he'd skip the beer altogether and go straight for the *real* intoxicating stuff.

A slight shuffle on the concrete behind him was the only warning he had that there was an intruder in his garage—and then it was too late to react.

As he turned, hand reaching for his sidearm, an explosion shattered the quiet of the night. A searing heat flared in his chest as the force propelled him backward and he fell. Hitting the floor hard, he lay on his back, vaguely aware of the figure dressed in black looming over him wearing a ski mask.

"You can thank your captain for your fate," the man said coldly. "If you live long enough. What goes around comes around."

The barrel of the gun lifted and two more shots exploded in the confined space. The gunman vanished and Taylor thought, *Cara. Please, let her be safe.*

Nothing but agony, in his chest and abdomen. Every breath he took was soggy and wet, and that was when it dawned—he was in real trouble.

I can't breathe. I'm dying.

"Taylor? What's going— Oh my God!"

Suddenly she was at his side, cupping his face, stroking his hair. Her beautiful eyes brimmed with tears as she touched him, frantic, trying to figure out what to do.

"Don't you leave me! Hang on, do you hear me?"

Then she fumbled for her phone, punched in a number with shaking fingers. Her voice faded in and out, but he heard her yelling for help. Begging for the police and an ambulance. His buddies were going to feel so fucking bad when they found out about this. He wished he could tell them not to.

The bastard had tricked them all.

"Cara," he whispered, clutching her hand.

"Yes, baby. I'm here." Tears were streaming down her face.

"Tell Austin. It was him. Their killer." His voice was a wheeze, and he coughed, afraid of the wet rattle. Knowing what it meant.

"No. Oh no." Grabbing him, she held him tight and started to cry.

"Love you."

"I love you, too," she sobbed. "Taylor, please stay."

"Trying."

"Try harder!"

But he couldn't fight the darkness, no matter how hard he tried. The last thing he saw was the red and white of the emergency lights cutting through the night all around him.

The last voice he heard was Cara's, crying out for him not to go.

Laura pulled into the parking lot at the Waterin' Hole, shut off the ignition, and debated whether to do this. She wasn't in the habit of chasing men, and she heartily despised women who did. Always had.

But wasn't there a difference between waggling one's tail like a bitch in heat and putting yourself out there? Letting the man in question see your fun side, that there's maybe no harm in taking a chance?

Yes, a big difference. Laura had made up her mind. Hell, she wasn't planning to throw him on the ground and have her way with him. She just wanted him to open up more, start to feel comfortable around her. It wouldn't hurt to try.

Walking into the club, she spotted him right away, seated at the bar. Even in the crowd, he appeared so alone, her heart went out to him. With new resolve, she approached and took an empty barstool on his left. His expression when he glanced over and saw her there was priceless.

"Laura! What are you doing here?"

"Coming out for a beer. What does it look like?"

"But you can't be here," he sputtered.

She frowned. "I beg to differ. Unless this suddenly isn't a free country, I most certainly can be here."

Leaning over, he lowered his voice. "No, I mean you can't be here with *me*."

"I don't understand."

"I'm working," he hissed in her ear.

"I— Oh. I'm so sorry." Crestfallen, feeling like an idiot, she started to climb off the stool.

Just then, Danny appeared next to them, shaking his head. "It's off anyway. He's not going to show."

They'd been on a stakeout for the killer, and she'd bumbled right into it. If the man had actually shown, she could've blown it, big time. Or put herself or the men in danger. Austin's glare said it all. *Shit.*

"I had no idea. Again, I'm sorry. I'll just go."

"You don't have to do that," Danny said, touching her arm. Which earned him an even harder glare from his friend.

Just then Austin's cell phone rang. He jerked it from his jeans pocket and frowned at the incoming number for a second before answering. "Hello? Hey, Cara, what's up?"

As she watched, his face was transformed from mild curiosity to horror. All color drained from his complexion, and he managed a few questions.

"When? Was he at home? Where are they taking him?" A pause, then, "We'll meet you at the hospital."

"What's happened?" Danny asked tensely as Austin ended the call.

"Taylor was ambushed in his garage tonight when he got home from the station," Austin said, his voice rife with pain. Anger. His chest heaved with emotion. "The monster was waiting for him, gunned him down."

"Is he . . . ?" Danny's question was filled with dread.

"Not yet. Cara said he's on his way to the hospital."

"Let's go. Jesus, we've got to tell the others. Especially Shane."

Laura knew the two were best friends. If anything happened to Taylor, Shane would be devastated.

"Come with me," Laura told Austin. "I'll drive you."

For once he didn't argue, a testament to how upset he was.

Outside, the others took the news about as hard as she'd expected. Especially Shane, who looked ready to pass out. Chris drove his cousin while Laura got Austin into her car and took off, praying the detective would survive.

Losing a friend and fellow detective to a murderer would tear a gaping hole in the group, and they might never recover from it.

Please, don't let it come to that. Let him live.

This is all my fault.

All the way to the hospital, the taunt repeated itself in Austin's brain. He should have known the killer would outsmart and double-cross him. He was probably laughing right now at the chaos he'd caused, the sorrow and pain.

I'm going to tear you apart. Someone else had better catch you first and put you in jail.

Once at the hospital, they found Cara easily enough. She was pacing the main waiting room, and when she saw them, she flew into Shane's arms. Her sobs broke everyone's hearts. Not to mention those of Blake, the nineteen-year-old whom Taylor and Cara had taken under their wing and grown close to in the past few months. The boy worshipped the ground Taylor walked on, with good reason.

"That animal shot him multiple times," she cried. "There was so much blood everywhere. He told me it was the same guy Austin is after."

Austin stepped forward. "Did he say how he knew that?" he asked gently.

"There wasn't time. But he sounded sure." Her body trembled. "I don't know what's happening. When the paramedics left with him, he wasn't doing well at all."

"I'll see what I can find out," Austin said.

At the desk, however, even his badge couldn't get him any information this time. Taylor was still in surgery, and that was all they could say. The doctor would be out when he could, and it looked like they were in for a long wait.

Cara took up refuge between Shane and Chris, Tonio hovering, and when Shane's wife, Daisy, arrived, Cara hugged the woman and cried in her arms. Daisy was a juvenile officer with the department, and a fine person. Austin told Laura as much.

"I don't know her very well, or Cara at all, but maybe I can remedy that sometime," she said sadly.

It seemed forever, and in fact it was hours before an Asian doctor came through the double doors looking for Cara as Taylor's listed next of kin. That didn't stop the rest of the detectives from crowding around, waiting to hear the news. Shane and Daisy were on either side of the woman, supporting her.

"Miss Evans?"

"Yes?" she said, voice tremulous. "How's Taylor?"

"I'm Dr. Chen," he said in greeting, expression sober. "I'm going to be honest. Detective Kayne is extremely critical at this point. He took three bullets, two to the chest and one to the abdomen. Both of his lungs collapsed and he nearly bled out, and we had to resuscitate him twice."

Cara's hand went to her mouth and a whimper escaped. "Will he make it? He will, won't he?"

Sympathy warmed the doctor's dark gaze. "I'm afraid it's going to be a long night. If he survives the night, he's got a chance. If he survives the next forty-eight hours, an even better chance. Every day the odds improve."

If he survives the night.

The realization on the faces all around Austin that their friend might not make it was almost more than he could take. There had been too much loss already. This absolutely could not happen. No way.

Dr. Chen finished by saying that they could see Taylor after he was moved to the ICU, but only two at a time for ten minutes each. Then he left with a promise to come back later. Nobody wanted to leave, and it was obvious his team was heartsick.

When at last Taylor was moved to a room in ICU, Shane offered to take Cara in first. They stayed twice as long as their allotted ten minutes. When they returned, Cara's face was red and blotchy, and Shane's eyes were red as well. There would be no easy way back for one of his finest detectives. A good man who didn't deserve this.

Daisy and Chris went next, returning fifteen minutes later. Austin steeled himself and Laura squeezed his hand.

"Go ahead with your detective. I'll be here when you get back."

"Thank you." He gave her a small, grateful smile; then he and Tonio made the walk to Taylor's room. It was the longest of his life.

When they stepped inside, Austin heard a Spanish epithet from Tonio. He agreed wholeheartedly. Taylor was lying flat on his back, face pale as wax, a tube down his throat and just about anywhere else they could think to stick one. His messy blond hair was all over the place.

"He needs a haircut," Austin said gruffly. "Don't I always fucking tell him that?"

Tonio gave a watery laugh. "Yeah, man. He always looks like a surfer boy."

Taylor looked dead. And would be if not for the machines keeping him alive and breathing. Rage ate at Austin's soul. So many lives would be torn apart if this man didn't survive.

"We're going to catch this fucker," Austin told his companion, as well as the man on the bed. "And we're going to put him away. I promise."

"That's right, amigo. If we don't put him down instead."

Austin nodded. That was a distinct possibility as well. He had a feeling the killer wasn't going to go quietly.

As they walked silently together back to their sad little group, a new determination seethed inside Austin along with the guilt. It was a toxic combination, because he could do nothing to assuage either at the moment.

Shane spoke up as he and Tonio rejoined the group. "Daisy and I will stay with Cara a little longer. Then she and Blake are going home with us. It's not a good idea for them to be alone at the house right now."

That was something everyone agreed on. In fact, it germinated a seed of an idea that took root and refused to let go. He'd save that for later.

"Everyone watch your backs," Austin told them. Though he knew it went without saying, he felt better saying it. "He doesn't care who he hurts or how, as long as he gets to me. Safety first, guys."

Austin hugged Cara and said good-bye to his detectives, and Shane assured him one of them would call if there was any change in Taylor's condition. Laura passed out hugs also, and it warmed Austin to see her reaching out to his friends.

He and Laura walked back out to her car, and he offered to drive. She shook her head.

"I've got this, Captain. Sit back and relax. I'm taking you home, and we'll go back to the club and get your truck tomorrow."

"Sounds like a plan."

He slumped in his seat and his eyes drifted shut. Instantly he fell asleep to the soft melody on the radio and Laura's hand in his.

Laura couldn't help but glance at Austin now and then as she drove him home.

The man was running on empty. Her heart went out to him for all he'd been through, and his ordeal was far from over. Slumped in his seat, his head tilted back, dark lashes fanned on his cheeks, auburn hair in disarray. His broad chest rose and fell evenly in the sleep of the truly exhausted. You had to trust someone a lot to sleep like that, right?

So he trusts me? She thought so, deep down, and that gave her a jolt of pleasure.

When she finally pulled into his driveway, she hated waking him. No help for it, though. She reached over and shook him gently. "Austin, we're here."

Grumbling, he sat up and blinked in confusion. "What?"

"You're home. Considering what happened to Taylor, I'll make sure you get inside before I go."

That caused a deep frown to crease his brow. "I don't think I like the idea of you going home alone. Not tonight."

"Are you suggesting I stay here?" Her pulse sped up.

"I think it's a good idea. Don't you?"

"It's probably not necessary." She wanted to stay, more than anything. But not from a sense of obligation on his part to protect her.

"Maybe not." He paused, gorgeous eyes boring into hers in the darkness. "But what if I want you to?"

"Then that would be different, wouldn't it?"

"Yes, it would. Stay?"

That one word, spoken softly from his lips with such hope, caused a ripple of desire through every cell in her body. "There's nowhere else I'd rather be."

They got out of the car, and a bit of unwelcome reality returned when he palmed his gun and placed himself just in front of her as he went to unlock the door. He never stopped scanning their surroundings until they were safely through the door.

Once inside, he disarmed the alarm and checked every room. Satisfied, he armed the house again. "We're set for the night."

"Are we?" He didn't miss the double entendre.

His smile nearly brought her to her knees. "Oh yes. We're set in every way."

She laughed as he started tugging her toward what she assumed was his bedroom. "You don't seem so tired anymore."

"I'll sleep later. With you in my arms."

She liked the sound of that. Liked it even better when they entered his room and he turned her to face him, started peeling off her clothes. He made removing her blouse into an art, slowly undoing every button, eyes heated as he studied each one. Then the blouse hit the floor and he got rid of the bra, flicking the clasp in the back.

As she let the bra slide off, exposing herself to his hungry gaze, he made a very male sound of approval in his chest.

"Beautiful," he said. Reaching out, he cupped her full breasts, grazing the nipples and hardening them to taut peaks. "So full and lush."

"Your turn." Taking the hem of his T-shirt, she pulled it up over his head and tossed it to the floor. Bare chested, sprinkled with a fine bit of hair on a muscular chest, a six-pack down below, he was a mouthwatering vision. "Damn. All for me."

"Yes, all for you."

Framing her face with his big hands, he took her mouth, and the kiss was every bit as electric as it had been before. More so. This was intimacy on a whole new level. Two people exposing themselves for the first time. Not just their bodies, but their hearts. She didn't kid herself that this was just sex, and knew he wasn't the type, either.

Which made it even better. Finally, he toed off his boots, pushed his jeans and underwear down, and kicked them off. His cock stood hard and proud, and she reached out, wrapping her fingers around his thick length.

"Shit," he hissed. "That feels so good. It's been too long."

"For me, too. You feel wonderful."

He was all silk and hardness, wrapped in one. She loved cupping and manipulating his heavy balls underneath, and watching the bliss in his expression as she played. It made her feel powerful, but also connected to him. He was hers to touch and explore.

"Let's take care of these." He went for the button on her pants, making short work of it.

Then he helped her as she kicked off her own shoes, slid off her pants and underwear. She let him guide her onto the bed and got settled on her back. He crawled over her like a starving panther, eyes glittering. She couldn't wait to be devoured.

Lowering his body over hers, he ate her mouth, and

she relished their heat pressed together. The weight of him felt so right. So good. Then he moved downward, laving each nipple, lavishing them with attention. She buried her fingers in his thick hair and caught a hint of silver in the strands, especially at his temples, and wondered why she hadn't noticed before. She loved it, just as she loved everything about him.

His lips blazed a path down her stomach, and he stopped to tease her inny with his tongue, making her giggle. Grinning, he moved on, kissing the inside of each thigh and looking up at her in question. In answer, she let her legs fall open in invitation.

Gently, he parted her folds and teased her slit with his tongue. Little currents of pleasure shot through her sex to her belly, ramped up more and more as he licked her deeper. Finally he was tongue-fucking her, grazing her clit, and she writhed under his attentions, coming undone one nerve at a time.

"Austin! Please!"

"Need my cock, baby?"

"Yes. Fuck me, please," she whimpered.

In a heartbeat he was on his knees, reaching for a packet in the bedside drawer. He sheathed himself quickly, then brought his cock to her opening and pushed inside. Never had she been filled so completely, and tears pricked her eyes from the sheer joy of finally being with him. Making love with Austin.

Grasping her hips, he guided her as he pumped, the action causing the muscles in his chest and arms to stand out, showing off just what great shape he kept himself in. Driving into her with sure strokes, he took them both to the edge. Then he lowered himself on top of her, kissing her deeply as they made love.

His strokes quickened and she felt the telltale heat spreading through her. She couldn't stop the orgasm that washed over her and she cried out, clinging to his shoulders. With a few more strokes he followed, spasming and arching into her until they were both spent.

"Sweetheart, that was so good," he said into her hair, kissing her temple.

"It was wonderful. I haven't had sex like that in—well, ever."

He made a pleased noise and carefully pulled out. After a quick trip to the bathroom he returned with a warm washcloth, which he used to gently clean her. He tossed the cloth into the bathroom, then slid into the bed again, tucking her against his side. Content, she snuggled with her head on his chest. She'd just made love with the man she'd wanted for so long, she couldn't remember desiring anyone else. Maybe they had a future. Maybe not.

But for now, it was more than enough.

7

"Shane said Taylor survived the night." Austin pock-eted his cell phone and turned to face Laura. "But it was a near thing."

His new lover was leaning against the kitchen counter, looking delectable in one of his T-shirts and sipping a mug of coffee. Relief suffused her face. "Thank God."

"Yeah. He had a crisis, though. His heart stopped and they had to bring him back."

"Oh no."

"They discovered he was bleeding internally and rushed him into surgery again. The doctor thinks they've stopped it."

"God, I hope so."

"Me, too." He shook his head. "It was a damn terri-ble night—well, the first part, anyway. The last part with you was terrific. I wish I could just hide here with you the rest of the day."

"Wouldn't that be great?" She sighed, rinsing out the mug and setting it in the sink. "One of these days we'll have to make that a plan."

"You bet, sweetheart." She smiled at him, and it

eased some of the weariness inside him. "Damn, I've
got to get ready for work. Shower with me?"

"May as well conserve water."

Laughing, he tugged her with him. He wasn't sure
how well the conserving worked out, but the shower
was fun. Twenty minutes later they emerged, cleaned
and much happier. Ready to face whatever the day
threw at them. He hoped.

"I'll take you to your truck before I go home and
change clothes," she said. "Can't wear the same ones
had on yesterday."

"Well, you *could*. Technically."

"No, thanks." She tossed him a grin.

The ride to his truck was far too short. When he
kissed her good-bye, he knew the day would be far too
long. Despite his resolve to stay away, he was already
way in over his head with this woman. Probably had
been from the day they'd met.

A long day of running down leads didn't garner
much. Austin spent hours going over his list of people
he'd put away in recent years who'd be vicious enough
to kill for revenge. He pored over details of their where-
abouts, what they'd been up to. The fact was, very few
were still around anymore. The ones who were just
weren't good candidates to be the monster who was
after him now.

It didn't make sense. The killer held a huge grudge,
but Austin couldn't imagine what it could be. He was
missing something important.

He didn't get to go see Taylor until early evening, just
before the sun went down. He'd wanted to get to the

hospital sooner, but knew the best way he could help was to work on catching the killer. The detective had plenty of visitors in and out all day, especially from the station. Cara, he was told, had barely left her boyfriend's side.

He wondered, as he approached her warily, whether she'd blame him for what had befallen her lover. That notion was dispelled, however, as she flung herself into his arms.

"I'm so glad you're here."

"I'm so, so sorry," he whispered. "I'd give anything to take this from him, and you."

"It's not your fault, Austin. I mean that." Pulling back, she gave him a look of fierce determination. "This isn't anyone's fault but that monster who shot Taylor. Find him and make him pay for what he's done."

"I intend to," he assured her.

"Good. That's all I ask."

"Has his day been better than last night?"

"A bit," she said. "He's more stable and there hasn't been any more internal bleeding."

"That's great news. Mind if I go in?"

"Of course not." She smiled at him through her tears. "He'd like that. Maybe he even knows somehow that we're here. At least I like to think so."

"I believe he does. Can't hurt to keep talking to him."

With a last hug, he left her and walked to Taylor's room. Nothing had changed, except perhaps the man's color was better. Or maybe that was wishful thinking. He talked to the detective for a few minutes, updating him on the investigation and stuff that was happening around the station, even though he probably couldn't hear a word. He talked until a nurse came in to check Taylor's vitals and informed him that his time was up. Probably had been for a few minutes.

Promising Taylor he'd be back, he left. After saying good-bye to Cara he headed out to his truck. He was parked in the side lot, and many of the cars had cleared out. Alert, he scanned the area. There was a van parked a couple of spaces from his truck, but nobody seemed to be around.

He was prepared for a direct attack, palm on the hilt of his gun. What he wasn't prepared for was the sting in his shoulder, almost as though he'd been stung by a wasp. Startled, he looked down to see a needle piercing his shirt, stuck into his flesh.

"Fucking hell!"

Yanking the thing out, he flung it away, but the damage was done. His head swam and his legs were suddenly made of rubber. He fell, hitting the pavement hard, and heard tires squeal. Saw the van peel out of the parking lot, could have sworn he heard a man's maniacal laughter.

He tried to grab his phone, but his fingers wouldn't work. It was hard to breathe.

That son of a bitch!

He heard a car approach and stop. A woman's voice yelling in fear.

Then he knew nothing more.

Laura pulled into the parking lot of the hospital, looking for Austin's truck. She knew he was coming to visit Taylor after work.

Finally she spotted it in a side lot and turned in that direction. Just then a van rounded the corner and went screeching past, nearly taking off her front bumper.

"Stupid jerk," she muttered. Then she spotted a figure lying crumpled on the ground.

Her pulse leapt into her throat as she closed the distance and slid to a stop. She recognized the man right away, and terror seized her. "Austin!"

She ran to him and rolled him onto his back. His eyes were closed, breathing labored. Something glinted on the ground nearby—a needle, attached to what appeared to be a dart.

Even though they were in the parking lot of the hospital, she had no way to move him and nobody was around to help. Hands shaking, she dialed 911.

"There's a police captain down in the parking lot of Sterling Hospital! Please, we need help."

The first thing Austin became aware of was the pounding in his head.

"Jesus." A bass drum battered at his brain, which must have meant he wasn't dead. Other than that, he wasn't sure of anything.

He tried to move. Big mistake. The drum pounded harder, shooting waves of pain to every cell and nerve ending. An involuntary moan escaped his lips and a hand immediately curled around his fingers. Small. Soft and warm.

"Austin? Please wake up and open your eyes, sweetie."
Laura . . .

Had he said her name aloud, or only dreamed it? He

struggled to do as she asked, and her hand gave a reassuring squeeze.

"That's it. You can do it. Let me see those big green eyes."

"Laura?" To his ears, his voice sounded rough. Felt like it, too.

"I'm here. You're going to be all right—don't you worry," she said softly.

Really? After several minutes of effort, he managed to pry his lids open. As his vision adjusted, he took in the stark white ceiling, plain walls. The strong antiseptic odor, making him a little sick.

"Hospital?" he rasped.

Laura laid a hand on his shoulder, began to comb her fingers through his hair with the other. "Yes. Be still, and don't try to talk too much. You've been through quite an ordeal, Captain."

Jeez, no kidding. "What happened?"

"You don't remember?"

He shook his head and was instantly sorry; even the slight movement made it seem like it would roll right off his neck. But her fingers raking his hair, her gentle touch, felt soothing. Nice. She scooted closer to the bed, angling over him so he could see her without turning his head too much. He sighed, drinking in the welcome sight.

Her dark hair caught the sunlight streaming in through the crack in the curtains, gleaming almost blue-black. She'd pulled the tresses back into a ponytail, and hadn't bothered with makeup. Fresh scrubbed, dressed in a plain dark blue T-shirt and jeans, she looked much younger than her late thirties. Somehow, having her at his side, gazing down at him with concern, caressing him, made him feel a little better.

"You came here to the hospital to see Taylor last night. Do you recall that much?"

The memory returned in bits. "I remember visiting, hugging Cara. Talking to Taylor. Then nothing but a huge black hole."

"I'm not surprised. You had enough Rohypnol in your system to take down a man twice your size."

He blinked. "Christ. How?"

Laura took a deep breath, the shadows in her lovely eyes giving him pause. "You went down to the parking lot. The stalker darted you and left you there. I saw the van leaving, though I didn't know who it was at the time. I found you and called the paramedics, and they brought you around to the ER, where they did some tests to figure out what had been in the needle. He overdosed you."

Shock had him trying to sit up, but moving caused the room to spin. Laura eased him back onto the pillows.

"They didn't catch him, did they?"

"He escaped. I'm sorry."

"Shit." He thought for a minute and said, "You know, this was a warning, not a real attempt on my life. He was fucking with me. If he'd been serious, he would have tried what he did to Taylor."

"Your guys agree," she said. "They were here earlier and said pretty much the same thing. This was the killer posturing, letting you know he can get to you."

Laura withdrew, and the loss of her touch left Austin strangely bereft. She appeared miserable. Upset. She seemed to be taking this pretty hard, and he understood. It wasn't too fun from his position, either.

"When can I go home?"

"This afternoon, as long as you check out okay. The doc said you'd be fine."

Another thought occurred to him. "Crap—nobody called my parents, did they?"

She smiled and patted his arm. "No. Shane said there was no reason to scare them, and you could tell them if you wanted."

"Not fucking likely."

He shuddered to imagine their reaction. They'd been through enough on account of their sons.

"What were you doing at the hospital anyway? Looking for me?"

A flush pinkened her cheeks. "Maybe."

"Hmm. I think you were," he teased.

"I think you hit your head too hard. I don't even like you very much."

His smile widened. "Liar. Come here."

"What for?" The hungry look in her eyes said she knew damn well what for.

"I'm an injured man. I need comforting. Kiss me," he whispered hoarsely. More like begged, but he didn't care. He wanted to taste her again, needed her body against his. Reaffirming that he was alive.

"You don't appear to be *that* injured." Her expression warmed and she bent over him, careful not to jostle him. A whiff of French vanilla teased his nose; then her lips covered his. Gentle, giving. Taking charge of the kiss, she slipped her tongue into his mouth. Exploring, tasting. Driving him out of his mind, and doing much to ease his headache.

Laura's breasts brushed his chest through her shirt and the thin fabric of his hospital gown. He imagined suckling her nipples, spreading her legs, trailing kisses down her flat belly the way he'd done their first time . . . He groaned, aware that his cock had swelled, harder than a red-hot poker.

She pulled back, grinning at him. "All better?"

"Yeah," he lied. "It's a damn good thing I don't like you, because if I did—"

"You'd do what?" She arched a brow, brown eyes dancing with mischief.

"Whoops, sorry to interrupt, kids."

Laura jerked away from him, straightening to look at the man striding into the room. Shane came to stand beside her, his huge grin testifying that he was anything but sorry. In fact, he looked amused as hell. His sharp gaze took in Austin, however, and the humor quickly fled from his face. He squeezed Austin's shoulder.

"Good to see you back from la-la land, Cap. You scared the holy fuckin' shit out of us."

Austin tried to smile. "Good to *be* back. Now if I can just get the hell out of here, I'll be happy."

"I'll bet."

"How's Taylor?"

"Hanging in there, showing some signs of improvement. The doctor is cautiously optimistic that they can move him from the ICU in a couple of days. Maybe."

That was truly great news, but he was hesitant to celebrate too much just yet.

"So, this attempt," Shane said. "He could've had you. I think he was sending you a message."

"Yeah." His humiliation knew no bounds. And his anger, too. Not only had the bastard gotten one of his men—he'd done a drive-by and slapped Austin on the ass for good measure. It was tough to take.

"Hey, it's going to be fine. We're going to catch him and put him away."

"I know. It's just infuriating."

They talked for a few more minutes, until Shane spoke a few more words of encouragement and finally showed himself out. Austin tried—he really did—but the dark mood that enshrouded him was tough to get past.

He tried to encourage Laura to go home for a while, but was secretly glad she stayed until his release.

She was safer by his side, or at least he told himself.

Even if he was an inept fool.

Austin had been quiet for the last hour and a half. Too quiet. No snappy barbs, no cocky smile. No teasing glint in his beautiful green eyes. He sat mute, staring out the passenger window of her Mercedes, expression blank. No, not blank, exactly.

Lost.

He'd barely responded when the doctor had released him that afternoon with strict instructions to take his pain medication and rest. Hadn't uttered a single protest when Laura had helped him dress in a pair of sweats, a T-shirt, and tennis shoes, rather than the clothing he'd had on the night before.

Danny had brought them each a bag as well, and she was insanely curious when Austin said they weren't going back to his rented house. Instead, she was following his GPS directions out of town, into the country.

Laura stole a glance at him. By now, he must be dying for a shower and a couple of ibuprofen for his aching head. She'd see that he got both. The only outward sign of discomfort was his rubbing his temples every so often and, he'd admitted, a bit of nausea.

They'd been driving for about an hour when he spoke up.

"Take a left at the next gravel drive."

"Gotcha." Laura swung the car into the wide driveway, ogling the impressive black iron gate flanked by stone columns. A box on the driver's side boasted a security panel and intercom. "Wow. Where have you been hiding this place? Did you win the lottery and forget to tell me?"

"Nah." He sighed. "This place belongs to my parents, but they're rarely here. It'll just be us for a few days, if that's all right by you."

"Definitely fine by me."

Austin rattled off the code and she punched it in. With a pop, the gate slowly swung inward. As soon as the Mercedes was clear, it reversed direction. Pretty fancy. Turning her attention to the winding, treelined drive, she admired the view.

Rolling hills stretched as far as the eye could see, no neighbors around to spoil the view of the land and trees. When the sprawling stone, log, and glass structure came into view, Laura breathed a reverent sigh.

"Oh, Austin, your parents' place is gorgeous."

"Thank you. It's my sanctuary, too, whenever I need it."

"How long have they owned it?"

"Oh, about twenty years, back around the time I joined the police department. Once they bought the land, I moved here from South Texas. Took us about a year to finish the house, Dad and me and some hired help."

Pride lit his face, and she was glad to see him focused on a pleasant topic for the time being. "You helped your dad build this place? Wow, I'm even more impressed."

"It was a labor of love."

Austin Rainey was a financially stable man, no doubt about it. Maybe even wealthy, one day—not that she cared about that. He was a man who'd carved a peaceful niche in an often brutal world.

"Is that where you're from, South Texas? Are your parents still there?" she asked, curious about his roots.

"No, they live in Tennessee. My oldest brother, Johnny, runs a ranch down there along with our middle brother, Michael. He's also the sheriff of McMullen County, so he relies a lot on our younger brothers, Lucas and Sloane. He works too damn hard."

"Are any of them married?"

"No, they're all single."

Laura blinked. There were four more hardworking single Rainey men? If they possessed one drop of Austin's sex appeal, surely no female within a hundred miles was safe from their quadruple blast of testosterone.

"We had another brother, Phillip, who was killed in Desert Storm. His death nearly destroyed my parents."

"I'm so sorry."

"Me, too."

So much for the brighter mood the prospect of the house had brought. She pulled into the circular drive and parked in front. A wide, shady porch graced the length and wrapped around the right side, where it disappeared from view. Stepping out of the car, she walked around to Austin's side and opened the door, reaching for him.

"Here, let me help you."

He waved her off. "I can make it. I was drugged, not crippled."

Not hardly. He pushed out of the car with a groan and started for the house with a shuffling gate. Laura took his arm anyway, and he offered no further protest as she guided him up the porch steps. She didn't want him to get dizzy and fall. At the front door, a grimace suddenly etched lines around his mouth.

"Damn, I left my truck parked at the hospital."

"Not to worry." She smiled, happy to be able to ease his mind about something. "Danny and Shane got your keys from your jeans pocket and brought that big black tank of yours home this morning. It's probably parked around back. Here you go—I almost forgot." She fished his truck keys from her jeans and handed them to him.

"Thanks." He breathed in relief.

"Good friends, huh?"

That earned a small smile. "The best."

Inside, Austin disarmed the security system while

Laura admired the rustic interior. The foyer was dominated by a staircase ascending to the second floor. Braided rugs accented the gleaming hardwood floors, and chocolate brown saddle-stitched leather furniture graced the cozy living room beyond. Tasteful, and wonderfully welcoming.

"Your home is marvelous. I've always dreamed of having a retreat."

A strange look flickered across his face. "Maybe someday you will."

"Oh, I doubt it," she murmured. "My condo is plenty big enough for me and Max."

"Max?" he questioned stiffly.

"My cat," she said dryly. "Who were you thinking?"

He relaxed. "Oh."

"Yikes, I have to get someone to feed him."

"We'll get one of the guys to take care of him."

Worry nagged at Laura. He looked dreadfully exhausted, dark smudges under his eyes hinting at lack of sleep despite the pain meds. As much as she wanted him near, it occurred to her that he might already regret his decision to act as her protector. That he might appreciate an out.

"You know, there's really no need for you to go to the trouble of watching over me. I'm sure you'd rather recuperate in the comfort of your own home, and Danny assured me he's got no problem staying at my place until the danger is past."

An ominous frown marred his brow. "I'll just bet he did, but that won't be necessary. I created this mess, and I'll fix it. Besides, I can rest at your place same as I can here if it comes to that. But I *will* be watching over you."

"We've been over this. *You* didn't create anything. None of this is your fault, and I wish you'd get that through your thick skull. But, Austin, if the killer is watching both of us, are you certain it's a good idea for us to be together?"

He laughed, a harsh sound. "All I know is, my gut's telling me we're safer together than we are apart."

She felt the same, and immense relief swamped her. "All right, if you're sure."

"I am. And I really don't think he knows about this place. It's not in my name or anything."

"Well, that should give you a few days to recover and mull over the case before he makes another move."

"Exactly." Falling silent for a moment, he stared down at his shoes. "Mind if I shower? I feel filthy."

Her heart broke for him. If their situations were reversed, she'd scrub at that depraved maniac's foulness until her skin peeled off. Even though the killer hadn't physically touched him, he'd still been violated. She laid a hand on his hard biceps, secretly thrilling at the coiled strength that hinted at none of the vulnerability underneath.

"Take as long as you need."

"Make yourself at home. TV remote's on the coffee table, sodas and beer in the fridge if you're thirsty. Kitchen's through there." He pointed to a wide archway at the back of the living room. "I'll try not to be long."

Austin headed slowly toward the stairs, and Laura had to restrain herself from rushing to his side. He might benefit from her help, but the stubborn man clearly didn't want it. Although a line of intimacy between them had been crossed, she didn't know precisely how to proceed.

At loose ends, she treated herself to a tour of his living room. Without ever tipping into cowboy, the masculine wood and leather created a lushly rustic atmosphere, as one might find at a deluxe mountain lodge. A warm, enveloping treat to the senses.

A big stone fireplace with a split-log mantel graced a large portion of one wall. Two sofas, a square coffee table, and two recliners made an inviting arrangement next to the fireplace. An enormous flat-screen TV mounted on an adjacent wall provided the sole nod to high-end modern technology—and macho indulgence—within view.

She could easily imagine living here forever. Of never, ever wanting to leave. Thinking of her sleek high-rise condo, she shivered. Compared with Austin's home, her place had all the personality of his stale white hospital room. The thought of returning to that sterile box anytime soon depressed the hell out of her. Yes, she'd put some nice touches into Austin's rental home when he'd been in the hospital, but that had been a gift for him. She was rarely at her own condo enough for it to feel like home, so she didn't bother with decorating. She was glad to be staying here for a bit.

Idly, she wandered over to a table that held several framed photos. One was a studio portrait of an attractive fortysomething couple. Austin's parents. The man wore his auburn hair shorter than Austin's, but the distinctive strong jaw, chiseled lips, and clear green eyes were his.

The woman in the photo was stunning, with dark shoulder-length hair, full lips, and large brown eyes.

Her gaze roamed to the next photo, this one a more recent snapshot of five handsome, smiling men in worn jeans, cotton T-shirts, and cowboy hats, perched on a fence railing. One had shaggy dark hair, and three were blond. Austin was the sole ginger, laughing in the middle with two men on each side of him. These had to be his brothers. From the way they leaned on each other, arms looped across each other's shoulders, the Raineys must be very close.

The old, familiar ache knotted in her chest. As kids, she, Samantha, and Gray had shared that warm bond. A connection she'd once believed unbreakable.

But a vile monster had ripped that bond apart forever. The path Laura had followed to this day had been forged by the pedophile that left Grayson Eden an empty shell, their family in ruins.

Oh, Gray. Why did you turn from those who love you? We'd give anything to see you whole again.

She shook off the cloying sadness, casting it firmly aside. She and Sammie would get through to their big brother one day. They'd never give up on him.

Glancing at her watch, she noted that Austin had been upstairs for forty minutes. He must've had trouble getting undressed and showered. She should've at least helped him up first, made sure he wasn't still too loopy from the drug. Biting her lip, she debated whether to go to him. Did she dare risk their budding relationship by invading his privacy?

What if he was passed out on the floor? The awful

possibility got her feet moving. Laura took the stairs quickly, pausing on the landing to scout her surroundings. Five doorways were nestled around the loft area, three on her left, two on her right. Only the door in the far-right-hand corner was closed, so Laura went with the odds.

Walking over, she hesitated, raising a fist to knock. But before she did, a muffled sound froze her arm in midswing. The door wasn't pulled completely shut, and there could be no mistaking what she'd heard. If the door had been closed, she might've missed it altogether.

Another quiet sob reached Laura's ears, shocking her, searing her soul as nothing else could have. Without hesitating further, she pushed inside, the sight sticking her tongue to the roof of her mouth.

Austin sat on the edge of a king-sized bed in profile, head hanging low, left hand over his face, right arm tucked against his stomach. A discarded T-shirt lay on the bed next to him. His gleaming hair was wet from the shower. He'd pulled on a pair of fresh jeans, but they were unsnapped, and he was barefoot.

Silent tears rolled down his cheeks, dripping off his chin, and Laura went weak in the knees. *Oh God— anything but this.*

Austin Rainey, the tough cop who, just a few short weeks ago, had a good life and a baby on the way, was crying.

Eden men did not weep, even under the most awful circumstances, which was probably why they were so unable to purge old wounds and heal. Laura had no experience with grieving men, and no idea what to do with this one.

"Austin?" she ventured.

No answer. She walked a few steps closer, then stopped, torn between the desire to comfort him and flee like a coward. No, to hell with running. If he wanted her to leave, he'd have to ask.

She circled around to sit next to him on the bed and laid a hand on his broad back, stroking. "Sweetie, I'm here. Whatever you need."

Silence, long and agonizing. Finally, Austin raised his head, the stark misery in his eyes stealing her breath.

"What did my child do to deserve this?" he whispered. His throat convulsed as he went on. "That monster took his life before it had a chance to begin, and now he's trying to take everything else."

Tears stung her eyes. "Sometimes there's no reason beyond that some people are evil. They think everything is someone else's fault, like this killer. He blames you for whatever is wrong in his twisted head, but it wasn't your fault." *Stupid platitudes meaning nothing,* she thought helplessly. After her family's ordeal with Gray, she should know.

He gave a low, bitter laugh. "The hell of it is, I don't have any idea how to stop him. I feel so fucking clueless while he's dancing circles around me, *murdering* people."

"Oh, Austin." She lifted her arms to him, and he fell into the circle of her embrace, nearly knocking her over. His big body shuddered, gradually relaxing as she held him close. Tentatively, she stroked his damp hair, mur-

muring soothing phrases, a woman comforting a man's bruised heart.

The connection that had taken root between them the first time they'd made love was still there, and grew even stronger. It was more than sexual. It was a connection to a man she'd never experienced before. A certainty that this man had been made for her arms, her soul recognizing his on the most essential level. God, what an amazing, incredible feeling.

She pulled back and he lifted his head, gazing at her with such raw need, her insides quivered.

"Laura," he groaned. He dipped his head, capturing her lips with his. His tongue parted the seam of her mouth, exploring, tasting. A gentle, tentative kiss that continued as he cupped her cheek, stroking her jaw with his thumb. His fingers traveled downward, finding the vee of her blouse, brushing the curve of her breasts. Lingering.

"Don't stop—" She breathed between kisses.

"I don't want to. I want to make love to you again."

The confession made her want to shout with joy. "I want that, too. I've wanted you forever, it seems."

A ghost of a smile touched his sensual lips. "Damn, you're amazing."

"What took ya so long to figure *that* out?" she quipped.

That earned her a full-fledged, heart-stopping smile, one that chased the shadows from his eyes and made the butterflies in her stomach do the tango.

"I always thought that." He touched a finger to the end of her nose, a sweet gesture. "What are we doing, sweetheart?"

"You need an instruction manual?" she teased.

"Hmm. Not for some things."

And he kissed her again, hard this time, the way a man kisses a woman when he wants to curl her toes, turn her guts inside out. Make certain she knows whose lips belong on hers.

Oh, the man knew how to kiss. She wanted years to learn all the talents her captain had. Then she placed her palm in the center of his chest and urged him onto his back.

Scooting to the center, he arched a brow. "Plan to take advantage of me?"

"Is that a problem?"

"Not from where I'm at."

Giggling, she grabbed the waistband of his jeans and briefs, pulling them down together. His cock half pointed to the ceiling, flushed red, hard, and ready. She quickly took off his shoes and socks, letting them fall to the floor, then finished ridding him of the rest of his clothing.

Her own jeans and top went next, joining his. Then she positioned herself between his spread thighs and grasped his silken length. She enjoyed the way he sucked in a sharp breath as she licked up one side, then the other. He was so hot, he was like a brand in her fist. A pearly drop escaped the tip and she flicked it with her tongue, loving his salty taste.

As she took him into her mouth, began to suck, he moaned, raising his hips. Encouraged, she swallowed him deeper, her single goal to drive him out of his mind. From the sounds he was making, the way he writhed on the bed, she was succeeding.

"If you don't stop, I'm going to come," he said, panting.

She pushed him a little more, giving him a few more good sucks before he gently urged her back. Leaning over, he rummaged in the nightstand and came up with a condom. This time she did the honors, rolling it over him. Then she straddled his hips and lowered herself onto his cock.

The joy and wonder on his face were a sight to behold. There was so little of either in his life of late that he simply took her breath away. She moved over him, riding him, and had never felt freer. Their passion built until she was bouncing in his lap, so close. So close—

She came with a cry, clenching around him, fingernails digging into his chest. Tensing, he followed her over the edge, pulsing inside her again and again. Replete, she draped herself over him and he held her close, kissing her hair.

"God, what you do to me, lady."

"The same thing you do to me."

"You put a smile on my face, make me so satisfied I can't see straight."

The smile he gave her made her pulse stutter. "That makes two of us."

Climbing off him, she gladly let him tuck her into his side and they let their problems drift away. If only for a little while.

8

Rage chewed at his insides, a deadly virus determined to destroy its host.

"The Sugarland Police Department has no comment regarding the attack on Captain Austin Rainey, nor any possible connection to the ongoing murder investigation," Chief Byrne informed the clamoring media.

No goddamn comment! Slick bastards, with their half-truths and stinking lies.

Rainey would pay for committing such an unforgivable sin.

The problem was time. He'd taken a couple of days off, but the boss expected him in tomorrow. His schedule had been a bitch lately. Would everyone believe his story if he called in?

Who cares? Fuck them all. Nobody had a clue who he was. Now Rainey was actually finding happiness, and that couldn't continue.

Laura Eden, so fucking perfect. Beautiful, smart. "Goddamn you," he moaned, voice rising to a fever pitch. "Fucking whore. You're going to pay, too."

Rainey, you'll regret the day you ever stole from me.

*   *   *

Austin rolled over and blinked his eyes open to find himself greeted by his lover's beautiful face.

"Good morning. How'd you sleep?" she asked.

"Pretty good. You?"

"Like a rock." Reaching out, she combed her fingers through his hair. "How does your head feel?"

"A lot better, though I still feel kind of weird and out of sorts. I wonder if that's normal?"

"You may be that way for a day or two. Just get plenty of rest while you're here." She looked concerned.

"I'm fine, really. Just a little off."

"Are you hungry?"

"I could eat." His stomach rumbled at the suggestion.

She smiled. "How about some bacon, eggs, and toast?"

"And coffee. That sounds great if we have any."

"You do, actually. I snuck down there earlier and peeked in the fridge."

"I'll help," he said.

Deciding to shower after breakfast, they went down together and started the coffee. Soon the tantalizing aroma of bacon filled the air, along with the rest. Once the table was set they ate companionably, and Austin felt himself perking up with every bite. By the time they'd finished, he was much more himself.

"Want to go for a walk?" he asked as they cleared the dishes.

"I'd love to."

Once things were put away, he took her hand and led her outside, toward the back. A nice barn stood out there, and he took her to look at where the animals used to be kept.

"No horses?" The disappointment was plain on her face.

"Not anymore. Nobody's here enough to take care of them. Maybe someday that'll change."

Rows of empty stalls stood sentry on either side of the barn, and he could almost imagine his favorites sticking their noses over for a treat as in days gone by.

Leading her on, he glanced over at her. "Do you ride?"

"I've only done it a couple of times, through Girl Scouts. I'd love to again sometime."

"Hmm. Let me show you something."

At the other end of the breezeway, he took her outside again and over to a separate, smaller building. The doors were padlocked, so he produced a key and unlocked it. When he swung the doors open to show a large tarp covering something, she stepped forward in curiosity. Then he tugged at the tarp and it slid off to reveal two four-wheelers with camouflage paint jobs.

"Oh wow," she said, smoothing her hand over one fender. "Do they run?"

"They should. We keep them serviced. Want to take them out for a spin?"

Excitement lit her eyes. "That sounds fun, but I've never driven one."

He thought about that. "Tell you what. Why don't you ride behind me this first time, and we can give you a lesson later?"

"All right. Can we go?"

He laughed at her eagerness and thought she must not get away from her stressful job any more than he did. Of course, this meant they'd have to do it more often. "Hang on for a sec. I'll be right back."

Jogging into the house again, he searched the kitchen for a few items. For the second time this morning, he was glad they kept the kitchen stocked with a few necessities. Sticking them in a small lunch cooler he'd found in the pantry, he left the house again, locking up behind him.

"What do you have?" Laura asked, curious.

"You'll see."

First he stowed the lunch box on the back of the vehicle. Then, grabbing a couple of helmets off hooks on the wall, he handed her a smaller one and helped her fasten it into place. Once he fetched the keys off another hook and wheeled their ride outside, they were ready to go.

Austin climbed on first, scooting forward on the seat to give her room. "Okay, get on behind me and wrap your arms around my waist."

Grinning, she climbed aboard and scooted so that her front was so tight against his back, he wore her like a second skin. When her arms went around him, he knew nothing short of a major wipeout was going to dislodge her.

"I won't go too fast," he said. "Ready?"

"Yes!"

The engine took two tries to turn over, since the vehicle had been sitting for a few weeks. On the third try it caught, and he shifted into gear. Laura squealed as he gunned the speed a bit for effect, and he laughed. The sheer joy of it threaded through his soul, lighting places that had been dark for a very long time.

The rolling property made for great four-wheeling. He loved the wind in his face, the feel of the woman clinging to his back. Just being alive on a gorgeous day like today and having someone to share it with.

Is this love? The idea both excited and scared the shit out of him. He and Ashley had drifted apart and hurt each other so badly, getting over the loss of their marriage had taken a while. He wasn't sure he was ready to face getting hurt again.

He drove them all over the property, keeping their speed just fast enough to be fun, taking curves gently and slowing down over the bumps. It wasn't anywhere near the balls-out ride he'd be having if he was alone, but with his precious cargo on board he was extra careful.

Twenty minutes later he headed for the trees, to a dirt path he liked to take whenever he rode. The forest canopy formed a green tunnel and he slowed enough for them to enjoy the scenery. This was his favorite part, where the sun barely filtered through the leaves and played on the emerald carpet below. It was a world unto itself, almost untouched except for the path.

After a few minutes the trees began to thin out and the space around their vehicle opened up. Ahead of them was a slight clearing, and beyond that, a narrow stream that cut through the hills, lined by a rock bed. This was his destination, and he pulled up to the edge of the clearing near the stream, cutting the engine.

"It's beautiful!" Laura exclaimed. "I'm so jealous that you get to come here whenever you want."

The thought struck him that, if he got his way, she'd be coming here with him. Often.

"It is pretty incredible, huh? Hard to believe places like this still exist. Sort of like a heaven on earth."

She slid off the vehicle and he got off as well, taking her hand. He tugged her toward the stream, where they admired the clear water babbling over smooth oval stones worn by time.

He gestured to the brook and their surroundings. "I've always admired the simplicity of nature. It changes and yet it stays the same. A hundred years from now this might all look different. The stream might've shifted or even be gone, but if nobody comes in with a bulldozer, it'll still be breathtaking."

"That's a lovely thought. Poignant, too."

His lips curved in a smile. "I've always envied the creatures who live here and get to stay far away from the filth of humanity. They've got no problems out here."

"Unless you're small game that gets eaten by a predator," she teased. "Might not be so great, then."

He laughed. "Good point. Sometimes I forget Disney didn't choreograph this scene."

They strolled on, picking their way along the bank. Suddenly, Laura slipped on some slick moss, but Austin grabbed her arm just in time to prevent her from a dunking.

"Nice save, thanks." She smiled at him, a soft breeze blowing her dark hair around her face.

In that moment, he thought she looked younger and happier than he'd ever seen her. He wondered what she saw when she looked at him.

"You're welcome." Taking her hand again, he pointed to the flat grassy areas along the stream. "Right along there is a really good place to look for arrowheads."

"Really? Why there?"

"Two reasons. Some get washed down from the hills after it rains, but those found along or in a creek bed were left behind from the Native Americans hunting deer or other game. The creek bed was the best place to do that."

"Because the animals have to come get a drink," she guessed.

"You get the prize." He winked. "The best time to find them is after a gentle rain, when the soil is washed off the ones just under the surface. That's probably more than you ever wanted to know about arrowhead hunting."

"No, it's interesting," she protested. "I never get outdoors like this, and hearing you talk about stuff like that is great."

"I'm glad you think so. Ashley used to completely tune me out— Shit, I'm sorry. I didn't mean to bring her name into our conversation."

She squeezed his hand. "Honey, you're going to speak about her, and even your child. That's normal, and I wouldn't expect you not to."

"You're amazing—you know that?"

"Yeah, I am, aren't I?"

Pulling her into his arms, he decided to show her

how much he meant what he said. As he devoured her mouth she twined her arms around his neck, lithe body pressing as snug against him as she could get. Heat flared in his balls and his cock came to life, pressing against his zipper. She had to feel his arousal. No way to miss it, since she was practically riding his leg.

By the time he broke the kiss, his poor balls were about ready to strangle in his jeans. He gave her another quick kiss and then they continued on, shooting each other steamy glances now and then.

Conversation picked up again, and they talked about little things, like their favorite books and what kind of music they liked.

For such a classy woman, she was real, down-to-earth. He liked that there was no pretense about her, even though she drove a nice car and wore nice clothes and owned a condo. He got the sense that, to her, things were simply that—*things*—and didn't matter much in the grand scheme.

"Ready to head back?" he asked. "We've gone farther than I thought."

"Sure."

The walk back to the four-wheelers didn't take too long, and soon their spot came into view. Austin headed for the back of the vehicle and removed the lunch box from the carrier. Then he dug deeper into the pouch and removed a blanket just big enough for the two of them to sit on.

"You're full of surprises."

"I try," he said. "Shall we?"

"Pick us a good spot, my captain."

Her captain. Damn, he liked the sound of that.

After scouting around, he settled on a spot close to the stream but far enough from the bank that they didn't have to worry about getting wet or muddy. She helped him spread out the blanket and then they sat with the cooler next to them.

"So, what's the surprise?"

"Nothing much, just a few treats." Opening the lid, he pulled out two bottles of water and handed her one.

"Thanks! I was thirsty." She twisted off the top.

"You're welcome." Next he set out a couple of paper plates. Then came small baggies of cubed cheese, crackers, grapes, and strawberries. Plus one squirt can of whipped cream.

Lifting a brow, she waved a hand at the can. "What are you planning to do with that?"

"Put it on the strawberries, of course." Her smirk said she didn't buy his innocent act. Good thing, because he was far from innocent.

They munched for a bit, enjoying their companionship. Despite the innuendo, the whipped cream did end up on the strawberries. It just so happened to end up on other places, too.

He started it by squirting some on his fingers, then holding them up so she could lick it off. His curiosity about whether she'd play the game was answered when she curled her tongue around his fingers sensually, laving every drop. Then she sucked the digits as though deep-throating his cock.

"I think I like this game," he growled.

Another squirt to his fingers, and this time he

smeared the sweet stuff on her neck. Leaning over, he sucked it off slowly, making her squirm.

"You're a bad boy, Captain."

"You have no idea. What do you say we see how many places we can get sticky?"

After their clothes were discarded, that was exactly what they did. Austin took great pleasure in making whipped cream snow peaks on her nipples and sucking them off. Repeatedly. He liked the way she arched and moaned, causing the taut nubs to thrust into the air.

No way could he resist spreading some on her sex. That had to be the best treat of all, her flavor mixed with the creamy confection as he laved and tongued her almost into a frenzy. Finally she pushed at him and grabbed the can.

"Come here," she ordered. "I want to try some."

"Not about to argue with a lady."

Fascinated, he watched her cover his shaft with the cream. When she started to lick him like stick candy, he nearly came on the spot. She took him in her mouth and managed only a few sucks before he had to disengage.

"Want inside you, sweetheart," he said hoarsely.

"I want you, too. Fuck me."

Moving over between her thighs, he eased himself into her and sank deep. Nothing was so right as this woman in his arms. His cock was on fire as he began to stroke, slow at first. She moved her hips in time with him, fanning the flames higher. He was already burning out of control, and wouldn't last long.

Suddenly came the tingling in his balls, the quickening as they drew up tight. Then his orgasm exploded and he was hardly aware of his shout that echoed through the trees. Long legs were wrapped around his waist, her hot sheath milking him. Lowering his head, he kissed her until their release subsided.

After a few seconds, he moved off her and his slick cock slid from her—and he froze, eyes wide, staring down at her.

"Oh shit. Laura, I'm so sorry."

"What for?"

"No condom," he said, shame coloring his face. "I got carried away, didn't even think to bring one."

"Oh." Her voice was small, and she glanced away. "Well, I got caught in the moment, too. It happens. I'm clean. You?"

"Yes."

"And I'm on the pill, so . . ."

"Good! That's— I mean, good to know." He should have been ashamed of how relieved he felt that she was using birth control. But the thought of another woman being pregnant with his child, another innocent life being in danger, made him sick with fear.

A flash of something that might've been hurt appeared in her eyes and was gone. "Yeah. Been on them for a long time. They regulate my period."

"Ah."

Separating, they started getting dressed. Crap. Now things were awkward and it was all his fault. She helped him clean up and fold the blanket. Soon they were ready to go, no trace remaining of the pleasurable time they'd spent together.

Once he had her helmet secured again, he put his on and they climbed aboard the four-wheeler. On the way back, he took a roundabout route, trying to inject some fun back into their day. She laughed, and he felt a little lighter. Still, he felt he'd tarnished their outing somewhat.

Things seemed normal when they arrived back at the storage shed. He put away the vehicle, helmets, and keys, and locked the doors. Cooler in hand, he led the way back to the house and let them in.

Inside, he paused, looking around. Listening.

"What are you doing?"

"Habit," he told her. "Seeing if the house looks or feels different since we were here earlier. It's a cop thing."

It went without saying that his current situation figured into that as well.

"I'm going up to shower," she said, then hesitated.

He nodded. "You go on ahead. I'm going to make a couple of phone calls and I'll be up later."

"Okay." Tossing him a smile, she turned and headed upstairs.

Not before he'd glimpsed the disappointment on her face, though. God knew he couldn't get it up again so fast at his age, but he could at least have kept her company. Had some shower playtime.

She sensed him pulling away some, and he hated that. Hated himself for being weak in the face of a possibility that was partly his doing.

Tired, he stretched out on the sofa. He really did need to make a couple of calls and now was as good a time as any. The first one was to Shane, and his detective answered on the second ring.

"Hey, Cap. How's the rest and relaxation going?"

"Good. The aftereffects of the drug have me tired and feeling a little strange, but I'm fine."

"You sure you don't need another checkup?"

The concern in Shane's voice made him smile. Having a foster son had brought out the inner dad in the guy. "I'm sure. Any news on the case?"

"Nothing new. There were no surveillance cameras covering the lot you were found in. The cameras they do have show footage around the building, but you can't see that far out in the lot. Plus it was dark."

He cursed, even though that was expected.

"Sorry, Cap."

"Not your fault."

"Is Laura still out there with you?" Shameless prying, something all his men excelled in.

"Yes, she is. And I'm not telling you anything, before you start asking more questions."

The other man chuckled. "That pretty much tells me what I want to know anyway."

"Glad you think so."

"When are you coming back to the station?"

"I'll be in tomorrow," he said.

"Don't push yourself."

Austin rolled his eyes. "See you."

He ended the call. Then made the next one, to the Realtor who'd found him his current rental house. She seemed thrilled to hear from him.

"Captain Rainey, how are you? Everything going well with your house?"

"Yes, it's fine. I do have another matter I need your assistance with."

Emotion suddenly threatened to cut off his next words. He hadn't anticipated they'd be so hard to say.

"My actual home, the one I own," he said quietly. "I need to put it on the market."

Laura tried to tamp down the hurt that had speared her when Austin had been so relieved she was on the pill.

She told herself any man would feel the same. Their relationship was new and they hadn't come close to discussing how they would handle a slipup like an accidental pregnancy. His reaction was normal.

He'd been sort of distant afterward, though. After she had showered, he'd done the same. They'd just hung out watching movies and snacking, which was fine. Dinner was a quiet affair with sandwiches and soup from a can, and she didn't mind. He was good company, but it was a very different feeling from the joyous verve that morning on the four-wheeler.

Now they were about to leave and she didn't want to go. Something about this place called to her, and leaving felt as though she was abandoning it. Could a house feel sad? It seemed so, even though she told herself she was being an idiot.

"You ready?" Austin was waiting in the foyer.

"Not really."

"You like it here that much?"

"I love it," she admitted. "I don't think I've ever felt so at peace anywhere."

He nodded thoughtfully. "It has that effect on people. We'll be back—I promise."

Her spirits brightened. "Really?"

"You bet. Anytime you want."

She heard the truth in his tone, and knew he meant it. As they got into her car, she was glad to note that most of the tension of yesterday had faded away. Even better, as she pulled down the driveway, he wrapped his fingers around hers and didn't let go for a long while.

Back in town, they stretched the morning a bit by stopping at the diner on the square to eat breakfast. Everything looked good and she ate a breakfast fit for a lumberjack, complete with pancakes and syrup. Austin watched with amusement but didn't say a word; he apparently knew what was good for him.

As they were finishing up, a man a few years younger than Austin paused at their table and smiled. "Hey there. Good to see you."

"Oh, hey. Chandler, right?" Austin stuck out his hand and they shook. "Austin Rainey. Good to see you, too."

"Austin, right. Not working today?"

"Oh, I've got to go in. Just putting it off as long as I can." Austin gave the guy a smile. "You know how it is."

"I sure do. Well, I'll see you around."

"You, too."

After he had gone to his own table, Laura said, "Seems like a nice guy."

"Yeah. He's a bartender at the Waterin' Hole."

Their conversation moved on to other things. All too soon, it was time to go, so Austin paid their bill and they left. Laura drove him back to his rented house, which she secretly thought appeared pretty sad compared to his parents' wonderful place.

"Thank you for this weekend," he said, cupping her cheek. "I loved having you there with me, taking care of me."

"I wouldn't have been anywhere else."

"I'm sorry for my meltdown, too."

"Don't be." She shook her head. "You've been through too much. Forget about it."

"I'll try." He placed a gentle kiss on her lips. "I'll call you."

Then he slid out of the car and walked down the sidewalk, up onto his porch. He stopped and gave her a wave before going inside, which made her feel better.

She couldn't stand the idea of any sort of rift between herself and her sexy cop.

Austin had already burrowed his way under her skin. And into her heart.

9

After Austin changed clothes and got his truck, he made a detour to see Taylor.

He was met by Cara and some welcome news.

"Austin! Taylor's off the vent! He woke up last night!" Her eyes were shining, the shadows lifted for the first time in days.

"That's great news! Can I see him?"

"Sure. They said if he keeps improving they might let him go to a regular room in the next couple of days."

"That's great. Once they move him, you can stay with him."

"I know, and I can't wait. I don't like leaving him."

"Soon enough you won't have to."

Giving her a hug, he walked to Taylor's room and nodded to the officer stationed outside. He went in and found Taylor asleep, but now he was breathing on his own.

"Hey, Detective. Who said you could sleep on the job, huh?"

No flicker of an eyelid from the man on the bed.

Breathing on his own was a good sign, though. He was bound to wake up anytime.

Not while Austin was there, though. He stayed a few more minutes, then unfortunately had to get to work.

Cracking jokes about someone else's misfortune is always more fun when the object of everyone's humor is around.

Austin crossed the room to his office and spotted a tight knot of officers talking in low tones. Their laughter was good-natured, but he wasn't in the mood for their ribbing.

"Heard Rainey got tranked like an elephant on safari."

"True that."

Reaching his desk, Austin lowered himself into his chair, gut churning in humiliation. Sick to his stomach, he was wishing he hadn't eaten breakfast. The cup of coffee he'd had that morning soured and roiled, threatening to rebel, but he willed it down with an effort.

Shaking with anger, Austin fished his keys from his pants pocket. The heavy ring contained the keys to his desk, which he always locked whenever he left. The key ring slipped from his grasp and landed on the tiled floor next to his chair with a tinny *plink*. Cursing, he tried to bend over and retrieve them. The awkward position caused his head to swim, and he straightened again without reaching them.

If the abrupt cessation of merriment from the jerks outside his office was any indication, they'd noticed that the object of their teasing was seriously not amused. Whatever. It didn't matter.

"Jesus Christ," one muttered, a man Austin recognized as Jenkins from Patrol.

Austin raised his head and forced himself to meet their stares, allowing every ounce of his irritation to slap them in their faces. The men shuffled in embarrassed silence for a few seconds.

"Rainey," Jenk called, not quite meeting his gaze. "Glad to see you're okay."

A round of agreement from the man's buddies ensued. Not trusting himself to speak, Austin merely nodded. Red faced, Jenk and the others began to drift off in different directions.

Not one of them had the balls to apologize.

Once they'd gone, Austin heaved a weary sigh and returned to the task of bending over to get his keys. A large tan hand appeared in front of him and deftly scooped them up, saving him the trouble. He sat up with a groan to see Tonio dangling the keys, grinning like an idiot.

"Here," he said, tossing them onto the desk. "Fuck those ignorant assholes. They've been over there for twenty minutes, gossiping like a bunch of old women." He parked his butt on the corner of Austin's desk, taking in his captain's appearance. "God, you look like shit."

Leave it to Tonio to put his thoughts right out there. The man was nothing if not totally direct. "Believe me, I feel worse than I look."

"Ouch." The detective crossed his arms over his

chest. "You shouldn't be here so soon after what happened to you."

"Same goes. *I'm* not undercover," Austin reminded him. "If Romano finds out you've been within ten miles of this building, we'll be fishing your body from the Cumberland River."

"Aren't you a ray of sunshine?" Tonio smiled, letting the warning roll off his broad shoulders. "I can watch my back just fine. Go home, Rainey."

"I agree." Danny walked over to stand beside Tonio, sober expression betraying his concern. "The guys and I have things covered here. You need to rest. You're no good to anybody at half speed."

Bemused, Austin studied his two friends. The pair couldn't be more opposite. In some ways, Danny acted older and more mature than the dark, devilish Tonio, who was several years his senior. Though Tonio's girlfriend, Angel, had settled him down a lot.

"All right." Austin laughed, holding out a palm. "You guys win. I'll take my files and work on them at home. Satisfied?"

"Works for me," Tonio declared.

"By the way, Frankie Blair has called and apparently left a couple of messages on your voice mail," Danny informed him. "He finally got through to me this morning. He's been trying to return your call, and he was concerned when he heard about your, um, incident on the news. Told him you'd get back to him."

For the first time, Austin noticed the blinking red light on his phone. "Thanks. I'll give him a call and see if I can pay him a visit before I head home. I need to find out if he's acquainted with Matt Blankenship or Rick Yates."

"He is," Danny confirmed. "I asked him when he called. Rick Yates is the friend who put him in touch with Blankenship for a recommendation on the graphic design job."

Yes! A lead, albeit a small one. "Good work." Austin nodded. "Did Blair say anything else?"

"It was a short conversation. I told him we'd like to talk to him in person, and he was very cooperative."

"Good. Let's pay him a house call. See where that road leads."

Tonio stood, offering his hand to Austin. "I'm outta here. Watch your step with this crazy bastard. I can't afford to buy a suit for your funeral."

Austin shook his hand, grinning in spite of himself. "Gee, you're all heart."

"Tell it to my therapist."

On that note, Tonio swaggered off, earning several appreciative and envious stares in his wake, both male and female. The man was a freaking magnet.

Danny went to speak with Glenn about another case, and Austin returned Frankie's call. Blair said he'd be happy to meet with them on his lunch break. After getting directions to Blair's apartment, Austin thanked him and hung up.

He unlocked his desk and removed the file he needed, but found his thoughts drifting to Laura. Did she miss him? Had she even thought of him at all? He liked to think so.

Women. Who could figure them?

"I don't think of you every second of the day, sweet-heart," he drawled, testing the lie. It burned like bitter acid on his tongue.

Shit.

Danny offered to drive over to Blair's apartment, and Austin didn't argue. His head was throbbing, and he'd been forced to take a pain pill. He hated being less than one hundred percent on the job, but he disliked pain even more. Irritably, he slipped on his mirrored sun-glasses to cut the bright sun threatening to deep-fry his brain.

Danny and Tonio were right. He had no business working today. Damn, had he been allergic to that roofie shit? Woozy, he scrunched his tall frame into his friend's Corvette and leaned against the passenger door, at-tempting to get comfortable.

Scowling, he adjusted his position again. "Why would anyone drive a little beer can like this? My prick is bigger than this car."

"You're just jealous, my friend."

"No way. I prefer lots of space. Besides, my truck is practical. I use it to haul feed for the horses, concrete, whatever. Or I did before Mom and Dad sold the horses."

"Personally, I think guys who drive big, fancy muscle trucks are trying to make up for lack of size in another area," Danny said with a grin.

"You wish, needle dick."

Danny laughed, and they lapsed into companion-able silence. His partner eased onto the Sugarland Tollway, heading north. Austin glanced at him, noting that he'd grown pensive. Maybe a bit troubled. About the case, maybe? As hard as he tried, Danny wasn't good at hiding his thoughts.

"You'll never work undercover, pal," Austin teased, his attempt at humor falling flat to his own ears. "You'd be dead inside a week. What's on your mind?"

Danny snorted. "How does Tonio get away with it? I wonder."

"Because he's full of shit. Don't change the subject."

His partner hesitated, then shrugged. "I drove out to Dynamic Media Creations yesterday. Matt Blankenship's coworkers knew about his wild lifestyle. Even so, they were pretty shell-shocked about his murder. The guy was really well liked."

"He wasn't a pariah. Interesting."

"Nope, just the opposite. He kept his escapades out of the workplace. Meaning, he didn't play with coworkers. But he had lots of good friends, and while they laughed at his antics, they worried, too. One girl told me, 'Matt's the class clown who never grew up. His games just got more serious.'"

"Well, the coworkers are a dead end in any case. We need to connect with his club crowd. Maybe Frankie Blair is the link."

"Sure as hell hope so. We've gotta find something before the killer goes after you again. He hasn't called since you were sprung from the hospital?"

"No, but he will. He's stewing, working up to a rage. I can feel it." The knowledge sent a chill down Austin's spine.

"Jesus."

"Now, why don't you tell me what's really eating you?"

The corners of Danny's mouth lifted as he exited onto Wycliff. "Damn, what are you, a freakin' cop or something?"

"Danny." He was starting to lose his patience.

"All right! I asked Laura to dinner," he blurted.

Austin stared at him, lungs seizing in his chest. His friend hadn't made an idle threat the other day. He'd actually asked her. "When was this?"

"The day of your press conference, when you asked me to take her home. It was the evening the killer called you, the night before the stakeout."

"That was days ago, Danny," he replied tightly. "And neither of you bothered to mention it?"

"There was no need. She turned me down." His friend shot him an uneasy look. "But I've been thinking."

Austin's head started to pound again. He stared at his friend. Why hadn't Laura mentioned the invite? And where the hell was Danny going with this? "Christ, spit it out."

"I know you and Laura have a thing going now, okay?" He sighed. "I'm your friend and I'd never try to poach even if I could. You know that, right?"

"Yeah." He trusted Danny.

"So, sure, I wanted to take her out, but she picked you. That's cool." He paused. "But the thing is, the killer has probably seen her with you. So I'm thinking it's a good idea if he sees her with someone else as well."

"Let me guess. You?"

"Well, you have to admit the idea doesn't suck. You don't want the murderer's attention on her, and if she's seen with someone else, that might do the trick. He'll believe she's less important to you than she is."

He might trust his friend—but he still wanted to punch him at the moment.

"It's not a bad idea," he admitted.

"Then we're cool? You're on board with the plan? I don't want a problem between you and me."

"Sure, we're cool. As long as Laura agrees, that is."

"Good." The nervous tension in Danny's posture relaxed. "I sort of already asked her, and she agreed."

Really? Like that didn't chap his ass or anything. But maybe he'd hurt her worse than he'd believed after they'd made love by the stream. Had he blown any chance with her? Maybe this was for the best. Danny was a good man, one with no baggage, no broken heart to protect. He could make her happy.

So could you, a voice whispered. *Take the risk; you might just win this time.*

"I want protection on her for a while," Austin heard himself say, as if through a tunnel. "Since she doesn't want to stay with me . . ."

"I'll crash at her place, if necessary. That's up to the lady."

Danny and Laura. Under the same roof. Getting closer.

Common sense and knowing Laura better told him that she wasn't the type to jump from one man to another that way. That didn't stop a wave of sheer violence from surging through his blood, and he willed it down. If he'd screwed things up with her? *Nobody's fault but yours, Rainey.*

Wisely, they let the subject drop. Danny turned onto a residential street and parked adjacent to Frankie's building. The aging condominiums, hunkered among tall, beautiful trees, were well kept. Flowers and potted plants adorned the various stoops, and an assortment of classy sports cars, sedans, and SUVs boasted of middle- to upper-middle-class inhabitants. Austin had been to this area only once before, but he knew the residents were predominantly gay men, both singles and couples. From Frankie's halfhearted attempt to pick him up at the Waterin' Hole, he'd gotten the impression the guy was definitely single. And looking for Mr. Right.

Austin was no homophobe. Hell, everyone deserved to be happy. God knew there wasn't much else worth fighting for in this sorry world.

Frankie's unit, number 115, was located on the ground level on the opposite side of the building. He followed the narrow walkway around the corner to the small landing, Danny close behind. He rang the doorbell and turned to admire the clusters of multicolored moss roses edging the porch. Some of the condos were bare of flowers, so he figured Blair must've planted them himself.

The door swung open to Frankie's cheerful greeting—

"Hey, Rainey, long time no see!"—which ended in a startled gasp. "Oh my *God*! What's with the Samsonite luggage under your eyes? They make cold cream for that."

Austin couldn't help but smile at the comical expression on Blair's boyish face. "Hi, Frankie. Can we come in?"

"Sure." The younger man stepped aside to let them in, looking him over from head to toe, dark brow furrowed in concern. "I heard on the news about what happened. Drugged! Jeez, are you okay?"

"As long as I'm unconscious. Guess it'll take a few more days before I'm back to my old self." Getting to business, he gestured to Danny, who'd been hanging in the background. "Frankie, this is my partner, Lieutenant Danny Coleman. Danny, Frankie Blair."

"Mr. Blair," Danny said, offering his hand. "Nice to meet you."

Frankie looked past Austin, blinking as though noticing Danny for the first time. *There's noticing, then there's* noticing, Austin thought wryly. *Put those big brown eyes back in your head, Frankie Boy. This one's after my girl.*

Blair stepped forward, flashing Danny a dimpled grin, wiping his palm on his jeans almost self-consciously before shaking the other man's hand in a firm grip.

"Please, call me Frankie."

Danny's green eyes widened a fraction, a strange expression flickering across his face, then gone so fast Austin might've imagined it.

"Danny," he responded, his voice warm.

Danny? Not "Lieutenant Coleman"? Austin's brows lifted in surprise. In two years, he'd never heard his starched and polished by-the-book partner breach professional etiquette with a witness.

"Cool, *Danny*."

Three seconds of complete silence. As if realizing the handshake had lasted about two seconds too long, Danny released his grip as though he'd been scalded. He took a step back, putting space between himself and Frankie, his face unreadable.

Austin narrowed his gaze at his friend. *What in the ever-loving hell was* that?

Frankie cleared his throat. "Are you hungry? I, um, made chicken salad. I made plenty for three sandwiches, if either of you would care to join me. We can eat while we talk."

Austin held up a hand, shaking his head. "Not for me, but thanks anyway. This damn pain medication has my stomach turning flips."

"Since you're offering, I'd love one." Danny smiled. "I'm kinda running on empty."

"Fantastic!" Their witness-turned-host gestured to a couple of barstools that faced into the gleaming kitchen. "Sit. Fire away with your questions while I make the sandwiches."

As they settled onto the stools, Austin took off his sunglasses and laid them on the bar, noting Blair's pressed jeans and nice blue polo shirt. The wavy black hair framing his face was damp, as though he'd just

BRING THE HEAT   171

showered. "Where's the company uniform? I thought you were working today," he observed.

"Had to take the afternoon off," Frankie replied, fishing a Tupperware bowl out of the fridge. He set it on the counter next to a package of baguette rolls. "I've got an appointment this afternoon to meet with my adviser. She'll go over my credits and approve my application to graduate. It's just a formality."

"What's your degree in?" Danny asked.

"Art, specializing in graphic design. I landed the job at Dynamic Media Creations, starting at the end of May," he said proudly. "I'll be working on designs for advertisements."

"Wow, that's cool," Danny enthused, clearly impressed.

"I think so, too. Especially since it means I get to say 'so long' to the cable guy routine." He removed three rolls from the package and began to slice them in half.

"Congratulations," Austin put in. "This is the job Matt Blankenship recommended you for, correct?"

The light in Frankie's eyes went out like the flame of a candle, and his smile withered. "Yes, but I didn't know him. He did it because Rick got the idea to show him some of my work. Matt liked what he saw and thought I had potential. He put in a good word with his boss, and the rest was up to me."

"Rick's a friend of yours, or just an acquaintance?"

He paused, a wounded expression crossing his features before he mastered it. "A friend, that's all. I'll be honest. I would've liked more, but—" He shrugged, then laid out the rolls and began to spoon on the chicken salad. "Wasn't in the cards."

"Rick's not gay?" Austin pressed. He felt bad causing Frankie pain, but he had to know whether his initial impression of Yates had been on target.

"No. He was confused for a while. He's not now."

Ah. Rick Yates had cleared up his confusion at Frankie's expense. And obviously hurt him in the process. *Damn*. While Austin scrambled for a way to express his sympathy without intruding on the guy's privacy, Danny solved the dilemma.

"I'm sorry, Frankie. That totally sucks."

Blair's gaze snapped to Danny's, and his humor returned. "For sure. Ever felt like you're a fucking science project in a glass jar?" He mimicked a woman's falsetto voice. "Look, children, a gay man! *Homo sapiens Homosexuas*. Don't touch—it might bite!"

"Christ." Austin chuckled.

Danny, however, didn't laugh. He watched as Frankie finished with the sandwiches, slicing them in half and placing each on a plate. After garnishing them with chips, he slid two of the plates in front of his visitors.

"Oh, none for me. I'm not—"

"Eat," Frankie ordered, cutting off Austin's protest. "You're running around investigating on an empty stomach and you wonder why you feel like shit? Jeez."

"Well, okay. Thanks." He sniffed. It *did* look good. He picked it up, took a bite. Heaven. "Wow, this is great. I guess I was hungrier than I thought."

"Terrific," Danny mumbled between bites.

Their host grinned, pleased. "The chicken salad's homemade. I'm a pretty decent cook when I have the time, which unfortunately hasn't been often, with work and finishing college."

Frankie grabbed them each a soda from the fridge. They ate in comfortable silence for a minute before Danny brought the conversation back to the unpleasant subject at hand.

"Sounds like you don't get out much."

"Not very often, but that's all right by me. I've never been big on the club scene."

Danny cocked his head. "But you *do* go out occasionally. You told me on the phone you saw Yates and Blankenship the night of the murder. We need for you to tell us about that evening."

Austin shot his partner a scowl. Really? He didn't appreciate being out of the loop. And he goddamn well intended to tell Coleman so when they left here.

Frankie nodded. "It's been over between me and Rick for months, but we're still friends. I went to Spanky's that Saturday night to see his and Matt's band play. Or maybe I just have a masochistic need to torture myself." He sighed, running a hand through his thick dark hair. "Anyway, I went. Stayed for the whole evening, until after the last set."

Danny leaned forward, elbows on the bar. "Did you see anyone strange hanging around, either a man or a woman? Someone acting suspicious, watching Matt? Coming on to him?"

Frankie barked a jaded laugh. "*Everyone* in that part

of town is weird, and most of them are looking to score
something or someone. Picking out one weirdo down
there is like trying to spot a polar bear in a snowstorm."
He hesitated, took a deep breath, and dropped his
bombshell.

"But after the band was through and had packed up
their equipment, I saw Matt leave. With a woman."

10

Hot damn! Now they were getting somewhere. Glancing at his partner, Austin managed to contain his excitement.

"Did you notice anything peculiar about Matt before he left?" Danny asked carefully.

"Yeah, but it didn't hit me until the next day, when I saw the news about his murder. Matt seemed drunk, but that wasn't unusual, so I didn't think much about it then." His mouth flattened.

"Later I realized he hadn't hung around for long after their set, maybe half an hour. I specifically remember he didn't drink during their show that night, but he was weaving when he left on the woman's arm. I wondered how he'd gotten wasted so fast. Then I just figured he'd popped some ecstasy. According to Rick, Matt was notorious for doing that shit."

Danny looked at Austin. "That's when Matt was dosed with the date-rape drug."

The truth remained unspoken between them. Frankie had most likely been the last person to see Matt Blankenship alive—and on the arm of a killer.

Blair drew the awful conclusion on his own. "Av
fuck."

"Yeah." Austin paused. "The problem is, who's th
woman? Our killer is supposed to be a man."

"Damn," Danny muttered. "But remember, the lon
black hair found on Matt's body was synthetic. So th
killer could be anyone."

"True." Austin turned to Frankie. "After you saw th
news, why didn't you call the police and report wha
you'd seen?"

"Hell, I'm not an idiot," Frankie huffed. "Don't yo
think I was suspicious? I called the Sugarland Polic
that afternoon. Got the royal runaround and ended u
leaving a message on some detective's voice mail. No
body bothered to call me back, so I thought they didn
need my information. For all I knew, they'd alread
ruled out the woman I saw."

"Do you remember the detective's name?"

"Herrera, I think."

Austin slapped his hand on the counter. "Son of
bitch!" Herrera! By God, he'd roll up the case file an
shove it up the jerk's ass. "Call Herrera, Danny. Fin
out why he ignored a possible witness to a murder. Be
cause if I do the honors, I'll get called out on the ca
pet."

"Will do, with pleasure." He looked back to Frankie
"Can you describe the woman? If it *was* a woman."

"Tall, long black hair almost to her waist. She wor
a black dress that ended midcalf. I didn't get a goo
look at her face, but I thought she was a pretty larg
lady. Not fat, just big-boned."

"How tall?"

"Very. Statuesque. I'd guess Matt was around six feet, and I recall thinking she could look him in the eye. I only saw them from across the room as they were leaving. I doubt I could pick her out of a lineup, but if she came into the club again I'm pretty sure I'd know it was her."

Danny gazed at him a few seconds, worry clouding his eyes. "Do you go to Spanky's often?"

"Hardly ever. It's not my scene. Like I said, I rarely go out. If I do, I usually meet friends at other places that are more tame."

"Good. If I were you, I'd stay away from the night-life altogether for a while," Danny advised. "Just to be on the safe side."

Frankie set his can of soda down with a *plunk*, mouth dropping open. "You don't think the killer would come after me . . ."

"If a serial killer recognizes a witness, all bets are off. Lie low and don't take any chances." On that dire note, Danny stuffed the last bit of sandwich into his mouth.

"God."

Blair appeared so shocked and upset by the possibility that his life might be in danger, Austin felt sorry for him. Hell, he knew that fear too well. "Hey, it doesn't hurt to be careful, that's all. Don't sweat it."

"Right," Frankie drawled, rolling his eyes. "Just another day in the jungle. Does the PD put you guys through desensitivity training or what?"

"I'm a sensitive guy." Danny grinned. "Rainey's the asshole."

He scowled. "I am *not* an asshole." *Am I?*

They thanked Frankie for his hospitality. He waved off their thanks with a smile, then dumped their plates in the sink and checked his watch.

"Hate to rush, but I've gotta book out of here if I'm going to make my appointment," he said. "But if you need me for anything else, I'll be around."

Danny fished his wallet from his back pocket and removed a small card, handing it to Frankie. "The main number to our field office is on there, as well as my cell phone. Don't hesitate to call anytime if you remember something else or a problem comes up."

Frankie took the card and hesitated, cutting Danny a speculative look from under his dark lashes. "Sure."

Austin glanced from his partner to Frankie, amused by the very real supercharged undercurrent passing between them.

As they took their leave and headed back to Danny's car, the direction of Austin's thoughts threw him even more off balance than he'd already been. Putting them aside, he refocused on the most pressing issue first.

"You kept me out of the loop on Blair being a witness," he began.

"I didn't do it on purpose, and I only found out when I talked to him this morning."

"You could've mentioned it."

"Well, I didn't," Danny stressed, anger simmering close to the surface. "You're not exactly up to speed yet, and you know it. You show up at work half looped, about to fall over—"

Austin stopped in his tracks. His friend squared off with him toe-to-toe, not giving an inch. "I don't give a shit. If you know something, I know it five minutes later, unless I'm dead. Got it?"

"I got it," he snapped.

"And what the hell was that back there with you and Frankie?" Austin winced inwardly at how damn personal—and harsh—the question sounded.

Danny stilled, his eyes gone cold as chipped ice. "What're you talking about?"

Christ. He'd made a mistake bringing this up. "I don't know, partner. You tell me."

Every muscle in his friend's body went rigid, and his jaw clenched. "I resent what you're insinuating."

"I'm not *insinuating* the fact that Frankie couldn't keep his eyes off you and that it seemed mutual," he said. "Not that there's anything wrong with that, because there isn't. If there's anything you want to tell me, you can. You know that."

He'd stepped over the line. Danny's mouth fell open in shock, outrage contorting his face. A myriad of emotions swirled in his eyes. Pain, anger, and panic. He ran a hand through his hair, breathing heavily.

"Jesus, Danny. I'm sorry—"

In one step, his friend closed the gap between them and shoved Austin in the chest, hard enough to send him staggering backward.

"Fuck you, asshole!"

"Danny—"

Another shove, this one slamming his back into a

tree trunk. Sharp pain radiated through his back. Murder in his eye, Danny grabbed a handful of his shirt in one fist.

"Are you so goddamn jealous over my date with Laura that you'd accuse me of being gay?" he hissed. "Does it drive you crazy knowing you're such a dumbass she might end up being mine?"

He did his best to defuse the situation. "This isn't about you and Laura at all. I wasn't imagining the vibes I got in there—admit it."

His partner tightened his grip, clenched his free hand into a fist. He braced himself for a blow that never came. Instead, he watched something inside Danny wither and die, leaving a blank slate. No infectious humor, no rage. Nothing.

He cursed himself for handling everything so badly. And prayed he hadn't severed their friendship.

"You go straight to hell," Danny said, releasing him. He spun on his heel and strode for the car, leaving his partner to follow. Or not.

"Too late, pal." He sighed. "I'm way ahead of you."

Much later, as Austin stewed over Danny's impending date with Laura, it occurred to him that his pissed-off friend had never denied one word of his observation regarding Frankie.

Not one single word.

She hadn't heard from Austin all day, even after work. Not surprising, considering the plan he and Danny had cooked up. More Danny's idea than Austin's, and she had a feeling her lover wouldn't be too happy about it.

Danny had arrived and had driven her home so she could change for their "date." He'd even offered to drive her out to Austin's afterward, once he was sure they weren't being followed. She wasn't sure the subterfuge was going to fool a brutal killer like this one, but it couldn't hurt. Or at least she hoped not.

Laura stared at her disconsolate reflection in the bathroom mirror. She didn't like this at all. It felt wrong going out with Danny when she knew he'd hoped for more. A hot rush of tears stung her eyes, but she fought them back. Why the hell was she so weepy? It wasn't as if she wouldn't see Austin again.

She smoothed her black skirt and blouse, brushed out her hair, leaving it loose around her shoulders, and dabbed on some lipstick. Finished, she went to the living room, where Danny was waiting.

Hearing her approach, he rose from the sofa with a smile. "You look gorgeous."

"Thank you. So do you, handsome."

He did, too. A beautiful smile with straight white teeth in his boyishly handsome face. All that lush chestnut hair, falling like silk into sparkling green eyes and down to the collar of his coat.

He treated her to dinner at an outrageously expensive steak house. The man was fabulous company. Funny, charming, and mature beyond his years, he was just about as perfect as a guy could be. Exactly the sort of man any woman in her right mind would love.

Except he wasn't Austin Rainey.

As they talked and ate, both of them kept a sharp eye out for anyone who appeared to be watching them with too much interest. They spotted nobody suspicious, but that meant nothing.

Walking back to his car after dinner, Laura linked her arm with his. "I had a wonderful time, Danny."

"Me, too." Then he said, "You're falling for him, aren't you?"

The love in her heart was almost physical. She didn't bother to pretend ignorance. "Falling? No. More like fell, hard."

"I knew. Maybe because he's been sitting between us all evening."

She angled her head to look up at him. The corners of his mouth were tilted up, but she thought he seemed distant. Troubled. She pulled him to a stop, turned him to face her. "I won't lie to you. I've been in love with Austin for so long, I don't remember what my life was like before we met. I'm sorry if I've hurt you. I've screwed up, haven't I?"

He shook his head. "You haven't hurt me, Laura. And no, you haven't screwed up. I'd like for us to be friends."

"I'd like that, too." She paused, studying his miserable expression. "What's wrong?"

"I'm the one who's screwed up. Austin and I had a nasty falling-out earlier today," he confessed, studying his shoes.

"Oh no! What happened? Was it about me?"

"Among other things."

Lord, were those tears in his eyes? "Sweetie, you can talk to me."

A strange look crossed his face. "Can I . . . can I kiss

you? I know you're with Austin and I told him I wouldn't poach, and I won't, but . . . I have to know something."

The request wasn't what took her by surprise. It was the desperate urgency in his voice. The way he stared down at her, a silent plea etched in his face. As if she alone held the answer to unlock a mystery.

"All right," she agreed. "Just once."

Laura tipped her head up and Danny's strong hands cupped her face. Slowly, he lowered his head, covering her mouth with his. Boy, could he kiss. His lashes swept down as his lips captured hers, warm and soft. Heartbreakingly gentle. His tongue teased the seam of her mouth, but never invaded. Sensual, erotic. Perfect, for the right woman.

He didn't make the earth quake under her feet. Didn't set her soul ablaze with conflicting emotions that turned her inside out. Not like Austin.

Breaking the kiss, he opened his eyes and dropped his hands. "Seems I lost you somewhere along the way."

"Hey, you're gonna break somebody's heart with that kiss one of these days," she vowed, attempting to lighten the mood.

"You think so?"

He sighed, staring off into the night, looking so sad Laura wanted to cry. She touched the sleeve of his coat. "Danny, I didn't mean to make you feel used. Or sad, or whatever."

"It's okay, Laura," he whispered low. "Because I think maybe I used you a little bit, too."

*   *   *

In the end, Danny put an end to Laura's dilemma by ordering her to pack a bag. He was giving up guard duty and taking her to Austin's place, where they would either kill each other or work things out.

Danny never told her what the rest of his fight with Austin had been about, but Laura sensed it was bad. So bad he wasn't willing to risk putting more strain on their friendship by staying with her, even platonically, to act as her protector. There was nothing between her and Danny, but Austin didn't know that.

Though he should, she thought. Especially after the times they'd spent in each other's arms, making love. Did he really think she was that easy?

Danny drove like a bat out of hell the entire way. He said the sooner he got her to Austin, who'd most likely worked himself into a towering rage by now, the better. Laura thought he was exaggerating a tad.

Until they arrived.

Danny pulled into the circular driveway, parked in front of house, and killed the ignition. "His truck's here and the living room lights are on. Ready?"

She swallowed her nerves. "I'm not so sure this is a good idea."

"Me, either. Got a better one?"

"Not at the moment."

"All right, then." He waggled his brows. "Into the lion's den."

They got out and walked up the steps of the porch together, Danny shouldering her bag. Laura rang the doorbell, and they waited. She rang it again, and they waited some more.

"Let's try around back," her companion suggested. "Maybe he's sitting out on the deck."

The porch wrapped around the ranch-style house, disappearing into the darkness. Danny led the way and she followed, their footsteps clomping noisily on the creaky boards.

At the back of the house, the walkway widened into a small deck sporting a large redwood picnic table and dotted with lounge chairs. Danny halted so abruptly she almost collided with his back.

"Jesus Christ."

Laura stepped around him. Austin was reclining in one of the loungers, staring into the gloom. In spite of the chilly spring night, he was shirtless. A large bottle was nestled between his blue-jean-clad thighs. He never turned his head, remained still as a statue, as his low voice caressed them.

"Go. The fuck. Away."

"Austin," Danny began. He paused, uncertain.

Austin began to laugh, and the eerie sound sent a shiver through Laura as he lifted the bottle. A tall, square bottle with a white label, only half full. Jim Beam, she realized, stomach clenching.

He set the whiskey aside, then pushed out of the lounger. He was steady on his bare feet as he turned to face them. When he spoke, his voice was low and dangerous. He might've been drinking, but he wasn't drunk, wasn't slurring his words.

"Have a nice fucking time, kids?"

"We stuck to the plan," Danny said carefully, as though disarming a bomb. "We had dinner and then I brought her straight here."

"Why?" That one word snapped her like the tip of a whip.

"Because this is where she wanted to be, dipshit. With you. Though you're being so nasty right now, I can't fathom why."

Suddenly Austin swayed on his feet, almost went down. Danny lunged and grabbed him, kept him from falling.

Laura gasped, moving forward to cup his face. His skin was clammy to the touch. "Honey, have you taken any painkillers this afternoon?"

"My head was pounding," he muttered, lashes drifting shut.

"And then you drank?" Danny sputtered. "You dumbass."

"I'm so tired, Danny. Tired of being alone. I lost Ashley 'cause she didn't love me. I can't fall in love again," he said sadly. "The killer will destroy me and the woman I love. What am I going to do?"

Love? Laura's heart leapt. Was he referring to her? Could he truly be falling in love with her?

"Don't let a lunatic dictate your life, that's what." Danny frowned.

"I'm sorry, Danny," Austin murmured, swaying on his feet. "What I said before? Forgive me . . ."

An instant later, his legs folded. Danny lowered him to the deck and they dropped to his side.

"Is he all right?" Laura cried.

Danny grabbed his wrist, checked his pulse. "Slow, but steady. Let's get him inside."

"Shouldn't we get him to the hospital? What if he's taken more pills?"

"I don't think so. He's been drinking, but from the looks of the bottle he didn't consume that much. You should keep an eye on him, though."

Handing Laura her overnight bag, he scooped Austin into his arms, grunting under the strain of his burden. She ran to open the sliding patio door for him, then trailed anxiously behind as he carried his friend to the bedroom and laid him on his bed.

"Damn, he's heavy." Danny panted, straightening to rub the small of his back.

She put her bag in a nearby chair, then sat on the edge of the bed next to Austin. She couldn't stop herself from touching him any more than she could stop her heart from beating. She ran a palm over the smooth planes of his broad chest, relishing the hard ridge of muscle under taut golden skin. What would it be like to have the entire length of his tall, gorgeous body pressing down on hers? Filling her?

Aware of Danny watching, she nixed those delicious thoughts. Somehow, it seemed wrong to drool over Austin when his friend had just shown her such a nice time. But hell, Danny knew how she felt.

She let her hand linger over his heart, gratified to find the beat steady and strong. Then she skimmed upward, stroking his face. His cheeks were shadowed with dark burnished stubble, long dusky lashes resting against them.

"He'll be okay," Danny said quietly, sitting on the other side of the bed. "He's just passed out, and he's gonna have a killer headache in the morning."

Killer. The word snagged in her mind, eliciting a terrible thought. "God, Danny! Do you realize what could've happened if we hadn't shown up? He might have passed out on the deck, completely vulnerable to that maniac!"

"Idiot. What a stupid thing for him to do. But I'll let *you* fuss at him when he wakes up. I doubt he'll want to hear anything I have to say right now, and the feeling is mutual."

"Wow. Must've been some argument."

"Oh yeah." He pursed his lips together, sending her the message. Subject closed.

"I'm sure everything will work out."

"Right."

He didn't sound convinced. "You can leave if you want. I'm sure he's out for the count. I'll be fine here alone with him."

"Alone with a passed-out cop who couldn't fend off an angry Boy Scout, much less an enraged killer." He arched a brow. "Do you know the code to set the alarm if I go?"

"Well, no."

"Do you even know how to fire his gun?" He gestured to where the ominous-looking gun lay discarded on the nightstand.

"I could probably figure it out."

Danny grinned. "You plan to ask the nice psychotic killer to wait a sec while you Google the instructions?"

"All right, smart-ass!" In spite of the situation, she

laughed at her companion's smug expression. "You win. What do you propose, Kimosabe?"

"I'll bunk on the sofa downstairs tonight. Just wake me when the beast arises so I can get out of Dodge before he spots me."

"Oh, *now* who's the weenie?"

"Retreat and live to fight another day," he quipped, rising from the bed. Danny got to the bedroom door, stopped, and turned. "He'll get over his fears—just wait and see. When he does, he'll be the luckiest bastard on the planet to have the love of a woman like you."

"Oh, Danny." Damn, her eyes were tearing up again. "You're going to find your special someone soon. I know it."

He threw her a sad, wistful smile, then strode from the room without another word.

11

"Christ."

Consciousness seeped into Austin's throbbing brain. Slowly. Painfully.

Don't move. Don't breathe.

He took stock, realizing that, other than his head, he didn't feel too bad. Even the pounding was starting to subside some. Struggling to rise, he was thwarted by something weighting his arms and legs, wrapping him like a tamale.

Sheets. His half-clothed body was tangled in bed-sheets, and he worked to disengage himself so he could hit the bathroom. Once there, he did his business and washed his hands, wondering how he'd gotten to his room.

The last thing he remembered was—what?

Sitting on his deck the night before, stewing over Danny and Laura being out together. Carrying out the stupidest fucking plan in the history of ever, and himself getting angrier about it as the evening went on.

A memory tugged at him and he recalled Danny and Laura. They'd showed up on his deck, and Austin hadn't exactly been his charming self. He winced at the thought of what he might've said.

"Austin?"

He froze. "Laura, what are you doing here?"

"Honey, are you all right?"

Heat crept up his neck, ignited his face. Unfortunately, embarrassment wasn't fatal. He turned his head to peer at Laura hovering in the doorway, and his jaw dropped. His libido gave a pathetic attempt to rise.

One hand braced on the doorframe, she was studying him, worry shining in her brown eyes, looking delectably tousled, raven hair forming a silky curtain around her face. She wore nothing but a huge red T-shirt, so big it hung past her knees, revealing only her toned calves and shapely feet. *His* T-shirt, the one that declared: *Save a Horse, Ride a Cowboy.*

He pointed an accusing finger at her and managed to find his voice. "Why are you wearing that?"

She glanced down at herself, then back at him, a faint smile teasing her gorgeous mouth. "I forgot my nightie. I hope you don't mind."

"Forgot your nightie? I thought you were staying at your place." He stared at her. What had he done last night? "Did we—?"

She arched a brow and her smile widened, a little cat toying with her prey. "Sleep together? Yep."

He closed his eyes and bowed his head, humiliation complete. How had she ended up here last night, in his bed, when she was supposed to be with Danny? "I'm so sorry. I don't remember."

"That's okay. It wasn't anything to write home about."

Boy, that hurt. The lady knew how to grab a man by the testicles and twist. "Go away and let me die in peace."

"Sorry, sweetie. You're out of luck on both counts. I'm not going anywhere and you're not going to die anytime soon. I will, however, go downstairs and make coffee while you shower."

Coffee? His belly cramped at the notion, and he groaned. For a few seconds, he thought she'd left, until her throaty voice drifted over him again.

"By the way, nothing happened between us. All we did was sleep. You mixed alcohol and your pain pills, so I stayed with you to make sure you were okay. Well, I was going to stay anyway. That's why Danny brought me here in the first place."

His head came up at that revelation. "Oh."

"Get cleaned up. I'll explain everything when you're finished. Can you manage all right?"

Austin sensed she wanted to come in and help him, but she held back. Maybe out of consideration for his bruised pride. Or maybe she believed he'd reject her aid. Whatever the reason for her hesitation, he was grateful. His self-respect had taken a serious beating and was lying prostrate at his feet, in dire need of CPR.

"I'll be fine, thanks." He gave her a weak smile, but she wasn't buying.

"See you downstairs," she said, shaking her head as she walked out.

Her consternation made him feel like a naughty teenager instead of a grown man, and rightfully so. Of all the stupid, irresponsible stunts to pull, sitting on his deck putting himself at risk. And then what? Damned if he could remember.

He'd needed to escape reality with a desperation that bordered on madness. To get away from everything. Memories of Ashley and the baby, loving and losing them. His stalker, arguing with Danny, falling for Laura.

Laura. She was the clincher, finally pushing him over the edge. The futile struggle not to fall for the lovely ME, because in the end he'd lose her, too.

What a clusterfuck. Weeks earlier, his life had been simple. A neat, tidy, isolated world, posted *No Trespassers Allowed*. He'd learned the hard way to compartmentalize the pain, to stifle the longing to hold the woman of his dreams. To live without love, the one weakness guaranteed to kill him the second time around.

Cursing, he went to the sink, then brushed his teeth. Removing his jeans, he turned on the shower, allowing the water to heat before stepping in.

The hot spray did wonders for soothing his attitude. His head didn't hurt as much as before and he found his mind was finally clearing.

Out of the shower, he toweled dry. Leaving his hair damp, he walked into the bedroom, retrieved a pair of black briefs from his dresser, and pulled them on. A fresh pair of jeans and an old, soft powder blue shirt made him feel more human. Then he headed downstairs in search of Laura.

The rich aroma of fresh coffee led him to the kitchen, where he found her sitting at the breakfast nook table, wearing his robe—and talking to Danny. They were leaning toward each other, whispering like a pair of thieves.

Wonderful. Wasn't this going to be fun?

"Morning," he murmured. Conversation halted as he walked to the coffeepot and took a mug from the cabinet. He poured the fragrant brew and joined them, taking a seat next to Laura, across from Danny. His friend nodded to him.

"How are you this morning?"

"I'm good, thanks."

"Did you know you're really heavy? I had to carry you to bed last night." His lips quirked.

He bit back the strong urge to tell Danny to fuck off, but couldn't keep the snarl out of his tone. "What are you two lovebirds doing here? And isn't that the same suit you had on yesterday?"

Danny's amusement cooled. "Your powers of observation are astounding. Yes, these are the same clothes. I slept in them—or rather, tossed and turned—here on your sofa. All damn night. To make certain my ignorant shithead of a friend didn't die of alcohol poisoning, and to be here in case Laura needed help."

Crap. He wrapped his hands around the warm mug, but didn't drink. "What happened?"

"I brought Laura over here to stay with you. We found you out on the deck nursing a bottle of Jim Beam, and you'd taken painkillers. You passed out and, as I said, I carried you to bed. My lower back may never recover."

"I remember some of it." Mortified, he dropped his gaze to his mug. "Thanks, Danny. I mean that."

"Yeah, well, don't pull an asinine stunt like that again. You scared the hell out of us."

"Don't worry. I doubt my brain would survive another round." He turned his head to peer at Laura, not quite daring to trust what he'd just heard. "I thought Danny was going to stay with you."

A blush stained her cheeks. "I changed my mind. I'd rather crash here, with you. If the offer still stands."

Relief washed through him like a tidal wave. He struggled to remain calm, to hide the stupid grin that wanted to spread across his face. "Of course, sweetheart. You're welcome to stay until this stalker mess is over, as long as you need."

How about forever? Then I'd never be lonely again and I'd make you so happy—

Danny rose. "I need to go home and get cleaned up before I head in to work. Walk me out?"

Laura took the hint and stayed behind to sip her coffee as Austin saw his partner to the door. In unspoken agreement, they stepped out on the porch together. Danny looked him square in the eye, wasting no time on what he had to say.

"I thought you deserved to know that before you passed out last night, you had a meltdown. I mean *really* lost it. Do you remember anything you said?"

"Jesus, no. Last night's a blank."

"Just as well. You were downright mean when we got here," Danny said flatly. "But that's beside the point. The only reason I'm bringing it up is because you broke down, starting moaning about Ashley in front of Laura.

Spouting a bunch of crap about not falling in love again. You get the picture."

Fuck, fuck, fuck! Now would be a good time for the earth to open up and swallow him whole.

"Has she mentioned it?"

"Not a word. If it hurt her, she's hidden it well." His friend leaned against the porch railing, crossed his arms over his chest. "Want some free advice?"

"Not particularly."

"Don't blow your chance. She's a terrific lady. Let the past lie. She wants you and you want her, so go for it."

"My stalker—"

"Is a convenient excuse."

"It's a little more serious than that."

His partner arched a brow. "So you're gonna drink yourself into oblivion every time you feel low? You're gonna push her away and she'll have no trouble finding the man who's all too happy to help her get over you."

"Like you?" he bit off.

"Not even close. Laura's a friend to me, nothing more. But make no mistake—if I had feelings for the lady, I'd fight the devil himself to have her."

Austin studied the open, honest expression on his friend's face. And something else lingering there, too. Remorse? No, that wasn't right. Damned if he knew.

"I hear you. To tell the truth, it's getting harder to remember why I'm fighting a battle I'll probably lose."

"Whether or not you'd be the loser is entirely a matter of perspective." Danny pushed away from the railing, throwing him a teasing grin that didn't quite mask the shadows in his eyes. "Gotta go. *One* of us has to make an effort to show up at work on time this week." He turned to leave.

"Hang on." Austin waited until his friend faced him again before continuing. "I owe you an apology for yesterday."

"Forget it."

"I can't. I was on edge, definitely not myself, but that's no excuse. I had no right to question your preferences. It's none of my damn business, and I'm sorry."

Danny slanted a look at him. "What if I *was* gay? Would it matter to you?"

"Are you?" he asked. "Is that what you're trying to tell me?"

"Just answer the fucking question."

Austin studied his unhappy friend. Now he got the expression he'd glimpsed on Danny's face. Total abject misery.

"No, it would not matter to me. Not one bit. You're a damn good cop, and one of my best friends. I've got your back no matter what. Understand? Nothing's gonna change that, so don't get all depressed and do anything stupid, for God's sake."

"I'm confused, not suicidal," he muttered.

"I mean, don't do anything impulsive."

"Like pay Frankie Blair a visit? You know, if we hadn't found you in such bad shape last night, I think I might have done just that."

"Aw, shit." Austin closed his eyes. How long had his friend been battling a load of inner torment? *Worse, how could I have been such a prick?* He opened his eyes. "What are you gonna do?"

Danny glanced away, jaw tightening. "I don't know."

"Whatever you decide—*if* you decide—Danny, be careful."

"This stays between us. I don't want the guys at the station getting wind of it."

"Goes without saying." Most, like Glenn's and Austin's detectives, would show their support. Some would keep a cool distance. And the rest, like the jerks he'd caught cracking jokes at his own expense, would turn on Danny like a pack of vicious dogs out for blood.

"Thanks. Catch you later."

Austin watched Danny trot down the steps and head for his 'Vette, shoulders slumped. Always so alone, he realized. Far too quiet and solitary for a man of twenty-six. The fact that he'd missed the signs of a good friend in serious personal crisis shamed him.

"I'll do better, I promise," he vowed as his partner drove away.

A cool spring morning breeze ruffled his hair, kissed his face. Goose bumps broke out on his arms, causing him to shiver. What was that?

Changes coming, the wind whispered against his skin. *Some of them sure to bring heartache. Be ready, Rainey . . .*

Great. He was losing his mind. Then again, taking a swan dive into the shallow end might not be such a raw deal. Funny little pills to keep you mellow, pleasant doctors in white coats, three squares a day.

But no Laura. A grim prospect that had become impossible to fathom. Suddenly, he needed to be with her more than his next breath. Ached to sit with her at his kitchen table, enjoying her company while she sipped coffee, wrapped in his ridiculous robe.

Danny's advice echoing in his brain, he hurried inside.

"Any big news in there this morning?"

Laura glanced up as Austin strode in and resumed his place at the table. Damn, how could the man look good enough to eat after all he'd been through the last few days, especially last night? There ought to be a law . . .

"Yep. Plenty of headlines, most of them negative." She flipped the newspaper closed. "Good news doesn't sell, and we know that better than most."

He propped his elbows on the table, pinning her with his green eyes. "How do you stand being immersed in other people's tragedies day in and day out without drowning?"

"And you aren't? What we do isn't so different, you know. You try to help people, and so do I."

He continued to gaze at her, as though working out the solution to a puzzle. "Your situations are always tragic, though. Yet you really believe you make a positive difference." An observation, not a question.

"I know I do." She lifted her chin. "And I have a three-ring notebook full of letters and e-mails to prove it."

"For example?" He cocked his head, appearing genuinely interested. Even encouraging.

She blinked. "Well, I received a letter from the parents of a little girl kidnapped right out of her backyard last year. The case was heartbreaking, yes, but the evidence I found on her body led to a career pedophile and rapist. The police were finally able to put him in prison before he harmed anyone else."

Austin smiled, clasping her hand. "That's wonderful, sweetheart. Not about the little girl, of course, but what you do to bring closure to families."

"Thank you."

Wow. She sucked in a steadying breath. The guy had no idea how badly she longed to jump his bones when he blinded her with those big pearly whites. Shaking herself, she went on.

"Successful closure on a case requires the whole team to be on their toes: my office, the community, the media, and the police. That's what I love most about my job, Rainey. As weird as it sounds coming from a medical examiner, I love being part of a happy ending. When it works, it's magic."

"Happy endings are rare. You're an amazing woman, Laura Eden."

"I hope you still think so when I tell you my idea." She paused, biting her lip. His exaggerated groan and comical annoyed expression might've made her laugh if she hadn't been so worried about his reaction.

"Oh no. Come on. You got something against us being happy for more than five minutes?"

"Promise you won't get uptight and we'll be dandy."

"No deal. The alarm bells you're setting off are jacking with my headache."

Laura took a deep breath. "Okay, I've been thinking—"

"Strike one."

"Hear me out." She threw him a scowl. He crossed his arms over his chest, a faint smile hitching the corners of his mouth, but remained silent.

"Your stalker has been quiet since his failed attempt to get you. Much too quiet, I think. He'll make a move soon, and when he does, there needs to be another trap in place. One guaranteed to shake him up, make him sloppy."

"Royally piss him off, you mean?" A spark of interest lit his face. "How?"

"We'll lure him out of hiding. Then you'll get him. I'm no expert on the criminal mind, especially not the psychotic personality. But I'm willing to bet he's on the verge of his rage spiraling out of control. It shouldn't take much of a shove to send him over. I can think of one scenario almost guaranteed to do the trick."

"I shudder to imagine," he said dryly.

"Aren't you tired of waiting for him to make an attempt on your life? What if he does see us out together after all? We really flaunt our relationship in his face. I'll arrange the publicity with Joan, make certain he sees us together. Maybe I'll do better as bait to draw him out, and when he comes after me, you'll get him."

Austin's humor vanished. His eyes turned glacial, and the sudden thunderous anger on his face damn near stalled her pulse.

"Absolutely not. Do you have any firsthand knowledge of what this crazy bastard is capable of? Really?" He slammed his fist down on the table, causing her to jump and sloshing coffee from both mugs. "*I* do, god-dammit! He's stolen my life!"

Austin broke off, breathing as if he'd been running for miles. Laura laid a hand over his fist and said gently, "I know. Let's get it back. Austin, I love you."

His face turned the color of chalk.

Jerking his hand from hers, he shoved from the table and left the room without a word. She sat unmoving, heard the sliding glass door to the patio open. Riddled with uncertainty, she waited a few minutes before going after him. Had she done the right thing by confessing? She knew only that witnessing his terrible struggle, she hadn't been able to keep it to herself.

She found him sitting on the steps of the deck, elbows on his spread knees, gazing across the small yard. He looked so lost, just as he had on the drive home from the hospital, and again last night. A shiver went through her soul.

He's stolen my life.

She sat on the steps beside him. Waited for the bomb to explode. But his quiet voice drifted over her, a silky caress.

"What do you know about Ashley?"

"Not much," she admitted. "Just that you two were miserable together."

"That's an understatement." He didn't look at her. "Though I did love her at one time."

"I'm sure you did. Is this about what I said? Do you want me to take it back?" She touched his sleeve. "I would never intentionally hurt you, Austin. Not for the world."

He did turn to her then, and the sheen of tears in his eyes stole her breath. Somehow they didn't spill over, probably from sheer force of will on his part.

"Oh, honey!" Laura cupped his face in her hands. "I'm so, so sorry. I didn't mean to cause you more pain. I know you must still be grieving for Ashley—"

"It's not Ashley." He paused, searching for a way to explain. "For weeks after she said it was over between us, I thought I'd die. God knows part of me wanted to quit. I saw a counselor for a few months. I got through losing her, eventually. Then we got pregnant, and things went sideways between me and her again, and you know the rest. But that's not even what's getting to me right now."

She combed a lock of auburn hair from his eyes. "If it's not the past dredging up your grief, what's upsetting you so badly? Talk to me."

"Your plan, in the kitchen . . ."

"I'm not following."

"I'm afraid, Laura."

"Of what, sweetie?"

"Of losing you," he whispered. "Because I love you, too."

And covered her lips with his.

12

Oh. Oh my.

Laura had no defense against this. A sexy alpha male with a gentle soul, stripping himself bare. Revealing the wounded, lonely soul underneath. Punctuate that with a searing, spine-tingling kiss designed to claim her as *his*, and she was toast.

He loves me, too. Yes.

He leaned into her, cupping the back of her head, his mouth hot. Demanding. She arched into him and skimmed her hands over his shoulders, nipples hardening against his wide chest.

Stolen kisses were no longer enough. Not with this man. She wanted everything he was willing to give. Truth be told, she always had.

"Let's go inside, Captain."

He pulled back, searching her face. Desire laced his deep, husky voice. "Are you sure?"

She traced a finger along his lower lip. "Oh *yeah*."

Giving her a lopsided smile, he stood, scooping her into his arms in one smooth motion. "My lady, your wish is my command."

"Put me down!" she squealed.

He tightened his grip, cuddling her against his chest. "I don't think so."

She laughed, reached up to stroke his face, loving the feel of his morning beard on his cheeks. He was all hers to touch, to hold. Happiness bloomed in her heart, spreading warmth to her fingers and toes.

Austin paused only long enough to close and lock the sliding glass door, then hurried through the house and to his bedroom as if she weighed nothing.

Once there, he laid her gently on his king-sized bed, then straightened. In record time, he shed his shirt and slid his jeans off, kicking them away. Laura drank in the sight of his naked body greedily. Austin was the hottest man she'd ever seen. Wearing nothing except a smile, the man was equal to none.

It hadn't been that long since they'd been together, yet it seemed like forever. She studied the startling green eyes set in the planes of his handsome angular face. Thick dark red hair framing his wonderful face, brushing his neck. She let her gaze drift leisurely to his broad shoulders and strong arms.

He was ripped with muscle, but not obsessively so. Strong and capable. A very light sprinkling of hair, a bit darker than that on his head, covered his chest, trailing downward past flat, hard male nipples. Finally, she allowed her attention to roam to his impressive erection, savoring the sight. Heat flamed low in her belly, between her legs. His engorged penis jutted proudly from a nest of dark curls, arching toward his washboard stomach.

"Still like what you see?" His smile told her he knew the answer.

"I want to touch you."

His eyes went dark, feral. "Your turn, sweetheart. All's fair."

Eagerly, she tugged his T-shirt over her head, pitched it onto the floor.

He climbed onto the bed to sit next to her and pushed her arms down to her sides. "God, you're beautiful. What did I do to deserve you?"

Laura's face heated, but she smiled. "Thank you. You're pretty damn handsome yourself."

"I don't know about that, but thanks."

Fascinated, Laura reached out to touch the broad head of his penis, swirling it with one finger as a drop of precum beaded the tip. Encouraged by his sharp intake of breath, she became bolder in her exploration, wrapping her hand around his cock.

"*Yes.*" He leaned back and closed his eyes, spread his long legs to encourage her journey.

She pumped him slowly, enjoying the texture of silky, baby-soft skin over such hardness. Next she moved her hand to cradle his testicles, reacquainting herself with the feel of his heavy sex. Marveling that such a powerful man could be reduced to jelly with a caress.

"Sweetheart," he gasped, removing her hand. "I'm not going to last. But I promise I'll make it up to you next time."

Quickly, Austin reached for the nightstand and removed a condom from the drawer.

"Is that even necessary," she asked. "I mean, we already blew that one."

Immediately she regretted bringing it up. A shadow crossed his face as he shrugged. "It was just the one time, so using one can't hurt."

She swallowed her disappointment, unwilling to let it spoil the moment. "Of course. Hurry up there, sexy."

After covering himself, he lowered her onto the pillows and stretched his big body over hers, settling between her legs. His erection pulsed against her belly as he captured her lips in a sizzling kiss, tongue licking into the seam of her mouth. Teasing, tasting.

He broke the kiss, moved lower, repeating his attentions on her breasts. "Perfect, so perfect. So *mine*."

His teeth grazed one nipple, tongue doing wonderful things to the hardened little pebble. Sending delightful shocks to every nerve ending. When he suckled the other nipple, she came undone, pulling at his shoulders.

"Austin, I need you inside me."

Moving up to cover Laura, his gaze locked with hers. The raw male heat, the *possessiveness* on his face made her quiver in anticipation.

He slid a hand between her thighs, fingers brushing the dark curls there. Pushing one finger inside, he stroked in and out, spreading the dewy wetness to prepare her. Lengthening the strokes, he rubbed her clit, setting her on fire.

"Now, please!"

Guiding the head to her entrance, he began to push.

"Oh! Yes, yes."

"I've got you, baby," he crooned. "You feel so good."

He pushed deeper by inches, letting her adjust to him. His gentleness brought a rush of tears to her eyes. The feeling of him filling her became a flame burning brighter. Desire ignited, being with him a joy she'd never known with another man. She wrapped her arms round him, skimming her hands over the muscles in his back as he seated himself as deeply as possible.

"Feel me?" he whispered into her hair.

"Yes." She raised her hips, urging him.

He began to move, slow, tantalizing strokes. "Are you mine?"

"Oh, Austin, yes! I'm yours."

He held her against his chest, made sweet, beautiful love to her. Sheltered in the safety of his arms, his body covering her like a warm blanket, she'd come home. This wasn't just sex with a gorgeous man. This was love.

That they'd said the words made it even more beautiful.

His tempo quickened, his thrusts filling her harder. Deeper. Faster. But even as he drove into her, taking them to the edge, he was careful not to crush her, protecting her while entering her with powerful strokes. Hurtling them higher, higher—

His release erupted, his big body shaking. She followed, the orgasm shattering her control, the waves pounding her senses. He shuddered again and again, until he lowered his forehead to hers, spent and breathing hard.

She lay unmoving, loving his weight on top of her, his musky male scent teasing her nose. Loving him.

"I love you, Austin Rainey."

"And I love you, Laura Eden."

You're mine.

One hundred percent pure, satisfied male. Her heart thrilled at the memory of the words that had come from the depths of his soul, and she cherished them.

That was more than enough for her to be happy.

Austin disposed of the condom and returned to the bed, gathering Laura into his arms. "Wow. I think my bones melted." He felt her smile against his chest, and liked it. A lot.

"Me, too."

He tightened his hold, kissed the top of her head. "Tonight, lady, you'd better be ready. I plan on making love to you all damn night, in every conceivable way."

She wiggled against him, teasing, "Ooh, promises, promises."

"Hey, cut it out," he growled playfully. "Never dangle a bone in front of a starving dog. I've been lonely far too long."

"I'm sorry," she said, running a palm over his chest.

"For making me so hard again that I'm about to go blind?"

Her voice softened. "I'm sorry you've been lonely."

Austin was glad he'd admitted it to himself and to her. His heart belonged to Laura. He wasn't just falling hard. *I love her. Completely.* But oh, God, he was still so afraid of the danger his love might place her in.

Carefully, he hugged her close and kissed her hair. "Baby, I'm not lonely anymore."

Another smile, and a hug. "Me, either."

They lay wrapped together in comfortable silence, because words weren't necessary. A perfect, rare, treasured moment of crystal clear understanding between a man and a woman. Too huge for them both, so he allowed the knowledge of their love to bring him life after a long, harsh drought. Curl tendrils around his heart and hers, so good and beautiful the sensation seemed almost painful. Like water, he thought, filling cracks in dry, thirsty earth.

After several minutes, he stirred with a reluctant sigh. "We'd better get ready for work."

"We're already late. Ten more minutes? Please?" She rested her chin in the center of his chest and gazed at him with big, sad doe eyes, poking out her bottom lip.

He barked a laugh and kissed the end of her nose. "How do women learn to do the pouty face?"

Laura arched a brow. "It's taught to us by our grandmothers and great-grandmothers as a form of mind control that works great on men."

"It works. The question is, does it work both ways?" He returned the pitiful expression, sticking out his lower lip.

She burst into a fit of giggles, then scooted up and kissed his cheek. "Touché. I can see I'll have to use the weapons in my arsenal sparingly."

"But not *too* sparingly," he said, grinning. "I think I could get used to bending to my lady's wishes. Maybe I'm a closet submissive."

A feline smile curved her mouth. "Oh, *yum*. I say we test that theory tonight when I have my way with you."

"Damn, this is gonna be a long day," he griped.

"Poor baby." She traced his lips with a delicate finger.

"Mmm." Content to be the object of her sympathy, he relaxed into the pillows, enjoying her exploration. She brushed her fingers over his lips, the lines around his mouth, his brow. He groaned in pleasure when she sank her hands into his hair, massaging his scalp, sending wonderful little chills all the way to his spine.

She paused, peering at him in concern. "How's your head?"

"Better, especially with those magic fingers doing the trick."

"Does it hurt much?"

"Yeah, but not because of the roofie. I think that's out of my system. It's mostly because of the whiskey I drank mixed with the pain pills," he admitted ruefully. "Not one of my finer moments."

She ignored his comment and moved off him to his side. With her palm, she skimmed his rib cage. "Most people would crumble under what you've been through."

"Well, it's not enough to keep me from jumping your bones," he joked. The desperation in his voice ruined the attempt at lightheartedness. *Please, baby, I don't want to talk about this.*

"Austin, have you seen a counselor?"

"I don't have time for that."

"I sort of thought talking with a counselor was required of a police officer or any other emergency worker after the sort of grief you've had to deal with."

"Technically, it is. I've been putting it off because Glenn hasn't mentioned it yet." He must've sounded as depressed about the prospect as he felt. Laura propped herself on one elbow and reached out with her free hand to stroke his hair.

"Hey, chin up. The sessions might actually help you, like you said they did before. You might only need one or two."

"Yeah, unless the doc decides I need ongoing therapy." Austin heaved a sigh. "I hate the thought of spilling my guts again."

Worry darkened her expression. "But, sweetie, you need it to heal. You're grieving the loss of loved ones. The stalker has done these terrible things to you. It's deeply personal. You're dealing with the loss of a part of yourself. Making peace with that won't happen overnight."

The slight catch in her voice made him curious. "Sounds like you know what you're talking about."

"I do. Promise me you'll be open with the doctor. Otherwise, your grief and anger will fester until—" She broke off and shook her head. "I'm sorry. This is really none of my business."

He frowned at the sudden sheen of tears brimming in her eyes. "Don't be ridiculous. I've got no secrets, especially from the woman I just made love to. Laura, what's wrong?"

"I've seen what happens to a person when a ravaged psyche doesn't heal. Don't bury your pain until it destroys you."

He rested a finger under her chin. "I promise I won't let it come to that. But we're not talking about me anymore, are we?"

"Yes and no." She paused, as if debating whether elaborating was a good idea. "Something terrible happened to my brother when he was a kid. The trauma left him emotionally damaged. No, more like ruined."

"I didn't know you had a brother."

She nodded. "Grayson. He's the oldest, never married. And I have an older sister named Samantha, happily married with two kids."

Austin stared at Laura. "Grayson—wait a minute. Grayson Eden. *The* Grayson Eden?"

"Yep. Famous NASCAR driver. Merciless scourge of the track, asshole extraordinaire." But the raw pain in her voice spoke volumes about her affection for Grayson.

Austin rolled to his side, facing her. "You love him."

"I love the man he should've been."

"He's a successful celebrity," he pointed out.

"Who's loathed by nearly everyone who knows him. One of these days he's going to get himself or someone else killed on the track."

She had a point. NASCAR's most recent bad boy made the late Dale Earnhardt seem like a lamb in comparison. "So, whatever he went through as a young boy is what makes him tick as a man."

"He's a walking time bomb and everyone knows it. But as long as he rakes in the millions, his sponsors are more than happy to spread the shit with honey."

He reached out, smoothed a tendril of chestnut hair from her anxious face. "I'd like to hear about your brother, if it's not asking you to break family confidences."

"No, it's not a secret. Gray was kidnapped by a pedophile when he was fourteen. He was out riding his bike one afternoon and simply vanished. We didn't see him again for three long months. Honestly, we thought he was dead, and in a way I suppose that's true."

"Jesus."

"We don't talk about it publicly, but that doesn't stop the media from bringing it up now and then. Gray *hates* the media. We can't hold a conversation without him bashing what my friend Joan does for a living, yet he owes his life to a reporter, in a very real sense. How twisted and ironic is that?" she said sadly.

"You mean a reporter actually found him?"

"No, but she kept the story of his kidnapping alive long after other stations had dropped it. A hunter came across a run-down shack in the woods. He recalled the story and investigated on a whim. He found Gray inside, starving, naked, and chained to a bed. We can only imagine the living hell my brother must've gone through."

Austin tried to picture the sheer horror that had damaged so many lives, especially her brother's, and could imagine it all too well. He took Laura's hand. "I'm so sorry."

She clasped his fingers tight. "We got him back, but he was catatonic for over a year. Gradually, he came around, but he wasn't our Gray ever again. To this day, he's never spoken of his captivity."

"They never caught the man who took him?"

"No. All we know about the scum and what he did to my brother was pieced together by the detectives working the case. The psychologist our parents hired eventually gave up. Gray has always claimed he doesn't remember anything. Sammie and I believe he's blocking those horrible months, and one day it's all going to come crashing in on him."

"Thus the ticking time bomb. The reckless jerk no one understands is really a man in torment. And watching him, not being able to help him, hurts you."

"Exactly," she whispered. "Which is why I don't want to see you fall into the same emotional trap. Please don't shut me out."

His heart squeezed. "Don't worry, sugar. Not gonna happen. I'm too damn selfish to risk not having you in my bed, in my life. I'll do whatever it takes to keep you there."

She smiled. "Good, because I could get used to this. You know, it's funny. Not so long ago, we were worlds apart and I didn't think we'd ever get together."

He grinned. "You drove me insane with lust. I wanted you so bad I couldn't see straight, but I didn't *want* to want you, and that pissed me off. And you were such a witch, turning up everywhere I went, at every scene, acting all cool and sophisticated."

"You deserved every barb I tossed at your thick hide," she huffed without any real rancor.

"I had a permanent hard-on because of the pretty

thorn in my side. Still do." He gave her a wolfish smile, his gaze dipping to her full, ripe breasts. His erection stirred to life again.

"Aw, too bad we have to get to work," she teased.

"Like you said, we're already late."

With that, he rolled Laura onto her back, pinning her arms over her head. Her merry squeal rang in his ears as he retrieved another condom, then settled over her, positioning himself between her thighs.

"Austin Rainey! You're going to get me into trouble with my staff! Tonight—"

"Is too damn long from now." He lowered his head, swirling his tongue around one perfect nipple. Suckled.

"But—"

"Shh," he said, and slid inside her. Right where he belonged.

"Ohh, Austin. Yes."

The phone rang. He ignored it.

He began to pump his hips, slow and easy. Loving her, driving them higher. Worry and danger fell away, and nothing existed except the woman wrapped around his body. Giving her heart, shielding his. He lost himself to the glorious joy filling his soul, something he'd never hoped to feel again.

They were very, very late to work.

Two weeks. Two frustrating weeks of no more leads.

Austin spotted Danny waiting for him as he arrived at work one morning, and had a feeling that was about to change. Danny was circling his desk like an angry shark, his frustration palpable. His partner paced, checked his watch, then reached for the cell phone in his jacket. He spied Austin striding toward him and replaced it.

"Hey, sorry I'm late."

Danny scowled. "Well, you're looking mighty chipper this morning."

"I'm great. Thanks for asking."

"You're smirking."

"Am not." Dammit, he was. He struggled to wipe the smile off his face.

His friend's brows drew together in suspicion. "Yes, you are." His mouth fell open. "Jesus, you finally nailed her!"

Austin stilled. Something feral, fiercely protective, surged in his chest. "Careful, my friend. Beating the shit out of you would screw my psych eval." Little did his friend know he'd "nailed her" many times at this point. Wasn't any of his biz, either.

"Chill, for God's sake," Danny drawled, holding up a hand. "No disrespect intended. I'm behind you guys all the way, remember?"

Austin forced himself to relax. "I know. You hit a nerve, that's all."

"Sorry. I'll watch my mouth from now on. But listen, we've got major trouble."

Ah, shit. "Please don't say what I think you are."

"Wish like hell I didn't have to." He ran a hand through his dark auburn hair. "We've got another dead guy, murdered in his apartment in the Laketree sometime last night. Derek Thompson, age thirty-seven, fits your physical profile to a T. I just got back from the scene."

Austin closed his eyes. "Fuck."

"Same scenario, with one big difference. Our killer is losing control."

He opened his eyes, fighting down the choking misery. "How so?"

"This killing wasn't as methodical as the others. He didn't just cut the guy and leave him to bleed out." Danny blew out a shaky breath. "He tore Thompson to pieces in a pure rage, stabbed him in the groin over and over. Carved the word 'sinner' across his chest, too. It's a goddamn bloodbath."

Sinner?

A chill crawled down his neck. "Son of a bitch. Where'd he hook up with Thompson?"

"Get this. At Spanky's, like Blankenship."

"Damn!"

"Think he's rubbing our noses in our failure to catch him?"

"No. He's a psycho who's pissed at you. A creature driven by emotions that have spiraled out of control. The killer went back there on impulse, because he literally couldn't take the time to formulate a better plan. That's my gut feeling, anyway."

"Makes sense. But what doesn't is how he's luring them—and the synthetic wig. We still thinking he's in disguise?"

"That would be my guess," Danny said. "Especially based on what Frankie Blair said. He saw Blankenship leave with someone who *appeared* to be a woman but I'm betting was our man. Where is this bastard? He's a freaking ghost. He's fixated on you, but you haven't heard from him since he got you with the roofie. Christ."

"I'm going to have a look at the murder scene for myself, then head over to Spanky's and poke around. You coming?"

"Sure," Danny said. "Let me get my jacket."

After his partner trotted off, Austin sat behind his desk and picked up the phone. Another person murdered. *Because of his rage at me.* Something had to be done. No leads, no options, save one.

The internal battle warred on, his fingers gripping the instrument so hard his knuckles whitened. Every instinct screamed against putting Laura in more danger. But hadn't he already done that by loving her?

Until he pushed his stalker into making another play for him, another innocent young victim would die horribly. And another.

He dialed Laura's cell.

"Eden." She sounded breathless, noise in the background.

"Hi, baby. Where are you?"

"At the scene of a fresh murder in north Sugarland, Laketree Apartments. Male. Nobody's telling me shit."

His insides warmed. This was his smart doc. All teeth, all business. "I'll confirm for you. Another murder connected to me. Derek Thompson, age thirty-seven. Do your investigation, but withhold his name pending notification of the family. That's all I can say at this point."

"On the record?"

"Yeah."

"All right, thanks. Hang on a sec." More racket as she covered the phone, barked an order at someone. "I'm back. Where the hell are you, anyway?"

"On my way. And, Laura, I need your friend Joan to cover the scene. Make sure she waits and interviews *me* on camera about the murder investigation, no one else."

"I'll tell her." The frown in her voice was evident. "What are you up to?"

"Afterward, are you free for a late lunch?"

"For you? Any day, hot stuff. Business or pleasure?"

"A little of both. You or Joan got any contacts with the *Morning News*? Someone who can snap a photo, cause a stir?"

"You bet. I'll call as soon as we hang up. You want him today?"

"Today. Make sure he gets a cozy shot of us leaving the restaurant. Medical examiner and the police captain mixing the business and pleasure you mentioned."

"Austin!" She gasped, excitement dispelling the sharp, no-nonsense attitude. "You're taking me up on my idea?"

"Wish to God I had a better one. Stay put until I get there."

Off the phone, he looked up to find Danny waiting, arms crossed, an incredulous expression on his face.

"You heard?"

"You've lost your frigging mind—you know that?" he snapped.

He turned and stalked off, leaving Austin to follow.

Nice. Thing was, he couldn't disagree. He was gambling with Laura's safety, and his own, to provoke his stalker into a jealous rage.

Austin could only pray the taunt didn't backfire, explode in their faces. A cold promise breathed in his ear.

His next mistake would be his last.

13

Austin appeared beyond exhaustion.

Laura spotted him emerging from the victim's apartment, stripping off a pair of latex gloves. He fished a small plastic Baggie from his suit, stuffed them inside, then shoved the whole thing into his pocket. Pausing, he swiped a hand down his face.

Fists clenched, he stood gazing into space. Tension emanated from the hard line of his body. Impotent anger.

Danny, Shane, and Chris emerged from the apartment, stopped to speak with Austin, expressions grave. Then Danny clapped him on the shoulder before the men dispersed.

Austin might've been the dead man inside. They all knew. All were worried. The reminder made Laura sick.

He turned his head and saw her standing next to Joan and the news van, and started in her direction. Despite his tired smile, there was no mistaking his joy at seeing her, the renewed spring in his step. Laura wasn't the only one who noticed.

Joan froze in the act of checking her microphone and whistled softly, arching a tawny brow. "Whoa. Laura, girlfriend, that man has it bad for you. I think hell just iced over solid. The earth started spinning backward, birds flying upside down—"

Laura punched her friend in the arm, surprised by the steely cord of muscle that met her fist. "Good grief. Give us a minute, please?"

"Anything for you, my friend."

Laura ignored Joan as she walked around to the other side of the van and pretended to find something else to do. All her attention was zeroed in on Austin. Tall, broad shouldered, mouthwatering in his dark suit. And out of it.

Bad kitty.

He closed the distance between them rapidly. Didn't stop coming. Laura's lips formed an O of surprise; then he was pulling her into his arms. Settling her against his chest, head tucked under his chin. Wrapping his strength around her.

"Austin, we're in public! There are two other networks over there! We shouldn't—"

"I need you." He was trembling.

"Oh, sweetie. I'm here, always."

"Promise?"

"That's an easy one, Captain. I promise." Her arms encircled his waist, held him tight. His heartbeat pounded a frantic tattoo under her ear. She couldn't begin to imagine how horrific the scene inside must've been to upset him so badly.

"I intend to hold you to that."

She pulled back, looked up at him. "What do you say we get the segment over with and get out of here? We still on for lunch?"

He nodded, lips turning up in a weak smile. Green eyes haunted. "I don't know if I could eat, but anywhere is fine as long as I'm with you."

"You smooth talker," she teased, laying a hand on his chest.

Joan cleared her throat. "You two lovebirds ready?"

Reluctantly, Laura let Austin go to ready himself for the segment. Joan smoothed her jacket, adjusted her microphone. All set, she looked at Austin, who was frowning at something in the distance. "Captain Rainey?"

He blinked at her as though waking from a trance. "Yeah, sorry."

"Here we go," Joan said. "Three, two, one . . ."

"This is Joan Peterson live at the scene of what the Sugarland PD confirms is another in a string of murders committed by the serial killer who began his spree with the murder of local man Matt Blankenship on April third. With me is Captain Austin Rainey, who's in charge of the case. Captain Rainey, what can you tell us about the latest victim and the progress of the investigation?"

Expression grim, Austin relayed the barest information, careful not to reveal any details about the killing. He acknowledged that they believed the murder of the newest male victim was the work of the same killer, and little more, concluding by saying the department was doing everything in its power to catch the perpetrator.

"We're going to catch this animal and put him away," Austin said in a strong, commanding voice. "Mark my words."

Only Laura, and perhaps his closest friends, would be able to read the strain in the lines around his mouth. His stiff posture, the total absence of the self-assured cop they all knew so well.

The interview didn't last more than two minutes, but Austin's shoulders slumped in relief the instant it was over.

Laura touched his sleeve. "Ready to go?" She followed his gaze to Joan and her cameraman, who were busy returning their equipment to the news van. "Why do you keep staring at Joan?"

Instead of answering, he asked, "How long have you known her?"

"A year or so, I guess. About as long as I've known you." Puzzled by the question, she studied the strange look on Austin's face.

"Do you consider her a friend, or an acquaintance?"

"We're on friendly terms, but I don't know her well enough to call her a good friend." She slid a glance at Joan, praying she couldn't overhear. Apparently oblivious, the newswoman paid them no attention as she straightened and then closed the van door.

"Hey, Ms. Peterson," Austin called, waving her over. "Could you come here a sec?"

"Sure." She joined them again, running a hand through

her short platinum blond hair. Curious blue eyes locked with Austin's. "What's up?"

Austin kept his tone casual. "Laura tells me you've been at Channel Eight for a year now."

If Joan thought his interest odd, she gave no indication, merely lifted her slim shoulders in a careless shrug. "About that. I left Channel Twelve and the armpit known as Los Angeles before settling here."

Austin smiled. Putting the lady at ease. "Can't say as I blame you. Only a year ago, huh? Funny, I was thinking of all the times I've seen you on the news, but I could've sworn I'd seen you before that, somewhere else."

He had? Why hadn't he mentioned this?

Either Joan didn't notice that the captain was blatantly pumping her for information or she didn't care. "I never forget a face," she said pleasantly. "I sure wouldn't forget yours. But you could have seen me at the gym or the supermarket or at any of the clubs around here. I like to have a drink on my downtime."

"Really? Me, too. Where do you go?"

"Oh, the Waterin' Hole, Junior's, Twin Peaks, and a place called Spanky's. That one's a bit wild."

A little jolt went through Laura. She looked at Austin. His smile was a bit stiff and his gaze was speculative. The subtle change was confusing, and Laura wondered about it.

Austin's low voice came out low, raspy. "How about that?"

Desperate to break the weird tension, Laura linked

her arm through Austin's. "Sweetie, I'm sure Joan has a million things to do. I'm starving, aren't you?"

A weighty pause. Something dark, dangerous flickered in Austin's gaze. There and gone. "Yeah, starved. Thanks so much for covering the segment for me."

Joan grinned. "Anytime at all."

Rainey stared at her hard. "Yeah. Well, we'd better go. Thanks for answering my nosy questions. Old habits, you know."

"No biggie." Joan nodded. She turned to Laura. "If you're in good hands, I'll see you around. Let's do lunch."

"I am, and thanks. Lunch soon." She waved as Joan ambled around to the passenger side. She waited until the cameraman started the van and began to drive off before asking Austin, "What on earth was the third degree all about?"

"Just what I said. She seemed familiar from somewhere besides TV, and I'm pretty sure I've seen her around. Is she single? Does she date?"

"I've wondered myself, but that's not the sort of question I've ever felt comfortable asking her. Oh no—should I be worried about competition for your affections?" Laura deadpanned.

"Ha!" He snorted, relaxing a bit. "I didn't spend all these months pining for you from afar only to let you go the second I finally have you under my charming spell."

"Charming! Well, I suppose you have your moments." Sobering, she dropped the banter and pinned him with a look. "Seriously, whatever line of thinking you've got going on Joan, you're way off base."

He gave a tired sigh. "I know. I'm grasping at straws. It just struck me that I've seen her locally, and she seems strong enough to commit the crimes our killer has done."

Her brows arched. "Austin, really?"

Pulling her close, he gave her a hug. "I'm sorry. At this point I'd suspect anyone, even the mailman."

She felt bad for him. The man needed a lead, badly.

A commotion across the parking lot interrupted their banter and she gestured to the crowd. "Whoops. Time to get the heck out of here. You've got more reporters making a beeline in your direction."

"Jesus." Grabbing her hand, he practically dragged her to his truck. No doubt, tongues were wagging as they made their dubious escape.

Let them wag. At long last, she'd caught her sexy hunk of trouble.

And she would damn well keep him, even if she had to kick some psychotic ass to accomplish it.

From his dark corner, he watched them having lunch. Grinning at each other stupidly, heads together. Whispering, stealing little kisses.

Laura, you bitch.

"Think you're so smart, do you?" he seethed. "I warned you, whore."

Laura would die, and Austin would be punished. Soon. The pair had no idea who they were dealing with.

"You'll bring me down, will you, Captain?"

No idea. None at all.

*   *   *

Yesterday had been a howling bitch. The kind of day that makes a weaker man throw in the towel. Jump off a bridge. Walk in front of a speeding bus. After seeing Derek Thompson's torn, mutilated body, the stark horror fixed on his gray face, and knowing it should've been himself, Austin might have given up.

Except for Laura. Without her to steady him—his life raft in the storm—he might've drowned.

Holding a mug of steaming coffee, Austin walked into his bedroom and stood over her. She was lying flat on her back, arms spread. Raven hair spilled around her angular face. Her mouth was parted in deep sleep, and a delicate little snore escaped, making him chuckle.

Austin's T-shirt rode at her slim waist. One slender leg rested atop the bedspread, bent slightly at the knee. Sweet nipples poked at the fabric of his shirt, begging for his tongue. Her sex was completely exposed, inviting his cock to come out and play. Who was he to refuse such a delicious invitation?

His erection strained at the fly of his jeans. She was so soft. Beautiful. One hundred percent woman, and all his. She'd turned his world upside down and made him forget his fears and loneliness.

Setting the mug on the bedside table, he pushed off his jeans and climbed naked into bed. Spooned her from behind. Enthusiastically.

Laura shifted, wiggling her rump against his cock. "Mmm."

He bent over her, raked her hair aside. Kissed her soft neck, nibbled the tender skin there. Breathed her warm scent, which smelled faintly of him.

He slid a hand underneath the T-shirt, splaying it across her flat belly. He liked the way his fingers looked stretched almost the width of her abdomen. He loved the way she fit against his body, like an all-knowing higher power had handcrafted her perfection especially for him.

His fingers traveled upward, found the taut pebbles of her nipples. He took one, rolling the peak between his thumb and forefinger. She moaned, arching her back, skin heating to his touch. More kisses at the curve of her neck and shoulder. Tasting, playing with her breasts.

"Oh, Austin." She turned and blinked up at him, her big eyes glazed with arousal. Needing, wanting him.

"Let's get these off."

He flung the bedspread out of the way, tossing it to the floor. The T-shirt followed. She lay on the pillows, gazing at him with heated desire that rocked him to his toes.

"Spread your legs." Lips turned up, she did. Making room for him. He knelt between her thighs, trailing kisses from the inside of one knee to her sex. "So gorgeous. So pretty and pink. Already wet for me. I could come just looking at you."

She whimpered, raising her hips a bit. With a low chuckle, he obliged, his fingers parting her. His tongue flicked her folds, dipped inside. He lingered, taking his time. Licking slowly, like a man enjoying his last meal.

Laura fisted her hands in his hair, urging him. "Please!"

He fastened his mouth to her sex, suckling the sensitive nub. She came undone, bucking beneath him. Lost in decadent pleasure. The sight of her writhing, mindless to everything but his touch, nearly made him lose control.

Holding back his release shredded Austin as she found hers, wild against his mouth. Her honey bathing his tongue. *Oh, God, so sweet.*

When the last of her shudders stilled, he moved to her side. Bent and kissed her lovely mouth. He reached into the bedside drawer and grabbed the last condom, handing it to her to do the honors.

She sheathed his rampant erection. Grinned. "Poor baby. We need to do something about this."

"Oh, we are," he promised, low and dark. "I want you on your hands and knees. I'm going to fuck you from behind, sweetheart."

"What are you waiting for?" Laura gasped, pupils dilated. He'd aroused her all over again. She rolled and pushed to her hands and knees. "Like this?" she whispered. Excited.

"Jesus, yes." He looked his fill. Savored the sight of his woman ready to give herself to him this way. Dark hair cascading down her back. Knees spread, the pink lips of her sex, pouting and slick from his attentions, ready to welcome him inside.

He ran his fingers along her slit, spreading her. Jesus, he wasn't going to last. Grasping her hips, he guided the tip of his cock to her and thrust deep. Buried his cock to the hilt. Her heat surrounded the throbbing length of him, squeezing, driving him mad. *Not yet, not yet . . .*

"Look at you," he rasped. "So beautiful."

She began to move back and forth, stroking him. "Austin, please, fuck me hard."

"God, yes."

He surrendered control. Gave himself over to the beast raging to do her. Hard and wild. Wrapping his fingers in her long hair, he pulled her head back and pounded into her with long strokes. Thrusting harder, faster. Joyous feminine cries reached his ears, erasing any lingering doubt he might've had about taking her so roughly. He'd tread the razor's edge, but he'd never, ever hurt her. She knew, and trusted him completely.

"Yeah, take my cock, baby," he growled. "So fucking sweet."

"Oh yes! Fuck me!"

The beast stood no chance against such heady stuff. With a hoarse shout, he impaled her one last time. Held her small body close, buried so deep he actually *felt* them become one heart, one mind. His release rocked him to the core. Branded his soul as hers, for always. Her climax milked him, on and on.

Covering Laura like a blanket, he remained inside her for a moment, sweating and shaking. He'd never come harder or been drained more thoroughly in his life. Had never before shared a shattering awakening, a fusing of hearts, with the only woman he'd ever love from this day forward. He'd never known this sweet ache, ever.

Not even with Ashley, as good and fine as it had been in the beginning. She was truly gone, and he found himself at peace at last. Not with her murder—

never that—but with the knowledge that he would be all right now. The memory of his wife and lost child had settled into a soft place in a heart that didn't have to hurt so much anymore. She wouldn't begrudge his happiness, and he knew she'd have liked Laura.

And so Austin let them go. A tremendous weight lifted, set him free.

He pulled out, laughing as Laura collapsed with an exaggerated groan. He trashed the condom and gathered her into his arms, settled her head on his chest. She snuggled into his side, skimming a palm over his stomach. He loved her touching his body.

"Wow. Good morning, Captain. Anytime you want to strip-search me like that again, do your worst." She pressed a kiss to his chest.

"Oh, I intend to, sugar. I'm gonna enjoy the hell out of making you lose control. Often." Even to him, it came out sounding smug and satisfied.

She raised her head, arching a brow. "Yeah? Same to you, buddy. You probably scared the neighbors. Made small children ten miles away run screaming for their mothers."

"Witch." He kissed her nose. "You drive me wild."

She beamed at him. "Good. Glad to know some things never change."

"And that some things do," he said, his voice husky. "I love you."

Hell, he'd made her cry. But they were happy tears, judging from the kisses raining on his face. She cupped his cheeks, covered his lips with hers. Soft, warm. Her tongue slipped into his mouth, playing with his. A slow, languid kiss. Giving, sealing their love. She drew back, face streaked, heart in her eyes.

"I love you, too, Rainey."

Smiling, he brushed her hair out of her face, wiped her tears. "A guy could get real used to this. A smart, sexy woman in his bed. Sharing his life."

She took his hand in hers. "Is that where you want this to go? Us sharing our lives together?"

"God, yes. As soon as I put this crazy monster behind bars, I'm yours, sweetheart. Any way you want me, for as long as you want me."

She gave him a watery smile. "Forever works."

"It had better," he warned playfully. "You're stuck with me, lady."

They fell silent, simply basking in the glow. He burned to make it official. Pop the big question. And he would, eventually. But he'd ask without the specter of his stalker looming over their lives. He'd wait until the perfect time, when no more threat existed to rear its ugly head and spoil the moment. Laura deserved the best.

She snuggled into his arms again. "Can I ask you a really personal question?"

Her voice was so hesitant, he tightened his hold in a reassuring hug. "I think you've earned the right, sweetheart."

"I saw how you reacted to Joan, and it seems like it was more than your wild suspicion that she might be connected to your case—there's some kind of story behind it. You didn't even want to deal with the media at first. Will you tell me why you hate reporters so much?"

He kissed the top of her head. "I guess my bias started with my aunt and uncle and ended with Ashley."

"Your aunt and uncle?" She raised up on one elbow, giving him a puzzled look.

"If you'd ever read any articles on the Internet about my family, you might have learned that my uncle was Senator John Rainey. He and my aunt died in a private plane crash on the way to a fund-raiser nearly thirty years ago."

She frowned, mentally calculating. "You were only a kid."

"I'd just turned thirteen. My oldest cousin, George, had just finished his degree in business and had to take on raising his younger siblings. My parents helped all they could, but he insisted on taking care of them."

"And since they were from a prominent Texas family, the media coverage was brutal," she guessed.

"Like you can't imagine. Suffice it to say, I grew up with a bitter taste in my mouth where reporters are concerned. When Ashley was killed, and I couldn't deal with my grief, the media made it worse."

Laura laid a hand on his arm, face etched with compassion. "Once again, they were in your face, turning private heartbreak into public fodder."

"I was their flavor of the month. Tracking criminals is my job, yet that didn't stop my wife and child from being murdered, did it?"

"Oh, honey. Her death wasn't your fault."

"I know that now, but for a while I imploded. You were there—you saw." He gave a small smile. "But I'm grateful I have you and my friends. I don't know what I'd do without you all."

She kissed the corner of his mouth. "Your men have been great to you."

"Especially Danny. Even if he did have a thing for you," he teased.

"Hmm. I'm not so sure about that now." As soon as the words left her lips, she wasn't sure she should've said anything. However, Austin nodded.

"I'm not so sure, either. I think maybe he was lying to himself."

The way Austin said it, the look he was giving her, said volumes. Her eyes widened. "Do you think he's gay?"

"I'm not sure, but between you and me, I know he's struggling with the idea. Personally, I don't care. I just want him to be happy."

"Me, too," she said sincerely. "He's a great guy."

"He may be interested in someone." Austin grimaced. "It would be a hell of a lot simpler if the man wasn't a witness in our case."

"Oh crap. That could be a tricky situation."

"You're not kidding. The witness, Frankie, saw Matt Blankenship get lured from the club by the person we believe is our killer. Which may also put Frankie in danger. We told him to leave town for a while, but I don't think he followed our advice."

A horrifying thought bloomed in Laura's mind. Once it took root, it refused to let go. "Austin, have you ever considered that this man, Frankie, might be your stalker? The killer?"

He stared at Laura. "Once, maybe, but just briefly. Frankie is harmless. That man is no killer, honey."

"How can you be sure? Remember John Wayne Gacy? Big, jovial-looking guys who dress as clowns aren't supposed to be serial killers, either. Nobody ever suspects the average guy."

"Jesus." He blinked at her. "I'm pretty certain Frankie isn't our man. Look, you said yourself quite a bit of strength was required to do the killings, and he's not a big man."

"I'm just saying it's *possible*. With enough force and the right angle, anyone can commit murder," she said gently.

"Okay, I'll grant that it's possible, I guess. But my gut says we're looking for a different man."

"You're probably right," she said. "I'm just thinking out loud—pay no attention to me."

He kissed her on the lips. "No, it's fine. I'll do some digging, see if I can find out more about Frankie's background. See if he told me and Danny the truth about what clubs he frequents and how often. I was going to go by Spanky's yesterday and never got the chance, so I'll plan on doing that tonight."

"Yeah, well. Lots of people go to those clubs. You've been there," she pointed out. "I'm sorry I brought it up."

"No, now that you did, maybe it is strange that he just happened to be in the same places, that's all. What if he's not just a witness, but he actually did the crime? He described the wig and that's not something the public knows."

She stroked his cheek. "You'll find out the truth. I'm sure it's just a coincidence."

"Glenn always taught me there's no such thing as a coincidence, that a cop who falls into that trap might as well put a gun to his own head. I have to check it out."

"I know." She smiled. "If you didn't, you wouldn't be the smart, super-stud captain I love."

He pulled her close, crushing her breasts to his chest. "Flattery will get you into my shorts, lady."

"You aren't wearing any."

"Lucky me." He lowered his mouth to hers, then drew back, frowning. "Damn, I'm out of condoms."

She twined her arms around his neck. "I don't care. Do you?"

"No. I'm healthy, you're on the pill, and I love you so damn much." He swallowed hard, aching for her.

She pulled him down and he sank into her. Made slow, beautiful love to his lady. Pumped his hips, filling her deeper, deeper. His balls tightened as she wrapped her legs around his waist, her heat scorching him. Stroking his burning cock.

With a cry, he exploded, jetting his seed into her, again and again, while she held him close, pressing kisses to his shoulder. Loving him.

An hour later, as they dressed hurriedly, Laura threw a glance at the bedside clock radio and squeaked. "Oh, you're *so* going to get me fired!"

He shrugged. "We'll live off my inheritance. Being the nephew of the late Senator Rainey has its advantages."

Her mouth fell open. "So that's how your family can afford to own a place like the ranch. I'd wondered how a cop could swing it, but I wasn't going to ask. You're from old money!"

"Nah. We're not rich, but not hurting." He grinned. "I could retire early, though." The look on her face was beyond priceless. His financial portfolio wasn't something he broadcast. Glenn, Danny, and Shane knew. Others suspected, but it wasn't any of their damn business.

Laura was different. He wanted her to be secure in the knowledge that he could more than provide for her. Much more. A stupid macho attitude, yet important to him all the same.

She buttoned her blouse, pulled on her skirt. "Why do you put yourself at risk working for the police? Why not do something else, like cruise around the world or start your own business?"

He zipped his jeans, then slowly worked a T-shirt on over his head. Their morning fun had reminded his healing body just how sore he was.

"For the same reason my brothers still work our family spread in South Texas when they don't have to. I love what I do, sweetheart. My job is crucial. I help crime victims and their families find closure after the most horrible event of their lives. Isn't that why you told me you became a medical examiner?" he pointed out.

"Yes," she said softly. "You're exactly right, and that's why I love you."

"Back atcha, beautiful." He crossed to her in three

strides, pulled her into his arms for a hot kiss. After a long moment, she groaned.

"Ease up, Captain. If I don't get into work soon, my boss is going to have my ass on a platter."

"He's out of luck. That's my territory." He cupped her bottom and squeezed.

"Stop it!" She wiggled out of his arms, laughing. "I'm serious. I've got a marathon day ahead. In fact, I'll probably have to work until late tonight."

"Damn," he sighed, raking a hand through his hair. "Just as well, though. I've got plenty to keep me busy until you're ready for me to pick you up. Just call me at my desk or on my cell when you're done, and I'll be there."

"Will I have a tail?"

"Yeah, Danny. He's pulling a long shift watching you, but there isn't anyone else available. When you're at the office, he'll be staked out in the parking lot in a blue minivan. If you have to leave, make sure he sees you so he can follow."

"And who's going to protect *you*? I'm willing to make a bet that our psycho will read this morning's paper. Once he spies the article and the picture of us leaving the restaurant all lovey-dovey, he'll go totally Norman Bates on your ass."

He smiled to mask the chill in his bones. "I'm counting on it. I want to push him into making a mistake, and when he does, he's toast. I can take care of myself, baby."

"Promise me you'll be careful. I think maybe I'm the one who made the mistake in suggesting we push his buttons. If anything bad happened to you—"

He curled a finger under her chin, tilted her anxious face to meet his gaze. "Nothing bad can touch me now. Not when I have you."

Wrong. But with Laura in his arms, he managed to forget that you should never taunt cruel fate with thoughtless clichés.

That he'd likely shoved a psychopath over the edge, and he'd soon shove back.

14

Austin rubbed his eyes, which were just about crossed after staring for hours at the files spewed across his desk. He'd also made a ton of phone calls, left messages. First with Frankie's school, then with the cable company, looking for his boss. Trying to speak to an actual human being at a cable company was like shouting into the wind.

The third call had gone to the manager at the graphic design company who'd hired Frankie, contingent on his graduation in May. Austin was careful to tread lightly, not giving away too much information. Nor did he want to cause Frankie to lose the job if he was innocent.

The manager said that, yes, Matt Blankenship had brought Frankie's work to his attention because of a mutual friend—Rick Yates. Frankie and Matt weren't friends per se, as far as what Matt had told him, and the manager had given Frankie the job on his own merits. If he thought of anything else that might be helpful, he'd give Austin a call back.

There was no motive for Frankie to murder Blankenship. The guy had helped him get a job, and they weren't in competition.

Except that Blankenship resembled Austin.

Son of a bitch.

Round and round in circles. A dog chasing his tail.

Austin couldn't shake the notion that he was missing something vital. Right in front of his nose. The club was a connection, but he needed the tie to his killer.

Another call, this one to the lab. Would they rush the fucking DNA samples from the murder scenes, *pretty fucking please*? "Sure," the overworked lab tech had sneered. "I'll just put you in line ahead of the woman who's waiting to find out whether the man who's been arrested for her husband's murder is the culprit. All righty?"

Fuuuuck.

Austin stared at his desktop, head in his hands. A copy of this morning's paper was abruptly slapped onto the desk, in front of his face.

"'Local Police Captain Mixes Business with Pleasure'?" Glenn snarled. "How in the hell did this happen?"

He raised his gaze to the man he counted a good friend. Except when Byrne had to rein in the troops as chief. Right now, he was addressing Austin as his *boss*.

And the boss was *pissed*.

"How did what happen? The business or the pleasure?" Glenn's face darkened in anger. *Whoops, wrong tactic.* "Look, I'm—"

"Was this article your stupid idea?" he snapped.

A direct question, so he couldn't lie. "Laura suggested it, but I agreed."

Glenn's anger warred with bewilderment. He spread his hands. "Why, for God's sake? You got some kind of death wish?"

"I pushed the killer into making a move before. Next time I'll catch him." Boy, did that sound arrogant.

Glenn's mouth tightened into a grim line, his dark gaze pinning his friend. He tapped the picture next to the article. "This may have been Laura's idea, but it was your call. If this goes south, you'll have to live with the results on your conscience. If the crazy bastard doesn't kill you first."

Glenn straightened and strode to his office, slamming the door behind him.

Austin swore. *Your call . . . your conscience.* The rest of the afternoon and into the evening, Glenn's accusing words rode him hard. Concentration blown to shit, he stared unseeing at the files and waited for Laura's call. She gave him the rundown on Derek Thompson, then promised to be waiting for him at home tonight—the only part of this day he looked forward to.

Hanging up, he scrubbed at his bleary eyeballs, grinding them with the heel of his hand. Laura's report on Derek Thompson hadn't revealed anything new, except for the long strand of hair stuck to his bloodied body. Red instead of black. No surprise, since they'd figured the killer used wigs.

Like Blankenship, the man had been drugged, taken home. Tied down by somebody damn strong, probably a man, then mutilated.

A memory stirred, something about the attack in the parking lot of the hospital. Tried to pull itself forth. A man. Something about a man. The dark interior of the van. A face inside the van's open door. Long dark hair around a masculine face—

The killer. Good God, he'd just recalled a snippet of the stalker's actual face. But he couldn't remember the details, couldn't get a clear picture, no matter how hard he tried.

The roofie would've done that to his brain, erased the memory.

Pushing from his desk, he finally left work. Christ, he was so tired. Emotionally drained and running on empty. He had to make the stop at Spanky's tonight before he could go home, though. Checking his watch, he opted to swing by the hospital first as well. Visiting hours for Taylor would be over soon and he'd been busy the past few days.

When he arrived, he found Cara in her usual spot by the bed. This time, Taylor was sitting up, awake, watching the TV that was mounted on the wall. When he spotted Austin walk into the room, he brightened and flashed a big smile.

"Hey, Cap. How's it going?"

"It's going," he said, walking over and shaking Taylor's hand, then hugging his girlfriend. "About time I found your lazy ass awake for a change."

"I know. I blame all these good drugs they've been giving me."

"How are you feeling, really?"

Taylor sobered some. "Tired. Sore. Ready to get the hell out of here."

"When will they spring you?"

"Anytime now. I've been here for over two weeks, and I can mend the rest of the way at home just as good as I can here," he grumped.

Austin sympathized with the guy. Hell, he'd felt the same way before, in Taylor's position. "I hear you."

"Got any leads?"

No sense in bullshitting one of his own detectives. "No great ones, I'm sorry to say. All we've got are a bunch of threads that need connecting. They've got one common element and we can't figure out who or what that is yet."

"You will. I've got confidence." Taylor paused. "Go back to the beginning, back to your lists of suspects. The men you've put away. This is so personal, there *has* to be a connection."

"I agree, but damned if I can find it." It was beyond infuriating.

"You will."

They talked for a few more minutes, until Taylor's eyes began to droop. Then Austin patted the man on the shoulder and said his good-byes. "You take care and I'll see you soon."

"You, too, Cap. Watch your back."

"You know it."

All the way back to his truck, he mulled over Taylor's words, and deep down he agreed. There was someone in his past who was determined to make him pay for whatever transgression he thought Austin had committed. But he'd crossed the line.

"You'd better give your heart to God, you fucker. Because your ass belongs to me."

15

After Austin left Taylor at the hospital, his next stop was Spanky's, located in downtown Nashville, home of the weirdoes. A mix of the eclectic and extremely dangerous. If you couldn't find a drunk, pimp, pusher, whore, or rising music star in this part of the city, you had your eyes closed. More flavors than Baskin-Robbins, but a smart person wouldn't take a lick of anything this garbage heap had to offer.

Downtown didn't attract that many smart people.

Austin parked his truck under a burned-out street-lamp in the lot next to Spanky's, saying a prayer that he'd find it there when he came out. The idea of being stranded in this part of town at night without a ride gave him the willies.

So did the interior of Spanky's. Upon entering, guests were treated to a sign proudly boasting "Spank-a-Thons" held every Friday and Saturday night. The person who drank the most beer was punished—or rewarded—by Spanky's owner, an experienced dominatrix. The lucky winner got up on the stage and bent over bare-assed to receive his or her spanking in front of the audience.

"Thank God today's Thursday," Austin muttered, peering into the pitch-black cave. "Holy sheep shit."

Every surface—the walls, ceiling, and floors—was painted black. He suspected the major advantage and disadvantage of this charming motif was the same—he couldn't see a damn thing.

But Jesus, he felt his boots sticking to the floor as he paid the cover charge and found a crooked table in an equally depressing corner. Back to the wall, he let his eyes adjust, scanning the gloom.

The motley crowd was thin, but even on a weeknight the activity would pick up after nine thirty. Like a bunch of beady-eyed cockroaches coming out of the woodwork after everyone's asleep, he thought. *And what does that make me? Pest control?*

"Rainey! What gives?"

Austin peered at the advancing figure, but he didn't need a spotlight to know who was barreling toward him. "Thanks, Frankie. I was feeling *way* too inconspicuous."

Grinning, Blair took a seat without an invite. "Right. Like you don't stick out or anything." He rolled his eyes. "God, you're so vanilla in a place like this. All uptight in your cowboy threads, sitting over here like you've got a broomstick up your ass . . . or a nice big—"

"Spare me the creative analogies."

"Oh, what*ever*. Anybody who recognizes you will know what you're doing here, including Mr. Mega-Looney. What? You honestly thought the killer wouldn't know you're scouting for him? Or maybe you thought he'd just walk right up and introduce himself?"

"Goddamn." Austin rubbed his eyes, then stopped, lowering his hand to stare at Blair.

From the beginning, he'd noticed that Frankie was exceptionally pretty for a guy, gay or not. In drag, the man would make a knockout woman. He wasn't quite tall enough to fit the description of their suspect, but in heels? Maybe.

And so what? The description had come from *Frankie*. What if he'd made it up?

Blair's smile died. "What?"

Austin cocked his head. "What are you doing here? Your usual hangout is Junior's, right?"

"It is, and like I said, I don't usually come here often, but—" He sighed heavily. "To be honest, Rick was supposed to meet me here an hour ago."

"You said you were done with Rick."

He made a face. "Well, I'm stupid. What can I say? As you can see, I got stood up. Again. I'm a pushover, or at least I was. I'm finally done, though."

Two inconsistencies from what he'd told Austin before—being here and supposedly meeting Rick. Was Frankie lying?

"Man, I'm sorry. That sucks. I suppose I'll let you off the hook for not lying low like Danny told you."

"Thanks. Guess I'm a slow learner."

Austin turned Blair's words over. At some point, maybe his stalker *had* introduced himself. "Frankie, I need to ask you a few questions."

The other man eyed him warily. "Uh-oh. That sounds all official."

"No, if it was, I'd take you into the station."

"Like *that's* supposed to be comforting."

"Frankie, have you ever cross-dressed?"

"Ooh, you're filling my heart with hope, Rainey," he quipped. "Thinking of switching sides?"

"You wish. Just answer the question."

"Kidding." Sensing the seriousness of Austin's curiosity, he sobered. "No, I've never done that. Cross-dressing isn't my thing."

"Do you work out?" he asked, trying to assess the man's possible strength. Could he have strangled his victims?

"Some," the younger man said. "I'm no gym bunny, but I stay fit. I run a couple of mornings a week."

"Did you know a man named Derek Thompson?"

"No. Should I?" A frown marred Frankie's brow, then cleared as he gaped at Austin. "Wait a second. Are you—do you think I'm a suspect?"

"You're not an official suspect, Frankie. I'm just following up every possible lead I can," he said smoothly.

"Oh my God! That's why you're asking me these questions! You think I could do that? Kill people? I could never," he gasped, horrified.

"I don't want to think that. But I wouldn't have the track record I do if I believed everything people told me." He gave Frankie an apologetic smile. He truly liked the man and his instincts said this wasn't his killer.

"I get it, I do. But what I told you is the truth." Frankie leaned forward, speaking earnestly. "I saw Matt leaving here with a woman, or someone dressed as a woman, the night he was killed. I never saw him after that. The person Matt was with seemed familiar."

"You've mentioned that before. How so? Anything come to mind?"

"I'm not sure. I can't shake the feeling I've seen her, or him, somewhere before. There was something in her walk, her mannerisms, you know?"

"Yeah. Anything else?"

"No. I'm sorry."

"That's all right. Anything more you think of, call me."

"Will do."

One thing was for sure: he couldn't picture exuberant, likable Frankie as secretly twisted and in need of personal revenge against *him*. Dressing up to lure and kill people.

"Hey, how's Danny? When you see him, give him my best, okay? He seemed like a great guy."

"I'll tell him."

"And that medical examiner, too. She's your lady?" Blair asked.

Austin's gaze snapped to his. "How did you know that?"

"I saw your picture in the paper with her, and so did half the metroplex. Chill."

He raked a shaking hand through his hair, willing himself to calm down. "Of course. I'm on edge, to put it mildly. Yes, she's mine, and I plan on making it permanent when this shit is over."

"Good for you. I hope everything works out."

"Yeah, me, too. Thanks."

Blair made small talk for a few more minutes, then rose to leave, making Austin promise to keep in touch.

Reminding him to say hello to Danny. Austin reassured him on both counts. Hell, he liked the guy. Maybe they'd even become friends.

He sat for a long time after Frankie left, watching the swelling crowd. All sorts of characters from the average barfly to strange and downright dangerous. Pick your flavor.

But no sense of menace, of imminent threat. No one overtly staring, or approaching him. As Frankie had said, what had he expected? *Excuse me, sir. I'll be your killer this evening.*

Yet he'd taken the bait once before. He'd lured two men from this bar, for God's sake. And his control was disintegrating into frenzied impulse.

Two hours later, eyes and lungs burning from the thick buildup of cigarette smoke, Austin called it a night. He checked his watch and groaned. After eleven. The drive back would put him home close to midnight, running on no sleep.

By the time he pulled into his driveway, he had trouble staying awake. He pulled into the three-car garage and parked, hitting the button on his key chain to close the automatic door. Dead exhausted, he trudged inside, then remembered he hadn't checked the mailbox at the end of the drive in two days. Screw it, he'd walk out there tomorrow.

As soon as he entered the kitchen, a pair of arms slid around his waist and a soft kiss was pressed against his neck.

"I'm glad you're home."

Turning, he gathered Laura to him and held on as

though she was a life raft. He buried his nose in her hair and inhaled, loving her scent, the warmth of her pressed against him.

"I missed you," she breathed.

"Missed you, too. This is a nice surprise." Tilting her face up, he kissed her, slowly and thoroughly. When they came up for air, she worked a hand underneath his shirt and rubbed his chest.

"Well, I did tell you I'd be waiting. Remember?"

He smiled. "That you did. It's just been a hell of a long day."

"I'm sorry," she said in sympathy. "Want to talk about it?"

Holding her close, he snorted. "Let's see. I got blasted by Glenn for the picture I leaked of us to the paper, and I got no leads on our killer, including a visit with Frankie that produced nothing."

"Really?"

"Yeah. I went by Spanky's and he was there, presumably to meet a guy who keeps giving him the runaround. The guy stood him up, so we had a talk. I honestly don't think he's my murderer. That man doesn't have an ounce of hate in his body."

"I trust you. You've been doing this a long time and you have a feel for these things."

Her confidence meant a lot to him, especially when his own was sort of low. "Thanks, sweetheart." Lowering his head, he gave her a slow kiss. After they parted, he said, "Oh, and I went to see Taylor. He was awake and hoping to go home soon."

"That's wonderful news!"

"The best."

"That calls for a celebration. Unless you're too tired?"

He smiled. "I'm *never* too tired to demonstrate just how well you revive me."

With a grin, he tugged her into his bedroom. They shed their clothes in a hurry, but instead of leading her toward the bed, he got a different idea.

"Turn around and grab onto the post."

Her brows arched, but she smiled back at him. "Really?"

"And spread your legs, too."

Humming in appreciation of the idea, she walked over to the footboard and gripped one of the posts, hand over hand. Then she braced her feet apart, stuck her rear out enticingly, and gave him a sultry look.

"Like this?"

"Exactly like that," he growled. His cock thickened and rose to brush against his belly.

"You're a kinky boy, Captain."

"I can be."

"Lucky me."

"No, lucky *me*," he assured her, dropping to his knees.

Moving in close, he ran his palms down the outside of her smooth thighs. Her tantalizing rump hovered in front of his face, and he couldn't resist a few kisses. A nip, too, which made her jump and giggle.

Next he leaned in and spent some time savoring her sweet sex. Parting the lips, he licked her slowly, doing his best to drive her crazy. She moaned, widening her stance, so he figured he was doing a good job.

His fingers joined his tongue, working her channel

relentlessly, and soon she was writhing, begging for more.

"Please!"

No point in making them both wait. Pushing to his feet, he got into position behind her, gripping her hip to steady her with one hand. With the other, he guided himself into her welcoming heat, moaning.

"God, you feel so good around me," he murmured.

"Fuck me, Austin."

Those words, his name falling from her lips, boiled his blood in the best way. Set him on fire. As he began to thrust inside her again and again, he knew he wouldn't last long.

It was too good. The closeness, the passion. With Laura, the woman he'd wanted forever.

And now she was his.

Unable to hold back, he shuddered with his release. Filled her. With a cry, she joined him, reaching back to clutch his hair. Turning her head, she claimed his mouth as they came down together.

"Shower?" she asked, when they were spent.

"Sounds like heaven."

Reluctantly he pulled out of her. But the hot shower was worth it, and so was the shower gel fight they engaged in. It took ages to get all the soap out of their hair.

Once they were dried off, Laura blew her hair dry and then climbed into bed, where he was waiting. Opening his arms, he pulled her close. He was sleepy, but she was still wide awake for some reason, playing with his chest hair and giving a sigh now and then.

"Okay, what's wrong?"

Finally, she sat up next to him. Her expression was serious, and a premonition of dread coiled through him.

"I have something to tell you, and it's not the best timing."

Slightly alarmed, he sat up as well and took her hand. "What is it?"

"Austin . . . I'm pregnant."

"I— You're what?" he said stupidly. He stared at her, scrambling to comprehend.

"I'm pregnant with your baby." She bit her lip, waiting. Even in the darkness, he could see the glistening of tears in her eyes. "Say something, please."

"What do you want me to say?" All he could focus on was the fear. With the fear came the anger. "I'm not even over grieving for my son and you're telling me you're pregnant? I don't *want* another baby."

"This baby would never replace the one you lost, but—"

"Lost? I didn't *lose* him—he was murdered," Austin seethed. "Nothing can make the agony go away, ever. How am I supposed to go through that again? How could you do that to me?"

She couldn't have appeared more shocked if he had punched her in the face. With a sob, she slid from the bed and stood gazing down at him, a tear tracing a path down her face.

"I'm not asking for anything from you. It was never my intention to hurt you—this just happened. But this is my baby and I'm not giving it up."

Quickly, she started gathering her clothes and getting dressed, hands shaking. He could only watch, gutted, his emotions caught in a hurricane. How had things gone to hell so fast?

He couldn't bear the thought of loving and losing another child. The idea made him want to die inside.

So he could say nothing as Laura walked out the door. Maybe out of his life.

One thing was for certain: he never knew what lonely really meant until she was gone.

Laura cried all the way home.

And most of the night, too. By the next day she looked like a zombie and even her closest friends at work gave her a wide berth. The fact that she snapped at several of them probably didn't help.

Just after two, her cell phone rang and her heart leapt. It was only Danny, though, and her spirits sank again. "Hello?"

"Hey, it's Danny."

"Hi there. What's up?"

"I was hoping you'd tell me, because Austin won't," he said in concern. "I was just at his house and he's clammed up tight. Looks like hell, too."

As upset as she was, she hated to hear he was hurting. "He didn't say *anything*?"

"Just that you guys had a falling-out. He wouldn't talk about it."

Indecision tore at her. Normally she wouldn't discuss their business, especially with one of his friends. But her gut told her that Austin wouldn't go to his buddies for help or advice—he sucked at that. They'd have to go to him. Maybe Danny could help.

"Meet me for a drink after work?"

"Sure. When and where?"

She gave him the name of a pub in town with a nice bar. "Five thirty?"

"Works for me. See you then."

The day didn't improve. She had a body to retrieve, but at least it was a straightforward case. She had her examination finished and notes recorded just in time to meet Danny. Keeping busy had taken her mind off her sorrows for a while.

They returned full force as she pulled into the parking lot and shut off the ignition. She must've looked as bad as she felt, because Danny jumped to his feet as soon as she walked in, and gave her a hug.

"Okay, what's going on with you two?" he asked, seating her.

She wasted no time getting to the point. "I gave Austin some news last night that threw him for a loop. I'm pregnant."

Danny's eyes widened. "Um, congratulations?"

She gave a sad little laugh. "It would be a happy occasion if he hadn't completely freaked out."

"At the risk of sounding like an asshole, I can understand where he's coming from." He shook his head. "But he hurt you, badly. I can see that."

"Yes, he did," she said softly. "I knew he might take it hard, though. He survived a horrible loss not so long ago, and there I am reminding him of that."

"He's afraid."

"I imagine so. But that doesn't make it hurt any less."

"Do you mind if I try to talk to him?" Danny asked.

"Not at all. I'm guessing he could use a friend, and he's too stubborn to open up on his own."

"You've got that right." Danny smiled. "So, I suppose yours will be a nonalcoholic drink?"

She grinned back, feeling a little better. "Better make mine a Coke, on the rocks."

"Done."

Maybe things would be all right eventually. Austin just needed more time.

She really wanted to believe that was true.

He couldn't eat, couldn't sleep. Couldn't think about the case, or the dead ends.

Laura was on his mind day and night, every second, never letting him rest.

She's pregnant.

No two words had ever filled him with such wonder, and yet such terror. There was no changing that, and in truth he didn't want to. But he was just so fucking scared the same thing was going to happen to her. The monster would get his hands on her before Austin could stop him and—

A knock on the door halted his horrible train of thought. Walking over, he looked outside and saw Danny standing there. With a sigh, he opened up.

"Why do I get the feeling I know the reason for this visit?" he asked, stepping aside to let his friend in.

"Because you're a cop and you're smart that way."

Danny headed straight for the kitchen, pulled open the fridge. "You've got beer again! Say, is that a good thing?"

Austin followed him, leaning in the doorway. "I'm not an alcoholic. I was drinking to drown my grief, but I'm coping now."

"Hey, you're an adult. Just concerned, that's all." He twisted the top off a beer. "You want one?"

"No, thanks. But it's nice of you to offer me my own beer."

"Right." He took a swig. "Okay, you want the incoming lecture standing up or sitting down?"

"Let's sit in the living room. More comfortable to get my ass chewed on the sofa."

"That just sounded all kinds of wrong."

"Didn't it?"

Danny made himself at home in Austin's recliner and Austin flopped onto the sofa. He didn't have long to wait for the man to speak his mind.

"Do you love her?"

"That's easy—yes. I think I've been falling for a long time and I finally got lucky enough to catch her."

"And then you promptly fucked up."

"Whose side are you on, anyway?" He frowned, thinking that beer might sound good after all.

"I'm on both of your sides. I want to see you guys happy, but you gotta stop being your own enemy for that to happen."

"You don't understand how hard this is for me—"

"The hell I don't." Danny's eyes flashed with anger. "I stood by helpless when your grief almost killed you. But this is different. You have a second chance with a terrific woman who loves you, so if it's blown, it's your fault."

The truth of that statement couldn't be denied. He loved Laura, and he didn't want to lose her. But his fears were real and he had to work them out in his head before he could make things right with her.

"I hear you. Really, I do. But I have to do some thinking first. Get some things in order."

Danny nodded. "Just don't take too long. You don't want communication to break down."

The way it had with Ashley. No, he didn't want that at all.

"Feel like staying to watch the game?" he asked Danny.

"Sure. I'll order pizza."

Four days later, Austin finally worked up the nerve to call Laura.

She didn't totally let him off the hook, but she was more civil than he deserved. "Austin," she said in greeting, her tone wary. "How are you?"

Her first question was concern for him? His heart felt like it had been stabbed with an ice pick. "I'm good. No, that's a lie." He took a deep breath. "I miss you and I love you. I'm sorry I reacted the way I did, but I was scared."

There was a long pause.

"And now?"

"I'm still scared," he admitted. "But not so much that I'm willing to throw away the best thing to ever happen to me. Please say you'll let me pick you up for dinner."

"You hurt me," she said quietly.

"I know, baby. I hope you'll forgive me and give us

a chance, because I don't want to live without you or our child."

Another pause. Then she said, "I'll meet you there."

He was disappointed she wouldn't let him pick her up, but swallowed it down. She was in charge of how this would go, and he wasn't going to mess it up. "Okay. Italian Café, seven thirty?"

"That's fine. I'll see you then."

Before he could say good-bye, she ended the call. This might be even tougher than he'd thought.

The rest of the day was a serious strain on his thin patience. The hour of their date couldn't arrive fast enough, and he was dressed far too early, pacing the floor. The tick of the clock on the wall was driving him insane. When it was finally time to leave, he peeled out of the driveway so fast he left skid marks.

As he arrived at the restaurant, his carefully re-hearsed speech went out the window. All he could think was, *Please forgive me*, and other than that nothing else really mattered.

The hostess showed him to a nice table in a corner that was mostly private, with a candle burning in the middle for a little mood lighting. The waiter brought him a glass of water, but he held off ordering anything else until she arrived.

This had to go perfectly. She had to forgive him.

Trying to calm his nerves, he checked the time. And waited.

"Dammit!"

She was late. Only by a few minutes, but still. The

last thing she wanted was for Austin to think she'd stood him up.

Jogging out of the building, she waved good-bye to Toby Baxter.

"Where's the fire?" he called.

"I'm late for my date!"

Outside, she clutched her purse and hit the unlock button on her key ring. The Mercedes gave a cheery blip and she threw open the door and slid behind the wheel. Maybe she should go ahead and call Austin? She was about to dig her phone out of her purse when the passenger door opened and a man calmly got in, shutting it after him.

In his hand was a gleaming pistol.

"Wh-what are you doing? Who are you?" She stared at him in horror, heart pounding.

"I think you're smart enough to figure that out, aren't you?" He chuckled to himself. "Drive off, and don't even think about crashing us. I'll shoot a hole in you and save myself a lot of trouble."

The gun was aimed at her side. From the cold, hard look in his eyes, he wouldn't hesitate to do it. No way could she crash the car in her condition. And she certainly wasn't going to play on his sympathy by telling him she was pregnant; some attackers might be swayed by that, but look what this man had done to Ashley.

Terror gripped her heart as she drove from the parking lot. She could only pray that someone saw them, or the security camera got him on film. Her hands shook and her mouth was dry. She tried not to think about what this animal would do to her.

It would be a while before Austin realized she was missing. Longer still before a search got under way. It would be dark soon. Not good, any of it.

"Where are we going?"

"Turn up here, take I-49 out of town."

"Okay."

She stole a glance at him. He was maybe late twenties, early thirties. Muscular. Nice looking. What would make a man like this commit such horrible crimes?

"What's your name?" she asked.

"What's it to you?"

"I'm Laura, but I guess you know that." She'd heard sometimes if a kidnapper made a connection with his victim, that could help stave off the worst.

"Of course I know." He paused, turning a little in the seat to face her better. The gun didn't waver.

"Would you tell me?"

"Guess it doesn't matter. You can call me Chandler. Your boyfriend does."

"But that isn't your real name." It wasn't a question.

"No, and he'll never figure out my real identity," he stated, pleased with himself.

"Why are you doing this?" she asked hoarsely.

"Oh, you'll find out soon enough. And so will Captain Austin Rainey," he spat. "Right before I kill him."

16

When Laura hadn't arrived by eight, Austin was disappointed. But after he texted her and got no response, disappointment became worry. He tried calling, and got sent straight to her voice mail.

"Hey, baby. I'm at the restaurant and it's almost ten after eight. Did something come up with work? Call me as soon as you can."

Hanging up, he decided to phone her office. Even at this hour, somebody would be working. The line was picked up on the third ring.

"Medical examiner's office, this is Toby Baxter."

"Hi, Toby. This is Captain Austin Rainey with the Sugarland PD. I'm trying to reach Laura Eden. Is she still around?"

"Oh, hey, Captain Rainey. No, she left in a hurry a little before seven thirty. She said something on the way past me about being late for a date."

A chill crept down his spine. "You're sure she left the building?"

"Positive. Her car's gone. I was just about to leave myself."

"Okay, thank you."

"No sweat."

Ending the call, he stood and hurried for the door, giving his apologies to the waiter on the way out. He paused to slip the kid a twenty-dollar bill for taking good care of him, then dashed out. Laura wasn't coming. Something was wrong.

She wouldn't have stood him up. That simply wasn't her style. The man on the phone said she was on her way to meet him, and he believed the guy.

Panic rising, he drove the route to her office in Nashville, keeping an eye out for her car. He hadn't really expected to see the Mercedes, but he'd hoped for a miracle. There was no sign of her or the car. On the way back to Sugarland he phoned the troops.

Shane answered his cell. "Hey, Cap. What's up? Thought you had a hot date with your lady tonight."

Word apparently got around. "I was supposed to, but she never showed. Something's wrong. One of her colleagues said she left work to come meet me, but she never arrived and she hasn't called or texted me and her phone goes straight to voice mail."

"Maybe she went home?"

"No. She wouldn't stand me up. If she wasn't coming, she would've told me straight out."

"Okay. But I'll have a squad go by her place anyway, just to be sure."

"I'm heading in to the station. I need everyone who's available."

"You've got it."

"It's *him*, Shane," he said, unable to hide the fear in his voice. "I know it is."

"Stay strong. If it is, we're going to catch him. He's not going to get away with this."

Ending the call, he sped to the station. He no longer wanted to put this monster behind bars; he wanted him fucking dead. The bastard had taken enough from him. He wasn't going to take Laura, too.

At the station, Danny and Chris were already waiting for him in the conference room. Notes on the case were spread everywhere. Danny stood and pulled Austin into a brief hug.

"We're going to find her, my friend. Don't doubt that."

"I know. But we don't have much time," he said, voice strained. "He may keep her alive for a while to taunt me, but we can't be sure for how long."

Shane and Tonio arrived and they got down to business.

"Let's go through my list again. Odds are high one of these people I put in prison is trying to get revenge for my costing him someone he loved," Austin said, frustration rising. "But none of the suspects have panned out. The ones who lost someone while they were in prison are either still there or dead, while the ones who've gotten out didn't lose anyone while he was inside. What am I not seeing?"

They hunkered around the table and got to work. They sifted through all the names again from the beginning, with the same results as before. Hours and hours of work repeated—for nothing, it seemed.

It was almost three in the morning, and they were all exhausted. Austin was just about to suggest they get a few hours' sleep—not that *he* was going anywhere—when a uniformed officer knocked and stuck his head in the door.

"Cap? A squad just located Miss Eden's car a few miles outside of town. They took a look inside, found her purse with her cell phone still intact. They didn't touch anything."

"God," he rasped, trying to think. This was bad.

"Tonio and I will go out there," Shane said, standing. "See what we can find."

"Okay. Let us know, and thanks."

"Don't mention it."

Once they were gone, he looked to Chris and Danny. "Why don't you guys go home, get a few hours' sleep, and come back."

"You're kidding, right?" Chris shook his head. "I'm not going anywhere until we find Laura. That's final."

"Me, either."

A lump clogged his throat, but he kept his emotions in check. His lady was depending on him to keep his cool and find her. He wasn't going to let her down.

"Thanks, guys. In that case, let's try going through this again."

It was going on six in the morning before Shane and Tonio made it back to the station. Austin's exhausted brain snapped to attention when Shane entered holding a large evidence bag containing Laura's purse and related what they'd found out.

"There wasn't much in the car, and these were left

behind." He laid the bag on the table. "We'll check for prints besides hers, but that won't help much right now."

Austin wanted to yell or hit something. "Were you able to learn anything?"

"We did find a patch of flattened grass off the road, a few yards from where her car was found. I think he planned her abduction in advance and had a van or something out there waiting. He makes her drive, then ditches the car and retrieves his own vehicle."

"Makes sense." He checked the time. "Fuck! He's had her almost eleven hours. What are we missing here? *What?*"

"Well," Chris said slowly, "I can think of one thing missing from this list: women."

Austin stared at him. "The killer is a man. We know this, even though he dressed as a woman at least once, when he lured Matt Blankenship."

"Yeah, but what about the person he's avenging? My bet is it's a woman. Probably a wife or girlfriend."

Austin stood, brain whirling. "You're right. He *would* avenge his woman, and he blames me for something that happened to her while he was in prison."

"But none of the viable suspects lost anyone as far as we've been able to determine," Tonio said.

Shane blew out a frustrated breath. "It doesn't make sense."

The answer, when it hit Austin, almost took him like a bullet to the brain. "The killer is male. But what if *he* wasn't the one in prison—what if *she* was?"

The guys stilled, their eyes widening. Chris whistled

through his teeth. "Holy shit. That could be the angle we need."

Austin's mind raced. "Yeah, it could. Let me go through my case files from the last few years, and this time I'll list the women I've put away. There weren't nearly as many, so it shouldn't take long."

Leaving them, he retreated to his office, booted up his computer, and got to work. Time was critical.

"Hang on, sweetheart," he whispered. "I'm going to find you."

She and his baby had to survive. He wasn't going to accept any other outcome.

The first thing she became aware of was the awful pounding in her head.

Memory returned in pieces. The stranger jumping in her car. Forcing her to drive away. Then he made her pull over . . . and what?

She'd felt a sting in her neck and everything had gone dark. The bastard must've drugged her. The question was where he'd taken her.

The floor beneath her was cold, hard, and unforgiving. Listening, she caught the faint sounds of outdoors. Wind rustling in the trees, a few birds singing. Was it morning?

With an effort, she opened her eyes and blinked the room into focus. Well, not a room, really, so much as a dank space filled with junk. Rolling to her back, she looked around and groaned. Several feet above her was a small window she might be able to crawl through—if her hands weren't bound behind her back and if she could get some leverage to hoist herself up there. The dim light filtering through the dirty glass indicated the sun was just coming up, and a quick calculation in her fuzzy brain told her that if it was dawn she'd been missing almost eleven hours.

Austin would have the entire force looking for her. Of that she had no doubt. But she knew he'd been stymied by the identity of the killer, and he'd be searching blind. If she was going to get out of here, she couldn't wait.

She had to save herself.

Just then a door opened somewhere above with an ominous squeal of rusty hinges. Footsteps descended and the murderer Austin knew as Chandler sauntered over to her, looming large, a satisfied smile on his face.

He'd be handsome, she thought, *if he wasn't a vicious killer*.

"Well, good morning," he said cheerfully.

She eyed him warily, trying not to show her fear. Her mouth was dry and her tongue felt thick, thanks to the drug. "Better for some than others."

That made him laugh. "You know, I like you. It's going to be a shame to kill you."

"Waste not."

"True. But if I let you live, then your captain won't learn his lesson," he said, as if this were the most reasonable line of thinking in the world.

What a lunatic. "He's already learned it," she said in a soft appeal. "You took his wife and child from him. He'll never be the same, and killing me could never be worse than that loss."

Anger suffused his face, erasing all traces of hi good looks. "That fucking murderer won't be paid u until *I* say so. He took everything from *me*, so I'm no going to stop until I return the favor," he finished shouting, jabbing his finger down at her.

"Austin is *no* murderer." She glared up at him. "He' a police captain who does his job putting criminals i jail. *You're* the murderer."

For a horrible moment, she thought she'd gone too far. The very real desire to strangle her was simmerin in his eyes, in the clench of his hands.

"He took my woman and child from me, and I won' rest until I've destroyed his whole world. By the time kill him, he'll beg me to do it."

"How did he take them? What do you mean?"

But her captor had spun on his heel and was alread stomping back up the stairs. Immediately she went t work on her bonds. They were tight, not much give i the ropes that bound her wrists, cutting into her skin She'd need something sharp to saw them against.

Eyes skimming the basement, she searched for some thing—anything—that could be used as a tool. Mostl there were boxes overflowing with discarded house hold items, old clothing, cans of pesticides, and the like Disappointment settled over her—until she spotted th handlebars of something sticking out from behind a pil of boxes in one corner.

Please let that be what I think it is.

Before she pushed to her feet, she listened intentl for any sign of "Chandler" returning. Hearing nothing she got up and crept over to the corner and pushed a

he boxes. They slid out of the way with a noisy scrape
nd she cringed, ears trained for the killer's footsteps.
o far, so good.

One more push at the boxes, and her pulse leapt. An
ld lawn mower, the push kind that started by pulling
cord, sat there like a beacon of hope. She didn't think
er captor knew it was down here, or he would've re-
noved it. Now she just had to get it turned on its side,
rithout making a racket. No small feat with her hands
ed.

First, she sat on the filthy floor next to the mower
nd tried to use her feet, levering her toes underneath
ne metal frame to try to flip the thing. That was a
o-go; it was just too heavy. The mower barely budged.

Next she tried backing up to the same spot and lift-
ng the metal frame with her fingers. But the frame was
harp and the weight caused the edge to cut into her
esh. No dice.

"Dammit!" Gathering herself to her feet again, she
lared at the object. "One way or another, you're going
own."

This time she used her upper body to lean on the
andlebar. As soon as she did, the motion caused the
nower to essentially pop a wheelie, front half sticking
p. A bit more of a push downward and she could up-
et its balance, toppling it. Which wasn't going to be
uiet, but it couldn't be helped.

Finally, the mower fell over. It rolled to its side with
terrible clang, and for a few awful, heart-stopping
noments she stood frozen. But as minutes passed and
handler didn't appear demanding to know what she

was doing, she started to relax. He either was deaf or had left the house for a while. It was surely the latter.

Sitting once again, Laura backed up to the mower's blades. After some maneuvering to get the right leverage, she started to saw at the ropes.

And she prayed that time, and a bit more luck, would be on her side.

In his office, Austin scrubbed a hand down his face, rubbed at his tired eyes. He'd lost track of how many cups of coffee he'd consumed, but it was well past doing him any good and now was just making him jittery and sick to his stomach.

Midmorning. Time was running out for Laura, and going through the list of female offenders was a tedious process, even though the names were considerably fewer than the men. The stories were pretty much what he'd expected, except one woman on the list who had actually turned her life completely around and had become a social worker. A couple of the women had died after their prison terms, one from drug use, one beaten to death by her boyfriend. Others were still serving their time, or had been released and rearrested, but after all his research, he hadn't found a single one whose fate might inspire deadly revenge, or who even had a likely connection on the outside who would commit murder for her.

Then he came to a name that stopped him cold: Violet Johansson. As he recalled, a cold, hard bitch who was anything but the pretty flower she was named after. Violet was a dangerous criminal, a crack addict and drug runner Austin had arrested numerous times. The last time was enough to get her sent away for a long stretch.

Sitting back in his chair, he remembered that Violet was mean as a snake. The word on the street was that she'd cut the balls off a man who hadn't paid for his cocaine delivery, and then cut his throat. They'd found the man—the rumors about what she'd done to him were true—but had never been able to prove she'd done it. No, it was the drug charges that got her, and that wasn't nearly enough.

Picking up the phone, he made a call to the warden of the prison where Violet Johansson had been incarcerated. Fifteen minutes later, he hung up, grabbed the file, and jogged to the conference room, heart in his throat. He burst into the room, startling the exhausted detectives inside, who were instantly on alert.

"Violet Johansson," he said, slapping the file on the table. "Dangerous repeat offender. She died in prison after a fight with another inmate. And she was pregnant. The baby didn't survive."

Shane let out a curse. "This could be the link we're looking for. Who was the father?"

"She wasn't married, but her common-law husband was a guy named Douglas Bristow. I didn't have any dealings with him, never met him. The warden said he was extremely loyal, never missed a visit. He was also enraged when they informed him of her death."

"Motive," Chris said. "He snapped when she died."

Austin nodded. "He vowed to get revenge for her death, but the warden didn't put much stock in the threat. If he'd just picked up the phone . . ." There was no point in agonizing over that now.

Shane's gaze was sympathetic. "All of us in law enforcement get threatened constantly. It's easy to tune it out. Criminals are always running their mouths."

"Yeah," Austin agreed. That didn't make it hurt any less. "Anyway, Douglas has a minor record. Seems he left the heavy-hitting stuff to his lady."

"You got an address?" Danny asked. "A photo or description of him?"

"No, I came straight in here after I got off the phone."

Excitement shone in Danny's eyes as he woke up the screen on the laptop they'd been using. Austin and the others gathered around as he began a search for a current address. It took a few minutes of perusing city and county records, but the lieutenant got a hit.

"I think I found him. He's got a place just outside the city limits."

Austin noted the address. "It's out in the country a ways, but not too far. Let's check it out, but I want to find a picture of Bristow first."

Thanks to arrest records logged online, the mug shot was easy to find. And when Danny pulled it up, Austin sucked in a sharp breath, reeling in shock.

"Goddamn! That's Chandler, the bartender from the Waterin' Hole! That's what he *said* his name was."

"Well, he lied," Chris said. "He's probably been watching you all this time."

"Yeah. He started with a man who looked like me, then escalated to a woman who hit on me. Then he graduated to stalking the people I care for. He almost killed Taylor, and now he's got Laura." Rage boiled inside him, and his soul demanded justice. He had to find her.

"Everybody grab your vest, and let's move. We have a snake to catch."

Just a few last threads. She moved her wrists quickly, hoping she didn't slice her skin on the rusty blade, and the ropes were cut at last.

Rubbing her wrists and hands, she coaxed the circulation back into them. The pins and needles had barely started to abate when she heard the slam of a door from somewhere above. *Shit*.

Pushing to her feet, she wasted no time moving a large box underneath the window. Then she scrambled on top of it; it was sort of flimsy, but it would hold her weight well enough. Immediately she went to work unlatching and lifting the window. It was old, and perhaps had never been opened. Sweating with the effort of trying to force it open, she was considering breaking it when finally it started to inch upward.

And none too soon. Footsteps crossed the floor overhead—and the door to the basement opened. The clang of the killer's shoes coming down those stairs was the most frightening sound she'd ever heard.

"What the fuck?" he shouted, and took the last of the steps at a fast clip.

With a last shove, the window gave and she hoisted herself up. She was halfway out when she felt him grab her leg and try to drag her backward. Kicking, she managed to shake free temporarily and get in a good hit, hopefully to his face. His howl of pain gave her a spurt of satisfaction as she emerged on the other side and fell onto the grass.

Gathering herself, she turned and saw his enraged face in the window. He was simply too large to fit through. She took off running, having no idea where she was or where she was going. The house was totally surrounded by rolling, forested countryside. Just before she lost sight of the house, she looked back to see that his face had disappeared from the window. He was coming after her.

She ran as fast as she could, watching out for logs and holes hidden by foliage so she didn't twist an ankle. As she fled, she scanned the area for any sign of another house, somewhere she could beg to use a phone, get some help. There wasn't anything. She was completely alone.

Except for her pursuer, whom she could now hear crashing through the woods behind her. He shouted something, but she didn't care what. She kept moving.

A few steps later, a *crack* sounded from behind. A searing pain tore through her right shoulder and she stumbled, falling to her hands and knees, crying out. Her entire shoulder and arm felt as though they'd been lit with a torch. Looking down at herself, she was shocked to see the front of her blouse stained with red, and she touched the growing wetness with shaking fingers.

He shot *me. Oh God.*

The killer was closing in. His maniacal laugh drifted through the trees, getting her up and moving again. If she stopped, she was dead. And so was her child. This lunatic would deliver her body to Austin without one smidge of remorse.

A ridge with a cliff loomed ahead, and her heart sank. She could try to skirt it, in which case she'd probably get caught. Or she could go up. She opted for climbing. Maybe she could send a shower of rocks down on the killer's head.

Heart in her throat, she ran for the base of the ridge.

17

Austin and his men parked their two unmarked cars a short distance down the road from Bristow's house.

This place really was in the middle of nowhere, nothing but forest all around, bisected only by the old rutted gravel road. Keeping to the cover of the trees, they approached cautiously, guns pointed downward but at the ready.

All appeared to be quiet at the house. Interestingly, however, there was a truck parked at the side of the structure with the passenger door open. Austin and Danny crept up to peer inside while the others kept an eye on the house and started looking into windows.

"Groceries," Danny said, pointing to the few plastic bags that had been left inside on the seat. "Something interrupted his task of unloading them."

Leaving them, they joined the others. Chris had found a side door not far from the truck that was unlocked, probably the route Bristow had been using to unload the groceries. This was confirmed as Austin carefully eased the door open and looked inside. The other bags were sitting on a small table in the kitchen.

They stood for a moment, listening. No sounds reached their ears, and the house had an empty feel. Still, they had to search everywhere. Austin moved forward and motioned the others to follow.

Creeping out of the kitchen, he moved about a small living room, noting the signs that the house had been occupied. Magazines and newspapers littered the coffee table, along with a couple of fast-food wrappers. Austin walked over to the newspapers and his pulse sped up as he motioned for the others to take a look.

The papers were the issues that reported the killings, from Blankenship on to each victim. They were arranged in order by date, front to back. This was definitely their guy. Forensics would prove it. If they could find the knife he'd used on Blankenship or the gun he'd used on Taylor, even better.

"Bedrooms and bathrooms are clear," Tonio said.

Shane spoke up. "Hey, guys? There's a door off the kitchen. Looks like it leads to a basement."

Austin hurried past them all. If Laura was being held here, this was where she would be. He practically ripped the door off the hinges in his haste to get downstairs. At the bottom, however, he was met with an empty room.

Wait. Not quite empty. On the floor near a lawn mower that had been tipped on its side were some ropes that had been sliced through. And there was a big box sitting under an open window.

"She escaped," he said, hope warring with rising

fear. "He came home, realized she was gone, and went after her. We have to find them—now."

Quickly they jogged back upstairs and headed outside, around the house to the open window. Austin directed them to fan out and search straight back from the house, reasoning that she'd be inclined to get as far from the house as possible. Beyond that, he had no idea where she would go. The countryside out here was vast, but Laura was smart and resourceful.

Hang on, sweetheart. I'm coming for you.

Austin wasn't sure how long they'd searched before he finally started to see signs of broken brush, as though one or more people had passed that way. He was no expert tracker, but it seemed obvious. A few yards later, he spotted something dark on the leaves.

He knew what it was even before he knelt to examine the splatter on the leaves and the ground. His gut rolled with sickness. "Blood."

"Could be *his*," Shane said.

Nobody really believed that, but nobody contradicted him. Moving on, they picked up the pace.

Up ahead, a wall of rock loomed, giving them two choices: go around the ridge or over it. Just as Austin decided to skirt the ridge, he spotted Laura and Bristow. And his heart almost stopped.

"Oh Christ." The words came out as an agonized moan.

She was climbing up the rock face, Bristow in pursuit a few yards below her. Crimson stained her right shoulder. Her progress was steady, but Bristow's was faster. Austin knew the murderer could have shot her as she climbed and been done with it, but the bastard wanted to toy with her. That must have been the only reason he hadn't killed her as soon as he abducted her.

Austin had too much ground to cover in order to reach her, and not enough time. His gun was heavy in his hand as he ran, trying to gauge whether he had an opening to shoot Bristow if necessary. The bastard was closing in on her, though. By the time Austin got within firing range, Bristow would be too close, and he couldn't risk hitting her.

When he reached the base of the ridge, he tucked the gun into his holster at his waist and started to climb. The rock face wasn't straight up, and there were hand-holds and footholds, but the going was still plenty strenuous. He knew he'd feel every single one of his forty-two years tomorrow.

"Better climb faster," Bristow taunted her from above. "I'm gonna yank your ass right off there and watch you fall."

He'd do it, too. Austin's blood ran cold and he pushed faster. Angling his head back, he scanned the area above him just in time to see Laura finally heave herself over the top. His relief that she'd made it was short-lived. Bristow reached the top seconds later and disappeared from view as well.

With a curse, he climbed as fast as he dared. When he reached the top, he flung himself over and rolled to his feet, searching for Laura. She was sprinting toward a waterfall, Bristow hot on her heels. As Austin ran, the killer caught her in a flying tackle, taking her to the ground. Then he flipped her onto her back, pulled a fist, and punched her in the face.

"Bristow!" Austin shouted. The murdering bastard looked up just in time to see Austin barrel into him, taking him to the ground.

The fight was vicious, neither man willing to lose. Bristow's own gun had skittered across the rocks, and now he was determined to get to Austin's. They rolled, delivering hard punches and kicks, and Bristow finally managed to slam his fist into one of Austin's kidneys, taking his breath away.

Before he could stop him, Bristow grabbed his gun. Austin seized the other man's hands and a life-or-death struggle for the weapon was on. Bristow's dark eyes seethed with hatred as he gazed down at Austin.

"Just die already, murdering cop!"

"I didn't kill Violet! I arrested her! She got in a fight in prison and died, and I'm sorry about that." Breathing hard, he fought to turn the muzzle toward the other man's body.

"You kept coming after her! If you'd left her alone, she'd still be alive!"

"You break the law, you go to jail, and she knew that."

"You killed my woman and child, and I killed yours. An eye for an eye. But I'm not done yet." His lips twisted into a snarl. "After I finish you, I'm going to shoot your pretty lady in the head."

"No, you're fucking *not*."

He was done talking. If Bristow overpowered him, he was dead—and so was Laura. He couldn't let that happen. Using every ounce of his strength, he started to turn the muzzle toward Bristow's chest.

"Douglas Bristow, hands in the air!" Shane yelled.

Backup had arrived, but Austin's nemesis wasn't giving up. He sneered down at Austin and continued to fight for control.

"Bristow, release the weapon! Hands up!"

"Let go of the gun or I'll have to shoot," Austin hissed.

"Fuck you."

Bristow tried once more to turn the weapon back on him, and Austin had no choice. With one last burst of strength, Austin turned the muzzle and pulled the trigger. The gunshot echoed through the hills, the silence eerie as it died—along with the light in Bristow's eyes.

The man toppled over, crimson spreading over his chest. Shaking from exertion, Austin checked his neck for a pulse. There wasn't one. He couldn't have said he was sorry.

"Austin?"

At the sweet sound of Laura's voice, he pushed to his feet and stumbled over to her. Then he dropped down and gathered her into his arms. She tried smiling up at him through her split lip, and reached up to touch his face.

"You came for me."

"I always will, sweetheart." His voice choked with emotion.

Her face was pale as she stared at him, eyes glassy. She'd lost too much blood, he thought. They had to get help up there somehow.

"Somebody call the paramedics," he ordered, throat tightening. He couldn't lose her. Not now, after all this.

"Already on it," Tonio told him.

Using his thumb, he wiped the blood from her lip. "You're going to be fine, okay? I'm right here."

"Our baby?"

"He'll be fine, too." Tears blurred his vision. "I'm so sorry for how I reacted. Please forgive me."

"Shh. I do. Know you were scared."

"I am, but I want you and our baby. Don't doubt that."

"Good . . . love you . . ." Her lashes drifted shut.

"I love you, honey. So much. Laura?" To his horror, she went limp in his arms. A sob escaped his chest and he watched helplessly as his world fell apart. Again. "No—please don't leave me. I won't survive this—I *won't*."

"Cap, help is on the way," Chris said gently, crouching beside him. "The wound is through the shoulder, no vital organs located there. She'll be okay."

"What about the baby? I can't lose another child. I won't."

Chris's eyes widened. Belatedly Austin realized he hadn't told anyone about the baby Laura was carrying. They'd barely had a chance to discuss things themselves.

Chris laid a hand on his shoulder in support. "I have to believe the baby will be fine, too. I just can't imagine that fate would be that cruel twice. You have to believe that, too."

Turning his attention back to Laura, he nodded,

hardly aware of the tears that had escaped to stream down his face. He had to think positive. She and the baby would be fine. They had to be.

If they weren't, his friends could go ahead and bury him right next to the ones he loved.

The wait was damn near unbearable.

For over two hours, Laura had been in surgery. He'd called his mom and dad as soon as he'd arrived at the hospital, telling them not to come until he knew more. Of course, his parents were the people Austin got his stubbornness from, and they arrived a few hours after his halting phone call.

Right now he was grateful for their support. His men from the station were fantastic, but nothing could replace family.

When he'd told his parents about the baby, they'd been surprised at first, to say the least. Understandably, they were concerned that he wasn't ready to go through a new pregnancy, anticipating a child once again. What they really wanted to know, and weren't asking, was whether he was on the rebound from his loss and trying to replace the child that had been cruelly taken from him.

His answer was a firm no. His folks were relieved and didn't bring it up again. They seemed happy for him, and he knew they'd warm up to the idea of a grandchild again, too, in time. Austin wasn't the only one who needed to heal.

"Son," his dad said, nodding toward the double doors.

Austin shot to his feet at the sight of the doctor who walked through wearing clean scrubs. When the man smiled at him, he almost fell to his knees.

"Captain Rainey?"

"Yes. How's Laura?"

The doctor stopped in front of him. "She lost a lot of blood, but she and the baby are just fine."

"Thank God!" He sagged and his dad was right there behind him, along with Austin's detectives. "When can I see her?"

"She'll be in recovery for a bit while they get a room ready. Could be a couple of hours. Don't expect much out of her today in the way of being coherent, but tomorrow should be a much different story. We'll watch her for a couple of days, and if the wound is looking good, she can go home."

"That's great news," he said, relief draining what little energy he had left.

"Just make sure she gets plenty of rest for a couple of weeks, and don't let her do any heavy lifting."

"Oh, I'll make sure—don't worry."

The doc shook his hand. "I'm so glad things turned out fine. I'll have a nurse come and get you when she's in her room."

"Thank you."

Once the doctor had gone, Austin turned to his team. "Thank you, guys, too, for everything. I don't know what I'd do without you."

"Damn," Chris said. "I'm missing Taylor's smart-ass comments right now. This is where he'd say we need a group hug or something."

Austin chuckled in agreement, along with the others. "How's he doing, by the way?"

Shane spoke up. "He's improving every day. I'm going by to see him before I leave, give him an update."

"I'll go by, too," Austin said. "This evening."

The guys said their good-byes and drifted off to go home and pass out. Austin envied them, but there was nowhere else he'd rather be than at Laura's side.

Eventually he convinced his folks to go get some rest as well. They left with a promise to return tomorrow. Finally a nurse came and said Laura was in a room on the third floor. Heart pounding, Austin followed the directions to the room and eased quietly inside.

His girl was lying on her back, hair spilling around her like black ink. She appeared so frail and vulnerable when he knew she was anything but. She'd escaped a killer and led him on a merry chase through the hills, and had climbed up a cliff to try to evade him. She was one of the most courageous people he'd ever met.

Settling into the chair next to her, he wrapped his fingers around hers and let his head fall back, his body relax. Sleep deprivation and the knowledge that she was safe finally took their toll.

In moments, he was out like a light.

A gentle buzzing noise woke her from a deep sleep.

Her first thought was that somebody was outside using a Weed eater on the lawn. But no, that wasn't quite right. The sound was closer. Like, in the room with her. Snoring.

Who was snoring? What room?

Her ears caught other sounds as well. An occasional *beep*, a *whirr* of some sort of machine. Her body felt heavy, too. Especially her right shoulder and arm. *Wait*.

The memories came flooding back, and when they did, she heard herself whimper. Partly in fear, partly because trying to move caused a shard of pain to lance through her shoulder.

"Laura? Sweetheart, it's me. You're safe and it's all over."

Licking her lips, she croaked his name. "Austin?"

"Yes, honey. Can you open those gorgeous eyes for me?"

It didn't happen right away. But after a while her brain was awake enough to crack them open and get her first look at her lover since their argument. Quite simply, he looked wrecked.

His auburn hair was disheveled and his eyes were bruised, dark circles underneath. His clothes were wrinkled, as though he'd slept in them.

"Beautiful," she said, giving him lopsided smile.

"Now I know the drugs are still making you loopy." Smiling back, he clutched her hand. "What do you re-member?"

"Everything," she said, sobering. Then fear shot through her and her free hand went to her stomach. "The baby?"

"Is fine," he reassured her, bending over to kiss her lips. "You don't know how sorry I am or how much I regret acting like such an ass about our child. Please believe me."

"I do believe you, but I know you were scared." Her lips curved up. "Just don't let it happen again."

"I won't. I plan to spoil you as well, make sure you get plenty of rest when we get home."

"Um, we? And where is home?" Butterflies that had nothing to do with new life suddenly played in her belly. She wanted this, so much.

"Home to me is anywhere you are. I just want to be with you. Wherever you want to be."

Tears filled her eyes. "I want that, too. So very much. I love you, Austin."

"I love you and our baby. You're both the light of my life." He took a deep breath. "And I plan to spend the rest of my life showing you, if you'll have me."

"Do you mean . . . ?" She didn't dare hope.

"This isn't how I planned to ask you, but, Laura Eden, will you marry me?"

The tears finally spilled over. "I don't even have to think about it. Yes! I want nothing more than to be your wife."

"I don't know what you see in this old cop, but I'm so glad you're mine."

Carefully, he took her into his arms and held her close. Cuddling into his warmth, she breathed in his musky scent and knew she was truly home.

"I see forever with the man I love."

And she couldn't wait to get their future started.

Austin waited almost a week after Laura was released from the hospital to spring his surprise. Then he couldn't wait another single day.

One beautiful spring Saturday, he loaded her and their bags into his truck and took her for a drive. They had another week off together before reality intruded in their lives again. Then she'd be back at work on light duty, half days, for another week or so. He wasn't taking any chances with her and his child.

"You're not going to tell me where we're going?" she asked curiously.

"You'll figure it out soon enough." He gave her a wink.

As he'd predicted, she started smiling about halfway to their destination. She appeared extremely pleased when he turned down the driveway to the ranch.

"I knew it," she said happily. "We get to stay a whole week?"

"Yes, we do."

Once he pulled into the front, he unloaded their bags, flatly refusing to let her carry anything. Her shoulder was still healing and he was adamant that she not overdo things. With their stuff stashed in the master bedroom, he rejoined her in the foyer and then led her outside for a walk.

"I just love it here" she said happily. "I could stay here forever."

"Could you? Really?"

"This is what I've always wanted. A place in the country, plenty of room for kids and animals. I loved four-wheeling with you."

He gave her a quick kiss. "Well, we may not be doing that this time around," he said, to her visible disappointment. "Sweetheart, it's not safe with your shoulder, and I prefer you not ride one of those when you're pregnant."

For a few seconds she looked like she was going to argue, then relented. "If it makes you feel better, I won't."

"Thank you. We'll still go for long walks and visit our creek. Maybe even find some arrowheads."

"That sounds like fun."

They continued walking around the side of the property to the fence line, and stopped to lean on it and gaze over the rolling property. "I can almost see a few horses out there, can't you?" he asked, shooting her a sideways look.

"That would be wonderful. Too bad we can't have any." She sounded so wistful, the expression on her beautiful face so melancholy.

"Who says we can't?"

She turned to face him. "We'd have to hire somebody to feed them, and we could only see them on weekends, at best. It wouldn't be fair to them."

"Not necessarily, because I have a confession to make." He paused, taking both of her hands in his. "A few weeks ago I called my Realtor and placed my house up for sale—the one I shared with Ashley. It sold this morning."

"Oh, Austin," she said, squeezing his hands. Her face was full of concern for him. "Are you certain that's what you want to do?"

"Positive. I'm ready to start the rest of my life, and that life is with you. My parents said they'd give me a fair price for this place. I've got some money already, and with the sale of the house, we'll be set."

Concern slowly transformed to joy. "Are you saying . . . ?"

"I want us to make our home here, if that's what you want. You, me, and our children. What do you say?"

Suddenly his arms were full of bouncing, excited woman. Laughing, he gathered her close and held her carefully, mindful of her shoulder. When they pulled apart, he kissed her thoroughly. Loving every second of being with her, starting their new future.

"I take it that's a yes?" he asked with a grin.

"Yes!"

"Excellent. What do you say we make some plans? Horses, other animals, new furniture?"

"Yes to all that! And Max, my cat. We'll have to bring him."

"Of course."

Smiling, he wrapped his arm around her as they walked, and listened to her plans. He didn't care what she wanted—he'd give her anything at all. He couldn't believe he'd gone from being the saddest, loneliest man he knew to the happiest, in the space of a few weeks. He'd never, ever take Laura or this new life for granted.

He was a new man, reborn.

Thanks to the woman he loved.

Read on for a preview
of another Sugarland Blue novel

On the Run

Available from Signet Eclipse.

The stench reached his consciousness first.

Then the pain. All over, racking agony, which proved he wasn't dead yet, though he didn't have a clue how that could be.

Awareness of being trapped came next. Buried. But not in the dirt. As he tried to move, various items surrounding him shifted and rolled away. With his fingertips he felt . . . cans. Paper. Slime. Old food? Cold knowledge gripped him, turned his blood to ice.

After the bastards were finished with me, they threw me out with the garbage. Literally.

Move, Salvatore. Move or you're dead.

Using his hand, he sought the air. Pushed and clawed, twisting his body in the stinking refuse. The weight on top of him was heavy but not crushing. They'd meant to hide his body, completely confident he wouldn't awaken, or make it out even if he had. He tried not to think they might have been right.

At last, fresh air. But as he broke through the pile, the heap sloped downward sharply and he was tumbling sideways. For several feet he fell, being jabbed and poked by sharp edges until he landed in the dirt at the bottom, the wind knocked out of him. Breathing was almost impossible, his lungs burning. He was hurt inside and out.

His eyes opened to slits, and he tried to peer into the darkness. All he could make out was a sea of garbage. No moon or stars. Worse, little hope.

They'd thrown him into the dump miles outside the city, where nobody in their right mind would venture. *Don't give up.*

Drawing his legs under him, he pushed upward. His legs were like rubber, his strength almost nonexistent. He made it halfway to a standing position before crashing back to the ground with a hoarse cry. God, the pain. His entire body felt hot and cold by turns, and swollen like a balloon. Any second, he would split and spill onto the ground like the plastic bags all around him vomiting their guts. His skin and clothing were wet, too, from head to toe.

He knew it wasn't all from the slime of the trash.

Shaking, Tonio crawled forward on his belly, inch by inch. Time lost meaning. An hour or three might have passed, though he didn't think it had been so long—he would have already been dead.

Wetness ran down his forehead, down the bridge of his nose. Gradually, he grew cold. So cold he knew he'd never get warm again. What was he doing? Why had he been abandoned in this godforsaken place? Too much blood loss. Confusion. He tried to remember, couldn't. Knew it was the beginning of the end.

Anthony. I'm Anthony Salvatore, and I'm a cop. Have to get out of here, get help. Let them know—what?

Her name whispered through his mind like a promise. Or a nightmare. He didn't know which, and now he might never.

Angel.

Have to let Chris, somebody, know about Angel. Because if I fail . . .

Sister or not, Rab would kill her. He would show her no mercy, and she would end up here, in a grave next to Tonio. No matter what she'd done, her betrayal, he couldn't let that happen.

"Angel."

Her name was on his lips, her beautiful face in his mind, and the memory of her warm, supple body close to his heart when his strength finally deserted him.

Angel's or devil's mistress. Dark or light. He'd wanted years to learn her secrets, and been granted only weeks. It would have to be enough.

"Be smart, baby," he rasped. "Stay safe."

Against his will, his eyes drifted shut.

And Tonio surrendered to the darkness.

Five weeks earlier

Detective Tonio Salvatore leaned against the bar in his favorite dive, where the regulars only knew him by his first name, and sipped his whiskey, neat.

They didn't know what he did for a living, either, and nobody ever asked. He figured, if anything, they had him pegged for a dangerous thug of some sort, maybe into drugs or fencing stolen goods like three-quarters of the guys there. Because he was dressed as he always was when he came here, in leathers, a tight black Metallica T-shirt, heavy boots, a five-o'clock shadow on his jaw, and a bandanna around his short raven hair, it was a reasonable assumption.

It didn't hurt that he was six-four and muscular and looked mean, even though he wasn't unless he had to be.

Stroker's was a rough place with an even rougher clientele, but it suited him despite his job—or maybe because of it. It was the perfect place to keep his finger on the pulse of Cheatham County's criminal activity without risking being seen and recognized in his nearby city of Sugarland, Tennessee. He wasn't here in any official capacity, though. He just wanted to relax, incognito.

And maybe see some action that involved the weapon in the front of his leathers and not the one strapped to his ankle.

Taking another sip of his Dewar's, he savored the smooth flavor and recalled the sweet little piece of work from last weekend. The blonde—what was her name? Trish? Tess? Didn't matter. She'd been all over him from the minute she spied him at the bar, and it hadn't taken her long to maneuver her way between his legs as he sat on the stool, then proceed to check his tonsils with her tongue.

His cock stirred as he remembered giving her a ride on his Harley to the motel down the road, his go-to for one-night stands, which provided him and his chosen partners with relief. No way was he taking any of them home. He wasn't stupid.

The blonde had hugged him tightly from behind, pressed her breasts against his back, her hot crotch against his ass, and he'd nearly wrecked trying to get them to the motel. Inside, they'd been naked in seconds, and he'd eaten her out, enjoying the moaning and breathy little whimpers coming from her throat. She'd dug her fingers into his short hair and held on for the ride as he'd thrown her onto the bed, slid his cock deep, and fucked her so hard, the headboard had cracked the plaster on the wall.

Looking around, he hoped she'd be back tonight.

"Another round?" the bartender asked. The guy's name was Rick, and he was as tough as anyone here. Had to be to work in a place like this. Tonio knew for a fact the man kept a baseball bat behind the counter and wouldn't hesitate to use it.

"Sure," he answered. Fuck it, he was off duty tonight.

"Comin' up."

His night improved when the little blonde with the perky bust and tight jeans strolled through the front door. He turned back to his drink, making sure not to clue her in that he'd noticed her arrival. As he thought she might, pretty soon a warm body sidled close to him, and a woman's voice whispered in his ear.

"Fancy meeting you here, Tonio." Small teeth nibbled at his ear lobe. "Buy a girl a drink?"

"You bet." Damn, what *was* her name?

"Hey, Tess," Rick said in greeting. "What's your poison tonight, baby girl?"

Settling on the stool beside Tonio, she brought a long

manicured nail to her lips in thought. Then she grinned. "How about a Screaming Orgasm?"

Rick snorted and winked at her, then smirked at Tonio. "Don't think you need me for that one, but whatever the lady wants."

While Rick mixed her drink, she swiveled to face Tonio. Leaning over enticingly, she showed every bit of the rosy nipples under her plunging blouse and eyed him like a cat ready to pounce on a mouse. They both knew she wouldn't have to work real hard to catch him.

"Watcha been up to, sexy?" she asked.

He shrugged. "Not much. Messing with my bike, doing a little business to keep a roof over my head. The usual." All true, even if he'd just effectively skewed her perception of him possibly being a criminal even further. Why he was playing this game, he wasn't sure.

But they were both enjoying it, so what was the harm? He might learn something interesting.

"What do you do to keep that roof over your head, hmm?" She took the drink Rick slid over and took a healthy swallow.

He'd stepped into this willingly. But there was no question he had to develop a cover now. Besides Tess, Rick and a couple of other men were very interested in his answer and were trying to pretend they weren't. Who knew? He might luck onto a case that would lead somewhere, eventually to arrests for drugs, or who knew what else? Sure, his captain would have his balls for going out on his own, but if it led to something big, he'd forgive Tonio just as fast.

"I acquire things," he heard himself say. "For those who want them."

She arched a brow. "What kinds of things?"

"Whatever you want, for a fee."

"Anything?"

"Pretty much."

Tess wasn't fazed. "Good to know. I might be persuaded to pass that along."

"Up to you." Pulse kicking up a notch, he tossed back the rest of his drink, letting his demeanor say he didn't give a shit whether she did or not. But he'd gotten a nibble that might lead to something bigger, and the game was on. The high was better than any drug.

Almost better than sex. But not quite.

After taking another drink, she slid a hand up the thigh of his leathers and brushed her fingers across his tightened crotch. "I can provide something *you* want, too."

His dick was throbbing in his pants. Hot.

"Yeah?"

"Oh, yeah." Leaning into his chest, she took his mouth and tangled her tongue with his. Her nipples grazed his chest and peaked to tiny eraser points, rubbing. Driving him crazy.

"Want to get out of here?" he asked between heated kisses.

"Sounds like a great idea," a woman's voice said. And it wasn't Tess's.

Tonio and his hookup turned toward the woman who'd stalked up to them without either of them noticing—and Tonio's breath caught. The woman was several inches below Tonio's height—perhaps five-nine—long-limbed with a killer body that looked like she'd just stepped from the pages of a skin magazine. Long dark hair fell past her shoulders, almost all the way to her waist. Her eyes were large and green, and her nose was a sharp blade above a full, lush mouth made for sucking cock. Full, ripe breasts pushed at the snug cotton shirt, which had been cut with scissors or a knife to make it a low V-neck and sleeveless as well. She wore tight jeans and black ankle boots with silver conchos studded around them. Encircling her right upper arm was a surprisingly feminine Celtic tattoo. His mouth watered. The look, which would have come across as tacky on anyone else, was stunning on her.

Definitely centerfold material.

"What the fuck do you want, Angel?" Tess was clearly less than pleased with the other woman's presence.

"Are you really that stupid?" Angel stared at her, then shook her head. "You know this is Rab's territory. He's not going to be happy to find you here again, and he's not taking you back."

What? Stuck in the middle of Tess's trying to make another man jealous? Fuck.

"You think I give a shit what that asshole thinks, or what makes him happy?"

Angel sighed. "Look, I'm telling you this for your own good. My brother— Crap, too late. Here he comes now."

Angel really did look worried, Tonio had to admit. When Tess glanced toward the door, she did, too. Who was this Rab guy who had the women so nervous? Tonio followed their gazes and cursed inwardly.

The man who held their attention was a frigging tank, maybe even an inch or so taller than Tonio himself. He was about thirty or so and bald, and wore his tats proudly as sleeves down both thick arms. Several pendants bounced against his broad chest, and he wore jeans that emphasized his muscular thighs.

Rab headed straight for their group, a steely expression on his face. Tonio slid from his stool and planted himself slightly in front of the women on pure instinct. This wasn't even his fight, for God's sake.

"Bitch," the man growled, throwing his sister the barest glance. "What the hell are you doing here?"

Tonio's back went up. He absolutely *hated* any man who addressed a woman as *bitch*. Only bottom-feeders resorted to that kind of talk to make themselves seem like bigger men.

"What do you think?" she purred slyly. Curling into Tonio's side, she wrapped an arm around his waist. "I'm here for a drink, same as you. A little company, too. No harm in that."

"There is when you know goddamn well I don't want to see your face." His eyes were dark and cold, like black marbles. He hadn't acknowledged Tonio at all.

"Fine," she said airily. "I guess I won't introduce you to my friend Tonio here, who has a special talent."

That icy gaze settled on Tonio for the first time, and inwardly he actually shuddered. That didn't happen often. There weren't many people who scared him. But there was something about this man he perceived as dangerous. Even deadly. Maybe it was because he was too still, too calm. As though watching and calculating.

"What talent might that be?" Rab drawled, checking him out from head to toe, his disdain clear.

"Acquisitions," Tess said pointedly.

And here we go.

That caught the other man's interest. "What's your specialty?"

"Don't have one. Someone wants something, I get it." That was taking a risk, not specializing. It might have sounded too close to fishing on Tonio's part. Too suspect.

Rab studied him for a long moment. Tonio held his gaze, not backing down. *Never, ever volunteer more than you're asked. That's the first rule of being undercover.* Eventually, the other man spoke again.

"You got a last name?"

"Reyes," he lied.

"You got a number?"

Shit. He couldn't give out his real cell phone number—he'd have to get a burner, fast. And have an unpleasant conversation with Rainey first thing tomorrow. He was onto something here. He could feel it. The room had hushed, every single person there tense. Belatedly, Tonio noted all the men dressed in a similar fashion who'd risen to their feet and moved subtly behind Rab. None of them appeared to be the stereotypical bumbling backwoods yokel. They looked tough and serious. He'd bet most of them had done hard time.

This man was no small-time player.

"I'm around," was his only reply.

Several men flexed their fists. Looked to Rab, who held them off with a slight flick of a hand. *Jesus.* He'd escaped getting the motherfuck beat out of him by the skin of his teeth, and all he'd wanted was a cold drink and a hot woman. In that order.

"I expect you will be," Rab said, his warning unmistakable. "Same time tomorrow night. Here. We'll talk."

Dismissing Tonio, the man strode away, taking up residence at a table in a corner of the bar. The only vacant table in the place, which must have been reserved for him. Angel stepped closer to Tonio and tilted her head toward the corner.

"You've got his attention," she said, sounding less than pleased. And still concerned. "I hope you know what the hell you let in when you opened that door."

"Interesting way to talk about your own brother."

A second of unease flickered in her jade eyes. She glanced around and apparently decided Rab's men were no longer listening. "My advice? Don't come back."

"Noted." Angel warning him off. He was even more intrigued than before—and he knew he'd be back.

About the Author

Jo Davis is the author of the popular Firefighters of Station Five series (*Ride the Fire*, *Line of Fire*), the Sugarland Blue series (*On the Run*, *In His Sights*), and, as J. D. Tyler, the Alpha Pack paranormal romance series (*Chase the Darkness*, *Wolf's Fall*). A multiple finalist in the Colorado Romance Writers Award of Excellence and a finalist for the Bookseller's Best Award, she has captured the HOLT Medallion Award of Merit and been a two-time nominee for the Australian Romance Readers Award.

Connect Online

jodavis.net